D0257772

MY DROWNING

ALSO BY JIM GRIMSLEY

Winter Birds

Dream Boy

MY DROWNING

A NOVEL BY

JIM GRIMSLEY

FOURTH ESTATE • *London*

Many thanks to the Ucross Foundation, which provided support during the writing of this book.

669583
MORAY COUNCIL
Department of Technic
& Leisure Services
F

First published in Great Britain in 1999 by
Fourth Estate Limited
6 Salem Road
London W2 4BU

Copyright © Jim Grimsley 1997

10 9 8 7 6 5 4 3 2 1

The right of Jim Grimsley to be identified as the author of this work has been asserted by him in accordance with the Copyright, Designs and Patents Act 1988.

A catalogue record for this book is available from the British Library.

ISBN 1-84115-134-3

All rights reserved. No part of this publication may be reproduced, transmitted, or stored in a retrieval system, in any form or by any means, without permission in writing from Fourth Estate Limited.

Printed and bound in Great Britain by
Biddles Ltd, Guildford and King's Lynn

For Faye Araiza

CONTENTS

THE LOW GROUNDS

I CAN STILL remember the whiteness of my mother as she slips beneath the surface of the river. Years later I am standing in my clean kitchen when the memory returns. We are somewhere near the Holcomb River in the shade and my mother wears a white slip that flutters up in the water. She is very pale and fat and the blossoming of the slip makes her seem immense. Kneeling in the river, submerged to her shoulders, she turns her face to the sky. The fat of her arms sways in the air, dips into the dark water. She takes a breath and closes her mouth. From me, from all of us, she slides away.

I am hardly old enough to know how much like drowning this is. Why have we come to the river when it is swollen with rain, when it is running so hard and fast? The reason is lost; I remember nothing. Since I am wearing shoes, this must be autumn or winter. The world shows brown and dry. Only the daughters have come; my older sister, Nora, stands with me but none of my brothers has followed. Why not?

Mama rises out of the river gasping, throwing water from

her hair. Her breath rises in trails of steam. The surprise of seeing her move so freely still echoes in me years afterward. Her large, flat breasts lift, the yellowed bodice of the slip clinging to the high flesh. She says something, I can't remember what it is, something about the cold. But she addresses the air above my head, not me. Another person stands behind me, I can't remember who. How can such a vivid memory be so imperfect?

In the present I am standing in my kitchen with the light on. I am alone in my house but I am seeing everything around me in a strange way. All the objects have a patina, a film of iridescence. I am seeing a river at my feet as if it is flowing darkly there; I understand this is happening because I am old and all the rivers of my memory are rushing toward the sea, unstoppable. I understand that I am prone to remember the most ridiculous things, same as Nana Rose when she died. I have grown old enough that a memory becomes as real as the real thing.

Mama steps ashore. She stands over me, shivering and dripping, and I see the outline of her heavy belly, her rolling thighs. She looks down at me with the blankness of a cow. I am so in love with her, every part of me aches. The feeling returns vividly, an electric current running through me. She scoops me up, her arms are strong but soft; I burrow into them. I weigh less than the wet slip.

She holds me almost level with her face. Her eyes are blank and blue. She sets me onto the ground abruptly, having forgotten why she lifted me in the first place. The wet fabric of the slip heaves as she steps away from all of us.

I have seen and will see these simple images again and

again, in memory and dreams. We have come to the river, Nora and Mama and me—Ellen—and Mama in only her slip. We stand out in the cold while Mama sobs in the woods.

WE LIVED IN the Low Grounds, in a house with a fireplace, a wood stove, a well outside where Nora pumped water. We had a bed in the kitchen for Uncle Cope. We had kerosene lamps for light and an outhouse for shitting. My daddy was a tenant farmer on this land. He was thirty-two, my mother, the same.

I was hungry, watching the fire, wishing for something to eat. We would have biscuits soon, I could smell them, but I never ate fast enough to fill my stomach, and afterward there was never anything left over. So I huddled in Mama's lap and watched the fire and felt the hollow fist in my belly.

The smell of the biscuits filled the house, drawing my brothers, Carl Jr., Otis, and Joe Robbie, slouched like dogs along the walls. The smell awakened Daddy, who shuffled from the bedroom pulling a flannel shirt over his thin shoulders.

He spooned sugar into his coffee and said nothing. When nothing but biscuit appeared to eat, he stared into the top of the table. He chewed the biscuit as if he were grazing in a pasture.

I got half of a biscuit. The sensation of warm bread in the stomach made me happy, and I was allowed to eat in Mama's lap. We were eating, all of us. We crowded near the fireplace. No one talked.

I SLEPT WITH Nora. We had a bed in the same room with the boys; they slept across the room. At night Nora tucked me against her like a warm brick, and we breathed peacefully while our brothers snored.

Early every morning Mama woke Nora by pulling her feet, under the covers, from the foot of the bed, and Nora slid away from me with the groan that meant she knew better than to linger. Mama hovered, a large round shadow at the foot of the bed. I could see the softness of her eyes in the light of the kerosene lantern she carried. "Get on up, now."

I slid out of the bed with Nora. The floor struck cold at the bottoms of my feet, and I ached. I slid into clothes in the cold while Mama with the lantern sailed toward the door.

Nora had already dressed and stumbled after her.

We made a fire in the stove in the kitchen and another in the fireplace in the adjacent room where Daddy would sit to take his coffee and eat his grits. The fires had to be lit before Daddy would rise. Mama and Nora crept into the kitchen to build the fire in the stove, because Uncle Cope slept in the kitchen, and they were afraid of him. They heard him breathing in the dark while they fumbled with the wood. Once the fire was lit, Nora began to make biscuits. She ladled water, pumped the night before, and scooped lard from the tin. She measured by eye and kneaded the white dough carefully. She shivered in the cold kitchen, the kitchen fire only beginning to throw its circle of heat. She stood near the stove, warming as the oven awoke.

She made coffee. She boiled water for grits. She added wood to the fire from the firebox. I stood near the stove along the wall and watched. I fetched and carried whatever I was told.

Uncle Cope, when he lived with us, got out of bed and

roamed the house on crutches from the time Nora lit the fire in the stove. He woke, the first of the men, after the fire began to make heat. Mama and Nora had said over and over not to be alone with him, so I never was. If he came into a room when I was alone in it, I left. Even in the morning he smelled like whiskey, and he never shaved; he buttoned his shirts crooked, and his belly hung over his belt. His teeth were dark and bluish and had jagged shapes. I did not like him. Uncle Cope busted his leg to splinters when he fell off a truck, drunk, a long time ago, Mama said. He lived with Daddy part-time since Daddy was his brother.

WHEN THE SKY lightened and the coffee began to boil, Mama headed to the bedrooms to wake up Carl Jr. and Daddy. By then biscuits were baking in the oven and grits boiled in a pot. Daddy's shaving washpan waited in the warm room for the water we heated on the stove. Nora gave me biscuit dough when Mama was out of the room. I ate it greedily, raw. Hardly morning, and I was already hungry from the night before.

Carl Jr. stumbled out of the bedroom, pulling on his pants. The rest of his clothes he carried in his hands, dropping them on the floor near the fireplace, where he stood shivering and rubbing his hands together. He hurriedly pulled on an undershirt and buttoned another over it.

When he washed his face, he took care to use no more of the hot water than Daddy would be willing to spare. Carl Jr.'s beard hardly required daily attention, though he rubbed his palm along his throat as if he longed for thicker growth. He would carry this gesture, and this wispy, blondish beard, into manhood.

Daddy glided out of the back of the house, thin and sharp as a blade. His small, round head shone, the hair thinning at the top, wispy as Carl Jr.'s beard. Carl Jr. carried away the washpan and emptied it while Daddy backed up to the fire. Daddy fingered the buttons of his overalls. He knelt and laced up his boots. When Carl Jr. delivered the washpan, Nora filled it with the hot water and they both looked at it before Carl Jr. carried it back. That morning hot water satisfied Daddy, and the minutes passed quietly.

Odd, the detail that a person remembers among all those that lie forgotten or pass unnoticed. I remember the red-checkered oilcloth we had when I was very young, scored with dark holes where cigarettes had burned it. Daddy always rolled his cigarettes and smoked them sitting at the table. What makes the memory particular? The oilcloth was finally thrown away when there was more burn than cloth, and we never had another. But I remember kneeling in a chair and running my hands along the oily surface, counting the bright checks, sticking my fingers through the burns.

What do I fail to notice? What do I continue to forget? Why this particular morning?

Mama emerged from the back of the house. She had pulled a pair of socks over her feet and walked with her shuffling gait, holding her knees wide apart. In the kitchen she stirred four spoons of sugar into a cup of coffee, hot and strong. She carried the coffee to Daddy herself this morning.

He took the cup and swallowed. Satisfaction spread through his features. The fire warmed him sufficiently, and he found comfort.

Out the window dawn climbed in the sky, a purple light behind the pine trees. I stood at the window beside the stove, near Nora's skirt. Objects emerged from the murky outside, becoming the chicken house, the toolshed, the outhouse. Tobacco barns leaned to the side in the distance. In the morning a pale mist glided over the yard, between the trees. The sky flushed every color of the rainbow, but mostly it burned like fire, especially along the tops of clouds.

I was cold, but I avoided the fire. I would warm myself when Daddy left.

"Go put on some socks, Ellen," Nora whispered, "before you catch pneumonia," and I nodded and skipped into the cold bedroom. None of us knew what pneumonia was, but we were all agreed it would be bad to catch.

In our room the boys were still sleeping. I walked on tiptoes so only a bit of my foot touched the cold floor. Mama would wake up Otis soon, since he had to get dressed for school. Joe Robbie would lie in bed as long as he liked, and Mama would bring him a biscuit and some sugared coffee later, when everyone else left the house. But right now the room was still dark, and I found my way between shadows. I grabbed socks and returned to the kitchen. There were spooks in the dark; they would get you if you lingered.

In the kitchen, by the stove, I slipped the socks over my feet, hopping to avoid having to sit on the floor. Nora smiled at me from the side. Carl Jr. joined Daddy with his coffee and they drank together by the fireplace, sitting in the two chairs. Nora served them biscuits. We had syrup, and today Daddy poured syrup on one of the biscuits, to get him started, he said, and Mama laughed. She brought the syrup, kept on the top shelf out of reach of us little ones, as if it were a holy object. The stream of syrup oozed over the biscuit in thin, lacy trails. My mouth watered. Daddy smiled, showing the gap where a tooth was missing.

Daddy's face had paled from its summer bronze. His forehead was deeply creased from days in the weather. He was thin as a rake but strong as wire. He possessed, in my opinion, huge hands and feet. The feet could strike as swiftly and unexpectedly as the hands, and even Carl Jr. had no defense against Daddy's kicks and licks. An offense could be major or minor, even an offense as insignificant as moving too slowly across Daddy's striking range. I stayed on my toes around Daddy, I had learned that. I kept my back to the wall.

Carl Jr. left for work when the truck came. I had no notion when or why the truck arrived, only that it did. A dark round-hooded pickup truck with wooden rails at the back pulled up beside the ditch and beeped. Carl Jr. leapt into the back, and the truck vanished down the steep curve of road.

Not long after, Otis stumbled through the kitchen ready to walk with Nora the half mile to the place where the school bus stopped. Nora's coat had grown tight across the shoulders. Otis wore an old coat of Carl Jr.'s, a little too big for him, but he looked warmer than Nora.

When they were gone, the house became quiet.

Daddy sat at home in the kitchen and poked around in the yard. For much of the day he stayed in the shed. Later I learned he kept his liquor there. Sometimes Uncle Cope trekked across the yard on his crutches, to sit on a crate and fold his arms across his knees with Daddy in the shed. We could hear them laughing.

Mama studied the building with her milky eyes.

In the winter, Joe Robbie and I played near the fireplace or in the kitchen or, at worst, in one of the cold bedrooms. Joe Robbie never walked on his own legs, because of something I did not understand. I never liked to watch him because of the way he moved, but he could be right much fun, sitting down.

Daddy did no work on the farm. Daddy refused to go with the loggers and earn more money. We ate biscuit and meat grease half the week, till Friday when there was sometimes money. Then we had meat in beans, and maybe rice. Daddy had quarreled with the man who owned the land, about money. I knew about the fight. But it was less important to me than Mama's dreams about the dead baby boy.

We awoke the night before with Mama moaning. Maybe this is the reason for memory. She was shuffling in the hall, screaming, and Daddy ran behind her yelling at her. I had never before heard fear in my Daddy's voice. Mama called out that she saw the dead baby's ghost again, that it wouldn't leave her alone. And she kept crying and screaming till Daddy beat her to shut her up, and then led her, exhausted, back to bed.

Mama told me the dreams that day, when Nora and Otis were in school. The baby boy lay under the house, crying. At first he sounded like a cat, but then she could hear him scratching at the floorboards, and she knew he was trying to get into the house, wanting to get warm again. She told me this and stood at the window watching the shed, wanting to see through the walls.

She told me she had seen the baby's ghost before, floating

in the air above her bed. She described it as if some angel had wrapped it in swaddling clothes.

MOST DAYS WE ate biscuit for the noon meal. In this we were luckier than the ones who went to school. They got nothing to take with them to eat and could expect nothing much when they returned home. In the afternoon Mama made beans, if we had beans. If we had an onion, she cut up an onion into the beans. If she had managed to save a dollop of bacon drippings from the weekend (if there was bacon), she spooned this into the pot. For meat we ate fatback, souse meat, pig's feet, when we could get it, from the Little Store or from an aunt or uncle. Mama ate lard in the biscuit sometimes, syrup others. She gathered wood for the fire when we ran out during the day. She made a slow job of it, and sometimes she required the better part of an afternoon to find enough. While I was too little to carry wood, it was my job to watch Joe Robbie and fetch what he needed. Even in my earliest memories I am tending him.

Daddy wandered in and out of the house. He played with the mule harness, pretending to repair it. He walked into the field with his straw hat in his hand.

We owed the landlord money. Mama loved to say so, to me and Joe Robbie. We owed so much money, she said, Mr. James would put us off the land. Daddy refused other work. She looked out the window at Daddy's spidery figure in the field. He won't go to work to save his neck nor mine, she said. His neck nor mine. She was prone to repeat words, as if she were her own echo. Her sentences trailed off, as if the words were thin and would soon die away.

THE DEAD FOX

DADDY STOOD IN front of the Christmas tree and blinked, as if he did not know what it was. The fire roared at his back. His shadow hugged the flames, his arms crossed behind him.

He carried a tobacco plug in his mouth. In a minute he would spit. But for the moment like a cow he chewed, a rolling motion of the jaw. Dreamy-eyed.

I was with Nora. Carl Jr. squatted by the fire between Daddy and us. Nora and I hovered at the edge of the heat.

Daddy spit into the fire, the embers hissing. "So your mama wanted a goddamn tree."

Sitting on the floor, Carl Jr. rolled a cigarette on the floor. "It's nothing wrong with a tree, Daddy. The littlest ones never had a tree."

"She's shaming me."

"No Daddy, that ain't right."

After long silence, in the face of Daddy's blank stare, Carl Jr. swore under his breath and walked out of the house. Chill swept from the back door. Nora took me into the kitchen, deep into the shadow.

"She's rubbing my nose in it. I know what she's doing."

Has he killed the fox already? Or does this happen before? Does he go hunting after Carl Jr. cut the tree?

So many pieces to the memory. If I place them in no particular order, no one should wonder why.

I WAS SUPPOSED to want a doll. Where this idea came from, I fail to recall. But the desire for a doll became, at some point, a condition of my being, discussed when we looked at the dog-eared copy of a two-year-old Christmas catalog someone gave us. Nora pointed to the pages of dolls. "See how Ellen is looking at these. You want you a doll like this, don't you, honey?" She pinched my elbow as if she were being very clever to guess this wish of mine.

Gaping at the page, I attempted to discern which were the dolls, and guessed, and pointed.

I wanted the catalog, the bright colorful pages. I wanted to have it in my lap and to turn the pages. I wanted to touch each of the pictures, like someone blind, learning each object by touch. The catalog was enough for me, I had never seen anything like it. But Nora talked about a doll, Nora pointed her finger at a picture of a doll, and soon even I was convinced I must want one.

Joe Robbie wanted a cowboy pistol. I wonder, now, if his desire were as fabricated as mine. Like me, I think it would have pleased him simply to have the catalog, to look at it. But Nora kept that for herself.

THE DEAD BABY slept under the Christmas tree. His bed of swaddling clothes lay hidden behind the thick branches at the back, but if you looked close you could see it. Through the shadowy cedar branches the pale baby hand sometimes appeared. He lived in this house now, he would never leave. Maybe Mama whispered this to me, or maybe I dreamed it. The baby boy had come to stay.

Mama still saw him, but after a while she stopped talking about it, except to Joe Robbie and me. She no longer woke in the night to see the baby floating above the bed. She no longer heard his crying in her dreams. Now she saw him in more ordinary ways. Sometimes he lay on the couch in a rectangle of sun, stretching like a cat. Sometimes he looked down at her from the high kitchen shelves where she hoarded Daddy's coffee and sugar. Sometimes he hid under the bed or in the back of the closet behind Daddy's boots. But over the days near Christmas, he made a bed of his burial clothing in back of the Christmas tree, and I was so convinced her story was true I could see him there myself.

What did the dead baby dream of? Did he get cold? At night, after we were asleep, did he warm himself by the shadow of the fire? Did he ever appear outside? Would he ever speak?

Was he my brother still? Was he here and under the ground at the same time?

If Daddy threw the tree in the yard, the dead baby would have to move again. I was afraid he would start sleeping in my room.

When school stopped for the holiday break, Nora and Otis stayed home all the time. During the cold days before Christmas we sat by the stove in the kitchen, all of us, hungry, while the wind rattled the windows.

Nora took me with her when she searched for wood. The memory of one such day returns in a vivid way. All the coats, even the hand-me-downs, hung on me like sacks, but I wore both my pairs of overalls and my dress, and two sweaters, one of them with the sleeves rolled up. Socks covered my hands. I had Otis's old hat on my head.

The wind struck like a knife across the yard, and I was afraid it would blow me off the porch. Nora gave me her hand. We kept our mouths closed. Her coat was too tight to button so she held it closed with her other arm. We walked close together in the wind. The steady thwack of Otis's ax resounded behind us as he, in another part of the yard, split more wood for the fireplace and the stove.

The world spread out flat and wide, colored ash and clay. The sky, a pale blue, almost no color at all, swelled endless and empty over us. Fields yielded to a bare rim of trees. Wind spoke with a voice, pressed like a hand. We offered no sound to compete with it.

In the yard Nora let go of my hand and adjusted the scarf against her ears. We searched methodically in the woods nearest the house, Nora avoiding the places she had already scoured. I held the smaller stuff. Some good branches had fallen in the wind; we needed to search only a little way into the woods. Nora dragged the biggest pieces she could. We delivered the wood to Otis under the woodshed and crossed the fields for another load.

By then we were nearly frozen ourselves, and we returned to the house.

Beans boiled in the pot on the stove. The smell made me

weak to eat. Nora tasted the beans for seasoning and threw in salt. We shivered in front of the stove.

Gathering wood kept us busy till dark. The weatherman on Carl Jr.'s battery radio predicted a cold, cold night; we needed enough wood to keep the fire roaring. The sky layered with clouds and then the bottom of the clouds flattened.

Carl Jr. came home with a bag of groceries.

I was standing with Nora in the yard when he headed toward us, near sunset. The grocery sack nested in the crook of his arm. Nora took the groceries inside, and Carl Jr. stayed to help Otis with the wood.

For supper, because of Carl Jr., we had hambone in the beans, and chunks of lean and fat to savor, and fried fatback. We crowded around the table. Nora made the biscuits, smooth and brown, fluffy inside.

That night we set the lanterns around the Christmas tree and sat in front of the fireplace. We had never done this before, and I expect, therefore, that this memory comes from Christmas Eve. We never burned so many lanterns. The tree cast eerie shadows in the dark.

I watched the corner for the baby boy to emerge. I dreaded that only Mama and I would be able to see him. Mama sat in her chair with Joe Robbie in her lap, his soft legs dangling. She smoothed his hair.

I am remembering, I am looking back. I am trying to see clearly, but I do not even know that what I am seeing is true. How can the memory of so small a gesture be genuine? The movement of my mother's thick, blunt hand through Joe Robbie's hair repeats itself. Why have I remembered that?

Maybe because of jealousy, because I wanted to sit in her lap myself.

The radio played Christmas music, news from other places, a radio drama about Christmas. I remember nothing specific about these, except the fact of the radio in the dim-lit room. Carl Jr. kept it by his knee, and adjusted the antenna when the station faded.

Daddy came in the back door and let in the cold and slung a dead fox across the kitchen table. Daddy's sharp eyes raked mine. For a moment I was very cold. I stood near the table at eye level with the dead fox. A pink tongue trailed out of its mouth. The gray-brown fur hung flat against narrow ribs. Through the hole in its skull, a dark jelly oozed.

"You can't leave it there," Mama said.

"I'm going to put it in the back room, it's cold back there." Daddy blinked at her.

"You been out there all day and that's what you killed."

"It wasn't anything else to shoot."

Mama stirred the fox leg. "You been drinking. I know it."

"I ain't."

"I can smell it."

"I don't give a good goddamn what you can smell."

They fell silent. They were both watching the fox.

"What you planning to do with it?"

"I might get it stuffed."

Mama touched her index finger to the fox's paw. She stood like that in the glimmering lantern light. Her mouth worked on words. "Well, get it off the table then, and let me get you some supper. Carl Jr. bought some groceries."

"Did he?"

"Yes, he did. We had us a right good supper, didn't we, younguns?"

The sound of general assent followed. Carl Jr., sullen and silent, remained behind at the fireplace. He adjusted the tuning knob on the radio, turned the volume louder.

"You ought to look at this fox I shot." Daddy raised his voice a little, clearly to reach Carl Jr.

"Right now I don't want to look at no dead animal I can't eat."

"You little son of a bitch. Come in here and get this fox and take it to the back room. And open that window back there so it can stay cold."

Carl Jr. after a while rose, stretched his legs, rounded the corner, grabbed the fox by the hind legs and looked across the table at Daddy. "I sure wished it was a rabbit." He sauntered to the back of the house, the dead fox swaying from side to side.

Daddy ate his supper methodically, chewing the pork lean with relish, spooning beans onto his plate, sopping the bean broth with biscuit. He drank a glass of clear whiskey, smacking his lips and shaking his head. Mama boiled coffee for him, and he spooned the sugar in heaps.

"Santy Claus comes tonight," he sang. He pulled the lantern toward him and lifted his Prince Edward tin from his pocket.

I remembered that I was supposed to want a doll.

"Hush and don't get these younguns' hopes up."

"If Santy Claus don't come, it means they ain't been good."

"Nora, get in here and boil water for these dishes." Mama stamped off in a rage. Joe Robbie, sitting on a pillow near the fireplace, asked, "Will Santa Claus bring me a toy?"

"Santy Claus ain't bringing nobody around here nothing," Daddy said. "He don't know how to find this house."

Mama slammed the door behind her. The tree shivered. I slid next to Joe Robbie, leaned on his skinny shoulder. For once, he neither hit me nor pinched me. We soaked in the heat of the fire, without having to fight the larger ones for a place. The crackle and hiss of burning wood offered comfort.

Out in the world a dog howled, an owl crooned. We pulled the curtains closed as we always did at night. We feared strangers peeping in, tramps walking on the road. We feared the monster who lived in the woods around Moss Pond, who walked among the houses at night, according to stories we had heard. The curtains left a gap in the middle, enough for the width of an eye.

"These is good beans. Did you cook them?"

Nora had pumped more water and lugged the bucket through the kitchen door. "Yes, sir."

"Your mama can't cook."

"Otis, you better pump another bucket of water and bring it in the house. That well is going to freeze tonight."

"I don't want to go out there."

"You get your ass out there and pump water like your sister told you."

"Do I have to go right now?"

"Yes, you got to go right now. Now get out there." The rising sharpness of his tone lifted Otis from his torpor. He shoved his arms into the sleeves of his coat.

"Fill it twice," Nora said. "We might not can get no water tomorrow."

"I ain't going out there twicet."

"Yes, you are, Otis. I can't do it all by myself."

"I chopped that goddamn wood all day till I got blisters. I don't see why I have to do everything."

But Daddy said, "Get your ass out there like I told you." Otis stomped out the door, the screen slamming with a ringing echo.

"I need to beat that youngun's ass," Daddy said thoughtfully, sopping the last of his coffee onto a biscuit. "Give me some more coffee."

Nora poured. On the radio played a song I knew, I could hear myself singing it under my breath. Daddy rolled his cigarette and smoked it. He tapped the ash on the biscuit plate. The coffee steamed as he lifted the cup.

MAMA WENT TO bed. Nobody asked where she was. Everybody knew.

Sometimes, most of the time, Daddy would linger by the fire, and he and Carl Jr. sipped whiskey or moonshine, and smoked cigarettes, and listened to the radio. Sometimes, Daddy went in to Mama.

Tonight he stood by the fire awhile. Nora tended the flames to keep them burning, adding logs judiciously, mindful of our stock. Carl Jr. passed through with a last bucket of water. "Well's about to freeze, like Nora said it would."

Nora set the water tub near the stove to keep it from freezing. She would stoke the fire before we slept and let the warmth drain out of it through the night. She and I would sleep out here tonight, in Uncle Cope's bed, since he had gone to his daddy's house for Christmas. I liked the thought of sleeping in that bed. We would have extra blankets and the warmth of the dying fire, and clean sheets that Nora ironed.

I went to bed in my cotton nightgown. Nora slept beside me, close. I could see through the grates of the stove into the embers of the fire. The silver dishpan and pitcher caught the orange reflection. Either I slept or I became hypnotized. All night I dreamed of doors opening and closing.

THE BABY BOY drifts through the house on a current of air. I am riding behind him. The lifted edges of the baby's shroud lap my face. I have become able to fly through the agency of the dead baby boy, and we are one cloud together. I have the feeling I may be as cold as the baby. We float down the hall, over Daddy's work shoes, into the bedroom, where Daddy is lying on top of Mama in a strange huddle, and Mama sees us over his back, rises up, and screams.

ON CHRISTMAS MORNING under the tree, between the empty lanterns, appeared a toy pistol for Joe Robbie and a small doll for me. A bushel of apples stood among the lower branches. Otis got a toy, too, I forget what.

I held the doll in my hand loosely. Joe Robbie pointed the gun at my head.

He took the doll, and I sat beside him while he stroked the skirt.

I turned the pistol over and over in my lap. I liked the shape. Carl Jr. showed me how to hold it.

The fox had frozen on the shelf in the back room. I wandered in there when no one noticed. The rigid carcass lay on the flat surface, legs jutting straight in the air. A moulded pink tongue sprawled over yellow teeth. Frost had formed on the snout. Clearly dead, but for the eyes, which had a glint of fire.

We ate leftover beans with ham. We used syrup and sopped it up with biscuit. We ate twice, plus biscuits in the morning. Daddy drank coffee with sugar the whole day and never stirred from the fire. He sipped whiskey through the long afternoon, listening to the radio till the batteries were weak.

By the end of the day Joe Robbie screamed if I touched the doll. I sat dumbfounded beside him. The gun meant nothing to me, but, truth be told, neither did the doll.

The apples were the best gift. I ate until I was sick from them. I ate as many apples as I could stuff into my belly. Never before had there been so much of a food that I could eat all I wanted. I ate the apples until I could hardly move. I lay flat on my back through the cold afternoon, in an ecstasy of digestion.

Nora fought with Mama about my doll. Nora wanted Mama to take the doll from Joe Robbie so I could play with it. But any time anybody touched the doll, Joe Robbie screamed, and Mama couldn't stand to hear him scream. Mama decided Joe Robbie might as well keep the doll since he was puny and it made him happy. Nora huffed off and made Mama mad, and Mama reared back to slap her, but she remembered it was Christmas and contented herself to yank Nora's ears good and hard.

Not once did I ask Joe Robbie for the doll. When he kept the pistol too, I didn't mind.

I had been flying with the baby boy. I replayed the dream

in my head, and the memory kept me buoyant. The bushel basket still held more than half its apples. Tonight Nora and I would sleep in the kitchen again, with the ghost fire glimmering in the stove. All these were good things. But above all, I had eaten as much as I could hold. I had learned of the possibility of abundance.

WHEN THE WEATHER warmed, Mama carried the carcass of the fox outside, wrapped in burlap. She flung the softening corpse into the ditch. Daddy never asked what happened to it.

At night, across the room, Joe Robbie slept with the doll wrapped in his arms. I remained oblivious to the loss, but Nora carried the anger like a hot coal. She would get me another doll, she said, when she worked in tobacco this summer. This promise consoled her in some way. I did not care, myself. I would never want a doll.

NOT LONG AGO I drove to the Low Grounds, down that road where we used to live. I had begun to remember the Christmas of the dead fox, and I realized I was headed toward the place where that house had stood as soon as I slipped behind the steering wheel. I made the drive early one morning, after my slice of toast. The distance isn't much, only an hour or so from the place I live now, near Pinetops.

The road had been paved, Lord knows how long ago. Electric wires lined the pavement and now there was light in the Low Grounds, and more houses, most of them brick, with plain bare yards and pitiful scrawny azalea bushes. The house where my family lived collapsed long ago, and nothing remains except the chimney, lying on its side in the white dirt. I stood at the sidewise mouth of the fireplace. I closed my eyes and pictured the gray fox, the white biscuits, the specter of the dead baby boy. I remembered gathering wood across the bare field where now a brick house squatted. The countryside suddenly smelled of winter. I could not quite remember what year it was.

MOSS POND

WE MOVED FROM the Low Grounds to a house near Moss Pond. The house was small, four rooms, with a wood heater, a woodstove, and a hand pump for water in the backyard. An empty chicken house leaned precariously under a sycamore. The outhouse stood there too, in thick shade, with its narrow door hanging from the hinges and its plank seat with two holes cut in the surface for doing your business. We resorted to a slop pot only in the coldest part of winter. Otherwise everyone took the long trek down the path, except for Joe Robbie, who was allowed a pan and a jar.

Sitting suspended over the cavern of shit and piss, in summer with the buzzing of green flies, in the winter with cold fingers creeping from the wood along my nervous bottom, I felt a pure and memorable terror. I was small enough to drop straight down the hole, and I clung to the edges with my hands in fear of snakes and other creatures that lived in the woods thereabouts; I pictured them crawling along the planks toward my bare behind. The echoing of the hollow place beneath me sent a shiver of fear through me and I finished my business as fast as I could. I cleaned myself with soft leaves in summer and newspaper or comic books in winter, learning to rub the newsprint together until it softened and to grip the seat with one hand while cleaning with the other. I was fanatical in cleaning myself, frightened as I was of sitting there; Nora made fun of me for my fastidiousness.

If you walked far enough through the woods that surrounded the house, you came to Moss Pond, where the woods were full of bobcats, snakes, and even bears. Nora and I made the trip together. I savored the black surface of the pond, the reflection of pine and sky. Nora in general disliked my company but preferred it to that of our brothers. Carl Jr. and Otis never invited us when they went fishing, but whatever they caught, we cleaned. I learned first to scrape the scales from the sides of the fish and later to cut the fins neatly at the base. Spines in the fins were sharp as needles at the ends and drew blood from careless fingertips. I worked as hard as I could but nothing I did ever pleased Nora, who herself moved with neatness and efficiency that I admired. Nora sawed off the fishheads and gutted the silvered bodies, scooping out mysterious soft masses that clung to her fingers. Cats yowled and marked the door, trying to climb inside, whenever we cleaned fish.

Mama's belly had swollen with a peculiar roundness, hard and smooth like a ripe squash. Nobody told me why. Because it was summer, we worked on Albert Taylor's farm in his cotton field, or weeding in Ruby Jarman's garden, or topping and suckering tobacco for Mr. James Allison, whom everybody respected because he was rich. I worked along with the rest, weeding and plucking on my hands and knees.

Because I was so small, I could not hold a hoe to chop the cotton, but I pulled up handfuls of weeds that the hoe couldn't reach. At night we were all exhausted, but especially Mama, and Nora boiled hot water for her to soak her feet. Nora made supper, dry beans most of the time, maybe with fried fish, and we ate near dark or after dark, in the first cool of the day.

Mama began to talk about a new little baby in the house. She no longer dreamed about the dead baby boy, as if he had stayed behind at the Low Grounds. Nobody gave me the connection between the blossoming of Mama's belly and the coming of a new baby; I was left to wonder.

Daddy had quit being a farmer. People were after him for money, something about the farm, so when people came looking for him, Mama would say he wasn't home even when he was. Daddy became a logger like Carl Jr. and worked when he felt like it. Other times he sat in the house. Here he had no fields to wander in, only the white-dirt yard in which no grass grew. He wandered among the trees there, or walked to the pond.

Daddy and Carl Jr. listened to the war on the radio, between spells of country music. The war was a great thing, like a cloud. I was not sure which country was our country, but there was a lot of talk about what our army ought to do. My daddy and Carl Jr. pursued this discussion amicably and laconically, in their own manner.

"I think we ought to go over there and whip their asses."

"You're right about that." Daddy nodded his head as if he had thought about this a lot.

"Was you in World War One, Daddy?" Otis asked.

"No. I ain't that old."

The radio played as long as the batteries lasted. We listened to the Carter family, Grandpa Jones and his wife, Little Jimmy Dickens. Nora sang along with the music while she boiled water to wash the dishes.

Because I was older now, I had more chores. I hauled wood a piece at a time to stack beside the stove and fireplace. I climbed on an old chair to pump water, as much as I could carry in a bucket. I dried dishes and stacked them to put away.

On wash day I gathered clothes. Mama and Nora built a fire under the washpot and we filled the tubs with water while Otis chopped wood. Mama moved awkwardly, now and then placing a hand at her lower back. She and Nora sorted the sheets, underwear, workshirts, skirts, socks, all that we gathered from the bedrooms. Mama added the clothes as the water heated, tamping the cloth into the pot with a tobacco stick. The boiling took a long time, and Mama tended the fire with my help, directing me to shove logs here and there; meanwhile Nora continued to pump water for washing and rinsing, and scrubbed the clothes on the washboard once they had boiled, churning them in the soapy water. Mama rarely helped with the scrubbing, and I was too small to be much use with the larger items, like Daddy's heavy overalls or the cotton bedsheets. I carried the clothes to the rinse water and dropped them in. I liked the scattering of soap bubbles in the water.

We had neighbors here, though none lived close to us, except a few houses down the dirt road on which we lived. We lived on the west shore of the pond, through a strip of woods near the paved road from Luma to Kingston. Near the turnoff for the dirt road that passed our house, a bridge carried traffic across a narrow neck of the pond, and on our side of the bridge the Jarman family ran the Little Store. The Jarmans had built and run the old mill when you could still grind corn up there, and Chalmis Jarman acted as the agent to form logging crews. The Jarmans owned a house back of the store, under a huge old weeping willow and behind high azaleas. I liked to walk to the Little Store with Nora. I liked the candy jars stocked with candy and the smell of salt meat hanging in the back. We bought beans out of a barrel or fatback sliced from the slab and wrapped in wax paper. When we had money, Miss Ruby never said anything, but when we had none we had to ask if we could charge. Sometimes yes, we could, and sometimes no, we couldn't.

I was young, but soon enough I could distinguish between the two states. I could feel the slight discomfort of asking for credit, even for the smallest sack of potatoes; I could feel the difference when Miss Ruby narrowed her eyes, set her mouth in a line and shook her head. "Send your mama down here," she said.

Nora, red from the neck up, nodded meekly, and we snuck out the door.

Mama never went to the Little Store herself except at times when we had money and she could pay down on the bill.

Across the road from the store stood a white wooden sanctuary belonging to the Church of God Congregation in Holiness. Sometimes, when we passed, I heard singing from inside.

My memories of those days are clearer, and hang together better than my memories of the house in Low Grounds. At times, as the memories pass through me, waves of water, I am astonished at how much I have kept.

The day my brother Madson was born, we children were sent to the neighbor's house. Nora and I waked out of a sound sleep, dressed ourselves, and walked along the dirt road to sit in the neighbor's kitchen. Otis and Carl Jr. came with us.

I remember the morning vividly. The neighbors, the McCarter family, included a sour, roundfaced daughter named Anna who glared at us across the kitchen table, shaking the bows in her braids. When Otis asked for water she showed him the dipper. The pump sat inside the kitchen, a fact I found close to miraculous; and with a sink and a drain right there, too. The pump was new and hardly needed priming. Anna watched Otis drink from the smooth tin dipper. I was gazing at the jars of canned vegetables that lined the shelves: butterbeans, tomato, and cucumber pickle. I had never seen so much food in one place. "Your mama is having a baby," Anna said to all of us.

"Hush," Nora commanded, pointing at me.

"But she is."

"We know that," Otis said, red rising from his collar.

"I mean she's having it right now. My mama went down there to help."

"You better hush your mouth, girl." Mr. McCarter's deep, booming voice entered from the other room and froze her. She shrank against the wall. She hardly said a word after her daddy spoke.

We sat in the kitchen for a long time. Then we asked if we could go outside, and Daddy McCarter, in his booming voice, answered that we needed to stay in the backyard.

Anna showed us the hog pen and the chicken house, riches I could scarcely fathom. In the vegetable garden hardly anything was still growing, but the rows lay neatly arranged and the bean poles still stood, with dry vine clinging to the poles. In the hog pen the mud had dried at the edges but the sow inside had found a wet patch in the shade for resting. As she slept, the fine edges of her snout trembled. I stared at her through the gap between the lower planks of the fence. I liked the texture of her skin and the droop of her ears. But people said a sow would eat a little girl like me, so I kept some room between me and the fence.

Carl Jr. had brought his cigarette papers and tin of tobacco and rolled a cigarette. Otis begged one for himself, and they smoked side by side, sitting behind the barn. By then it was late morning and we had hardly eaten anything. I could feel the familiar hollow place in my middle. I had learned that hunger followed its own curve, the pangs rising to a peak, then dulling for a while. I asked for a dipper of water, and Nora took me to the outside well.

We drank a lot of water. We each knew what we were doing, and why. The hunger dulled a little and my stomach stopped making noise.

When we went back, Anna had taken a place close to Carl Jr. They were watching each other with teasing expressions.

Crisp winds crossed the yard. Leaves were falling, faded green and yellow, from some of the trees. We stayed in the yard all day, till, late in the day, Mrs. McCarter returned and told us it was time for us to go back home. "You got you a new baby brother. Your mama is doing just fine." She spread her arms and planted her hands on her hips. Her ruddy face quivered with animation, a smile showing dark teeth. "Ain't that nice?"

"Yes, ma'am," Nora said, and took my hand, and hollered for Carl Jr. and Otis to come on. Otis ran from the barn. Carl Jr. followed more slowly, and Anna sauntered behind him.

Maybe I am adding to the real memory by looking backward at it from such a distance, but I have the picture of the neighbor woman glaring at Carl Jr., as if she knew he had been flirting with her daughter. I have the picture of Carl Jr. drifting past her, chewing a blade of dry grass. I cannot possibly remember so much. But my skepticism does not dim the picture.

At home, lying in bed, Mama cradled the new baby near her breast. Daddy had gone to the back porch with his mason jar of clear whiskey, and with a washed-out look of surprise on his face. The new baby could hardly be seen, its dark moist hair lying flat on its wrinkled head. No one was allowed to hold the baby except Mama, because Mama believed it would mistake anyone who held it, that first day, for its real mama. Likewise, the bedroom door must be kept closed to prevent the cats from getting close. Cats were well known to drink a baby's breath and kill it.

She named the baby Madson Polk Tote.

Mama lay white as the sheets on which she rested, with hardly enough strength to cradle the baby in her arms. Yet they were joined as if one body; it was a sight I will never forget. His mouth cupped her nipple, and the tip had grown long at the touch of his lips. The sight shocked me and filled me with small revulsion. I hated Madson from that moment, for lying with her like that, for putting his mouth on her nipple like that. Now he was the baby, and worst of all, a boy. He was already thriving.

Days passed. Mama's eyes grew sunken and dark as the baby hung at her tit. Because the baby came in autumn, she had the luxury of staying in bed while Nora and I ran the house. Madson lay with her, drank from her, and she held him with astonishing devotion. I had become invisible, except as a pair of hands to bring her diapers or something to eat.

But even more difficult to accept than his theft of Mama was his theft of Nora, who became caretaker for Madson as soon as Mama was strong enough to get out of bed. The baby slept in a low cradle, always near us wherever we were, and when Mama was not tending the thing, Nora was. Worse, Nora persisted in asking me whether I loved my little brother and then nodding her head as if answering for me, while giving me a vapid smile.

I hated him. I stared down into his cradle at his wrinkled face and sweaty hair. I filled with pure malice, with no thought but that I loathed him with all the force I could muster. I doubt I understood clearly what I was feeling, but the rage echoes down through all these years and I feel it now. I stood over his bubble of a chin and his pinched ears. I despised the blood clot in his belly button and the putrid smell of his diapers. Most of all I detested the sight of him nestled against Mama's breast, mouth working on her nipple. I became enraged, and the rage silenced me; I can hardly breathe, even now when I am only remembering. Maybe it was because his belly was full, and mine hardly ever was.

WHEN NORA CHANGED his thick cloth diaper, I watched. She lifted the heavy, damp cloth and folded the brown baby shit inside. She handed the diaper to me to take the stinking mess outside, and I carried it gingerly, as distant from my nose as my arms could reach.

But while Madson lay on the tabletop, legs kicking weakly, I saw the flap of meat between his legs. I stared at it, fascinated. The tiny thing jiggled and rolled as he kicked his legs. Nora washed his wrinkled bottom and spread powder there.

As I carried the diaper to the door, the impression of the place between his legs stayed with me. Nora had already told me what it was, his precious little wee wee, and because he had a wee wee, he was a boy. The boyness covered him like a special radiance that all could see; boys were shining things. Girls were dull, and they, like me, had only the flat slit between their legs that neither jiggled nor moved at all. When I asked Nora what to call what I had, she said it was my pussy, and Daddy, who was also in the kitchen, laughed. Outside, in the quiet, I dropped the baby turd from the edge of the porch into the white dirt. It plopped softly and flattened. I dumped the wet diaper in the bucket with another. I touched myself carefully between my own legs, the flatness and absence. I was a girl. No one looked at me as if there were any light covering me.

It was a thought that persisted. I was a girl, there was a difference. I had never thought much about this in conjunction with my older brothers, but now the baby made the distinction plain, and I saw it every day. Mama's love poured down on Madson like a waterfall, clear and sparkling. Daddy, too, displayed his pride in his new son, carrying him in the crook of a flannel-sleeved arm while he sipped his whiskey or puffed his cigarette. Daddy had never touched me that I could recall, to hold me, only to hurt me. For Mama, I had become a creature made to fetch and carry, not even particularly useful since I could not, as Nora could, take the baby from her and tend to its needs in her place. I sat quiet and hungry in corners, my thin dress tucked between my knees. The pale mass of Madson in his blanket accused me in some way I failed to understand.

Joe Robbie felt the difference too. When we were alone, during the day when the others were working or in school, I became his company and his help. I fed him biscuit when his arms were too weak to carry the food to his mouth. I fetched water, I sugared his coffee, I wiped the drool from the corner of his mouth. I propped the little doll where he could see it. He had forgotten the toy ever belonged to me, he kept it with him day and night. Whatever he saw when he studied the plastic body and glass eyes, I failed to understand.

"I don't want any more brothers and sisters," he said one day, when he had crept onto the porch and we sat with our legs dangling over the edge.

I agreed that babies were too much trouble. Inside, Madson wailed for food again, crying for Mama with his senseless voice that made no words.

"I hate how that baby hangs on her titty all day."

"You're supposed to love him," I said.

"Do you?"

"No."

"Me neither." He sighed and leaned against me. He was softer than the pillow on my bed. The unaccustomed tenderness carved the moment into my memory.

"I'm hungry."

"Me, too." I touched my belly, which would soon be rumbling.

"But I can't eat out of no titty like he can. I wished I was a baby."

Soon, though, Mama's belly grew again, and we learned that we would have another baby, another brother or sister, in the house.

LEARNING ABOUT THE MONSTER

FILLED WITH NEWS of war, the winter passed. For me, the radio and its stern, hard voices might have been describing a conflict happening up the road, and by the way Daddy and Carl Jr. talked, Europe, Japan, France, and Germany were more real than Moss Pond and the Little Store. I was growing, but I neither felt the growth nor understood the changes it would bring.

One day a monster appeared in the woods around Moss Pond, and the rumor drew visitors to the Little Store from as far away as Kingston and Goldsboro.

We learned the news from Mr. Chalmis Jarman, the owner of the Little Store, who came to the house to buy our sugar ration coupons. Mr. Jarman's bald head reflected the light from the kerosene lamp burning on the high shelf beside the door. He had come in early morning on an overcast day; he slouched near the doorway with one thumb hooked through a belt loop under the shadow of his swollen gut. He offered folding money that Daddy counted, and Daddy reared back in his chair beside the wood stove.

"You got any gas coupons?"

"Yeah. But I ain't selling them."

"You ain't got a car."

"I know what I ain't got."

"You're selling to Allison, ain't you."

"He pays a sight more than you do."

Mr. Jarman chewed his lower lip, displeased. "Well, I got the sugar anyway."

"I sell you my sugar and Allison my gas."

Mr. Jarman continued to chew his lip with a reflective tilt of the head. "They seen that monster again."

"Who?"

"Them niggers."

"Which ones?"

"Holberta niggers, back of the pond. Woman said she come up on it, gnawing the head off her dog. She run off. The woman."

"Oh, Lord," said Mama.

"What monster?" Joe Robbie asked, and we looked at each other.

"Hush, younguns." Daddy's voice cracked over our heads. He returned his attention to Mr. Jarman, who slouched against the door sill. Daddy said, "My sister Tula seen that monster one time."

"Did she?"

"Oh yeah. She was out dumping the slops and that thing come up on her back by this old shed we had. She said it didn't look like no natural man, it was all gray like."

"What did it do?"

"Well, the way she told it, she got her flat little ass out of there. She didn't give it time to do nothing. My daddy went back there with a gun, he didn't see nothing but some tracks. But I tell you what."

They seemed so little aware of each other, they might hardly be talking. But presently Mr. Jarman straightened. "That colored woman went back in the woods and drug out her dog. I seen what was left of it. Something eat the head right off it, I tell you what. I ain't never seen nothing like it."

"She brung the dog out?" Mama asked, leaning forward.

"That's right. Drug it near half a mile."

"Lord, I wouldn't have gone back in them woods for nothing. Not after I seen no monster."

"Is it going to get us?" Joe Robbie asked.

"Hush, younguns."

"Roe Yates and his boys is coming up to the store. We thought we would walk around looking for it. You and Carl Jr. might want to walk around with us."

Daddy spit snuff into the spit can. "I sure would love to catch that thing."

"I'd be satisfied to see it. I don't care if we catch it or not."

"You bringing a gun?"

"I ain't going after no monster with nothing but my pecker."

"Well, hell, I don't know if I want to be in the woods with you if you got a gun, you liable to shoot somebody."

They laughed, and Mama laughed, all the older brothers and sisters did the same. They were all around us laughing, and Joe Robbie and I were alone with the knowledge that there was a monster loose.

"Where is the monster?" Joe Robbie asked.

"Shut up, younguns." Mama heaved out of her chair and gestured to Mr. Jarman. "Would you like to sit down?"

He tilted his head and studied her quizzically. "I expect I better get back to the store, Ruby will skin me alive if I don't come on. You know the Japs is bombing us."

"That right?"

"That's right. On one of them islands. You ought to turn on the radio."

"Batteries is dead," growled Carl.

"Get you some at the store."

But he dragged his belly out the door before Carl could ask for credit. Mama hollered, "We sure appreciate the visit," and stood in the doorway to wave good-bye.

"Daddy, is it a real monster?"

"Shut the fuck up."

"You ought not to talk so ugly to that youngun." Mama spoke mildly, framed in the bright rectangle of the screen door. "He's scared."

Nora ran her hands through Joe Robbie's hair and gave him a big-eyed look. "If that monster was to get in here, you couldn't even run, could you, sweetheart?"

"Hush, Nora."

Nora smiled and ran her hands through Joe Robbie's hair some more. His head bobbed as he tried to watch her. I wiped the spittle from the corner of his mouth.

"It's not any monster," declared Otis, "that fat son of a bitch was lying."

"Aunt Tula seen it. That's what Daddy said." Nora leaned over the baby's cradle to pet its damp hair.

"Well that don't mean nothing, Aunt Tula is crazy."

Daddy snickered into his pouch of tobacco. He squatted in the light by the door, rolling a cigarette into a paper balanced on his knee.

"That colored woman seen it today."

"That colored woman is crazy too."

"Well, who eat off that dog's head then?"

"I don't know."

"Then you don't know everything, do you, smarty?" Nora and Carl Jr. were laughing.

"I know it ain't no real monster out there."

"Shut up, you little son of a bitch." Daddy licked the cigarette to seal the paper. "Carl Jr., get my shotgun."

"I'm coming too."

"I don't give a good goddamn what you do, get my shotgun like I told you."

When Carl Jr. rushed to Daddy's bedroom, where the shotgun rested under Daddy's side of the bed, Mama rose from her chair and shuffled toward the fire. "You can't leave me alone in this house with no monster out there."

Daddy regarded this sudden transformation of Mama. "Me and Carl Jr. is going off in the woods to hunt the thing."

"I know what you going off in the woods for, but I tell you what, you ain't leaving me alone with these younguns and a monster running around."

"There's no monster going to get you in the house."

"It might."

"You keep the doors locked and don't let nothing in while I'm gone."

"Willie, you can't leave me alone. I swear I mean it."

When Carl Jr. entered, carrying the shotgun and shells, Daddy took the gun. Mama began to cry and Daddy shrugged. The noises she made were inarticulate, and her sobs shook the loose flesh over her shoulders. Daddy stepped toward the door and she moved as if she wanted to block him.

His hand rose, sudden and sharp like a blade. The report echoed from the high ceiling and bare boards, first the slap and then Mama's cry. The hand rose again. Daddy stepped past Mama, who swayed.

Mama lunged toward the door, but Daddy's heavy tread had begun to fade; he descended the steps and crossed the yard.

"Don't you leave me here with these younguns." When she turned, tears were draining along her cheeks and sobs shook her. She sagged in her chair. "Nora, lock the door."

"Yes, ma'am."

We sat. Joe Robbie and I leaned against each other.

Mama pressed her palms flat on her belly and closed her eyes. "He shouldn't leave us like this. It ain't right."

"I know it ain't," Nora answered softly.

"I'm scared," whispered Otis.

"We're all scared."

"I can hear something," Joe Robbie whispered against my shoulder.

"Be quiet, Joe Robbie." Nora pulled her sweater sleeves over her hands.

"But I heard something."

"Shut up, Joe Robbie. You didn't hear nothing. You're just a sissy." Otis faced us fiercely, face flushed.

"You younguns hush, all of you." Mama rose slowly from the chair, taking baby Madson from the cradle, moving into the other room, scarcely lifting her feet.

In the dim kitchen we found ourselves suddenly alone.

Otis added a log to the fire and rubbed his hands. "I'm eating me one of these biscuits."

"There's not much left."

"I'm eating one, I don't care what's left."

"Mama will whip your ass."

"Mama ain't doing shit, scared as she is."

"You eat Mama's biscuit, she will whip your ass, and you know it."

From the back of the house Mama shouted, "You younguns hush that fuss right now. Don't, I'll come out there with a belt."

Nora tilted back her head and hollered, "Otis is about to eat the rest of the biscuits, Mama."

"Otis, you eat one mouthful, I'll get your daddy on you when he gets home." Silence, then, "You hear me?"

"Goddammit, Mama, I'm hungry."

"You'll be hungry and your ass will be wore out, both, if you touch one of them biscuits. Now let me lay down for a while and give me some peace."

The door closed to the bedroom. Joe Robbie whispered, "Mama."

From the window between the back door and the stove I could see the whole bare front yard. Wind seeped beneath the lower edge of the sash, past the rag that was stuffed into the crack. But along the road were marching black children and their mother, or at least children and some older woman, dressed as poorly as we, with bundles and bags in their hands. They were studying both sides of the road at the same time, vigilance fierce and visible. They passed quickly, and I guessed they were heading for the black Methodist church further up the road, to take sanctuary.

"Get away from that window before that monster gets you," warned Nora.

"I ain't scared."

"You better get scared. Before that thing reaches right in that window and snatches you."

"Come back here, sister," called Joe Robbie.

Whether or not I would have obeyed was to remain undecided, for suddenly Mama reappeared, wrapping a scarf around her head. "You younguns get your coats. Nora, dress Joe Robbie and put him in the wagon. We ain't sitting here by ourself, we're going down to that store and wait down there till they find that monster."

TO LEAVE THE house altogether, all of us, was unprecedented. We dressed hurriedly in coats. Nora and Otis lifted Joe Robbie into the wagon. Mama carried baby Madson against her breast. I wore the green coat that was given to Nora years ago by one of Daddy's sisters. Mama, flush with her bravery, set a brisk pace. Otis pulled the wagon, and Joe Robbie hung onto the sides with what strength he had. I walked behind, watching him shake and quiver with each bump in the road. I was left breathless to keep up, but I managed.

"You better keep a look out in them trees," said Joe Robbie, voice trembling with the vibration of the ride.

"Shut up, Joe Robbie, before I dump you in the ditch."

"You better not."

But we were all conscious of the woods on either side of the road. We crossed the path that led to the black Methodist church, and we heard the distant strains of voices. Mama rushed forward never daring to look from side to side, but along with her fear shone a gleam of exhilaration in her eyes. She had become illuminated, like the moment she stepped down from the riverbank into the water in the dream I had already begun to have. Mama rushed down the road, the baby Madson huddled in her arms and another baby asleep in her belly.

More people than us had decided to gather at the Little Store. The crowd swelled past the gas pumps to the edge of the road, and laughter drifted high over the glassy waters of the pond. Men in overalls and wool coats pointed their bottles of orange soda toward the clouds. When we approached the store, some of them watched us and some of them nodded to Mama, who ducked her head and nodded in return.

We bundled near Mama with the wagon and made our way through the crowd. Joe Robbie reached for my hand and stared at the ground. It was hard for me to walk so fast and let him keep my hand like that, but I tried.

Mama stepped into the store and Otis went with her. Nora stayed outside with me and Joe Robbie. Before the door closed, I could hear Mama at the store counter, "Hey, Miss Ruby, I'm obliged to you to pay down on my bill."

The store, the road, the pond, everything loomed larger and emptier with Mama out of sight. People were talking about the monster, which had been spotted again near the old mill. "I knew that monkster would come back. My daddy was one of the ones who seen it the last time. And didn't nobody believe him."

"My daddy always said that monkster lived around that old mill where the old man killed his wife. I wish the Jarmans would tear that contraption down."

The first man nodded and continued. "I always told Thelma, Thelma, I says, that monkster han't gone nowheres. It's right out yonder. A-creeping around in them woods. That's what I says. Ain't that right, Thelma?"

"Yup. That's what you said."

I was hanging onto Nora's skirt. Joe Robbie had a line of slobber draining onto the wagon from his mouth, and I held the cloth, paralyzed in all the noise and commotion. A truck parked next to the gas pump drew a crowd; men hung onto the sides, shifting their weight from hip to hip, swapping a paper bag with a bottle in it from hand to hand, drinking and hollering. Some of them held axes, shovels, or hoes, and one of them carried a shotgun like my daddy's. Women giggled and edged toward the men. Nora was looking around as if the clear space in front of the store had taken on a new scent. Joe Robbie made a sound like a puppy's whimper. His drool pooled in the wagon, and he hung his head. "Dry my mouth, Ellen," he said in his slurred voice, and I did.

Everybody was talking about the monster, snatches of voices hurtling through the air. They'd seen the monster near the Sumner Wells Baptist Church; two women coming to clean the church caught him creeping through the edge of the woods, right in broad daylight. They also saw the monster on Fork Road near the old depot, a teenage couple spotted him trotting across the meadow that runs along the air base fence. They got a good look at him, and described him as gray and shaggy-like, maybe with scales or maybe with heavy fur matted and greasy, but moving on two legs like a man. And big. The size of a bear, or bigger.

A woman at the edge of the crowd wore a blue dress the color of a clear sky, with a white belt and white shoes and white coat, and she had a white hat with a brim nested on her black hair, looking as if she had dressed for spring. She was beautiful like a bird, and I stared at her till finally she stared back, saw me with Joe Robbie and Nora, and frowned.

Sometimes others in the crowd watched us. An old woman with a gray bonnet on her head and one long yellow tooth hanging over her lip. A young man with a flannel shirt beneath his overalls. A girl in a heavy coat. We were standing apart from everyone else, and I was conscious of a new feeling. There was something about the people watching us I did not like.

Mama and Otis came back with chocolate drinks and packs of crackers and we sat down in the dirt and drank the drinks. Joe Robbie was happy and smeared wet cracker over his lips and cheeks. I got a whole drink for myself, and two crackers out of Joe Robbie's pack. The ground chilled my legs and I stood again.

"How do, Miss Tate," said Mama to a woman with a swarm of warts on her nose and cheeks.

"Hey, Louise. I see your younguns is all drinking chocolate drinks."

Mama grinned as if this were a great compliment.

"How is everybody?" Miss Tate asked, licking her lips.

"We're fine," Mama said, "but it sure is cold."

"It sure is. Where is Willem?"

"Out yonder with them men hunting that monster," Mama spoke breathlessly. "He took our gun and Carl Jr. went with him. And I come down here with the younguns because I was scared to stay at that house by myself."

"I can't believe Willem left you there."

Mama ducked her head, almost shy. "He's a hard one, all right. I told him I was scared but he blowed right out the door."

A moment of pained silence passed as Mama sipped her drink.

"Did you know Villa Ray Hawkins saw that monkster yesterday at her house? But she says she didn't tell anybody till today."

"No, I didn't know that." Mama wiped her mouth on the back of her hand. "Villa Ray will tell a lie in a minute."

"I know that's a fact."

"She stole five dollars from Willem one time. Right out of his pocket. I tell you what."

"Well, she said she seen that monkster before that colored woman did. She said hit snuck right up to her back porch, and was a-peeping at her over the washpot."

"Lord God, I would have died."

"And she said she rushed back into the house and the oldest boy got his daddy's shotgun and the thing was trying to get up on the porch, but he run it off shooting the shotgun, and that's when they knew it was the monkster." Saying so much set all Miss Tate's warts to wobbling at once. Her skin had fine, soft crinkles, some lined with pink talcum powder.

"She come down here and told Mrs. Jarman about it this morning."

Mama squatted with the baby beside Joe Robbie's wagon. She balanced her weight on her heels, as if in a cotton field she was about to start picking. I wished she would stand up. She cradled the baby against her. Madson reached toward her with small hands. "Villa Ray has always seen something ain't nobody else seen. And she steals. She took five dollars from Willem." Mama nodded, as if Miss Tate has challenged her, and was about to launch into the story, when a truck roared off the road and men jumped from the back shouting that they had just seen the monster around the north end of the pond.

Everybody pressed around the truck to hear the story, including Mama and Miss Tate. Nora edged toward the crowd with Otis. I sat on the edge of the wagon. The men swaggered off the truck, looping their thumbs in their overalls, grinning at the women. Many voices were telling the story at once, and the noise rose like a white wall.

Suddenly I heard Daddy's voice, and everything got quiet around it. Daddy roared something, and Mama came stumbling out of the crowd with Daddy kicking her backside. Mama stumbled toward the road and Daddy followed her, each kick heaving her forward. "Get your goddamn fat ass to the house," he shouted, "get these goddamn filthy younguns to the house," and Nora was running toward the wagon and I jumped up. The chocolate drink splattered on my coat.

Everyone near the store had got quiet. They watched Daddy chase Mama down the road, and Nora dragged the wagon along the edge of the ditch toward our house. They watched me run, with the chocolate drink bottle swinging by my legs, my coat and skirt flapping high. I heard some of them laughing. The sound echoed for a long time.

WE HURRIED TO the house. Daddy chased Mama all the way there.

"I didn't want to sit here with these younguns," Mama wailed, as Daddy whipped his leather belt against her legs. She was climbing the porch, hugging Madson to her, shuddering, while the leather strap cut red welts into her shins. "I was scared."

We watched from the edge of the yard. We were afraid to go closer.

"Get in the goddamn house." Daddy lashed the belt back and forth. Mama had almost climbed to the porch, and now the belt landed on her dress. She sheltered Madson against her, or else used him as a shield for her face. She opened the screen and slid through the door. Daddy followed, still roaring.

We hurried to the edge of the porch. We could hear him beating her inside. She cried far louder than when we had to go to the neighbors for Madson to be born. Otis stood close to Nora, who hung her head. Joe Robbie whispered for me to wipe his mouth again, and I stayed near.

After a few minutes Mama's yelling stopped, but suddenly Madson was screaming, and then Daddy rushed through the door and hurtled to the bottom of the steps. He glared at us, pointing his long thin finger. "Get your asses in that house and stay there. Now."

He stood there while Nora and Otis hauled Joe Robbie up the steps. I sneaked in front of them, afraid to be last.

Inside, Mama sobbed at the sink. Madson lay flat beside the washbasin, his forehead bloody, his cries piercing the house. "Your daddy hit him with the belt," she told Nora. "He hit him. Poor little thing."

She sobbed and wiped her forehead. Blood drained around her grimy ankles from the lashes on her legs.

Otis built up the fire. Nora washed Mama's legs. Madson calmed and slept. The belt had struck across his tender forehead, a tiny line of red. Dark, drying blood glistened.

YEARS LATER I went back to the Jarman's store in the '62 Impala I bought with my own money, earned by working in the elementary school cafeteria. My own children were with me, clean and neatly dressed, and I wore my hair freshly done from the beauty parlor. My dress was sky blue, with a wide white belt, and I wore white shoes, but instead of the white hat, I wore a white rayon scarf tied around my hair. I carried my purse into the store. The reflection of myself in that store window took me back, suddenly, to that day when the monster was loose and Mama walked us to the store for chocolate drinks. I could almost smell the same hint of clean dirt and rain.

Inside, Miss Ruby smiled at me politely though she never recognized me, that time. I bought drinks for all my children, and cold hot dogs, and a loaf of white bread, for the journey. She eyed me over like she might know me, she put on her glasses to work the new cash register and then eyed me over again. She was stooped herself, her skin gone all to pin wrinkles. She handed me my change. For a moment I wanted to tell her who I was. I'm Ellen Tote, I wanted to say. In a clean dress with a scarf on my hair. But I never said a word. She bagged my merchandise. I paid deposit for the drink bottles, which I hated to do, and drove away.

ALMA LAURA

ALMA LAURA WAS born in the house near Moss Pond, months later when the memory of the monster had faded. Mama swelled and sat as before, chewing biscuit through the long day. At the end of Mama's time, Nora left school to take care of her.

Alma Laura emerged from my mother's shrieks into the midwife's hands in midspring. Miss Rilla, the midwife, called us into the house near midafternoon, telling us we had a new baby girl this time. We saw our new sister in Mama's bedroom lying in the cradle. Blankets swathed her pink china face. My heart ached from the first moment I saw her, and she filled an emptiness in me, as if I had been expecting her. As if she were returning from a long journey. She was my baby sister, my own true love, and she erased the hard memory of Madson's coming. When Mama allowed her to suck on a tit, I felt the warmth all through me.

Even that very first day of her life, I sat by the cradle and watched her sleep till the shadows were long and dark. I sat so long and quiet I scared Mama and she screamed for Nora to take me away. I kissed Alma Laura's burning red forehead and hardly felt Nora's fingernails digging into my arm.

She was sick from the beginning. I could rarely stop thinking about her, I dreamed her at night. In the dream I remember her breath was like fire, and when I lay near her I inhaled the heat into myself, as dry as she. Someone moved the cradle to the fireplace and we slept there, she in the cradle and me kneeling beside her. The house was more silent than it had ever been, we were alone. The wind scoured the house, and I tucked the thin blankets around her. We were out of wood. I hollered for more. But the fire burned faster and I could find nothing to keep it going, and the cold soaked through the floorboards, my socks hardly helped at all and I could not find my shoes.

From dreams like this, I wakened into the cool of a spring morning, the wee hours before dawn, with the baby crying and Mama crying as Daddy cursed them both.

Mama moved to a pallet in front of the fireplace with the cradle beside her. Uncle Cope snored in the kitchen on his big bed. Daddy got his rest.

EVERY POSSIBLE WAKING minute I spent with the baby. I held the pins while Nora changed the diapers. I was strong enough to push the pins through the diaper when Nora held the diaper for me, except once I stuck her thumb with the pin and she slapped me sharp across the face. It hurt and I cried, but I really did not blame her, and she trusted me enough to let me try again. We changed the diapers neatly. I stroked Alma Laura's wrinkled forehead while she kicked her legs.

Sometimes I sat on the floor or on a stool and cradled her burning body against mine. She was hot as a coal, her face scarlet, her dark hair curled, plastered to her tiny face. I had no images, no fantasies that she was my child, that we were together anywhere but in our kitchen. I simply held her and felt her life. A raging love coursed through me.

"A shitass girl," Daddy said, "and this one too puny to live."

"She's fine, Willie. She's gained some weight. Nora and me both think so."

"Puny," spat Daddy, "a runt. Look at her."

"She sucks at me till I'm sore," Mama rubbed her elbow over her blouse, "she'll get bigger."

"You should have had a boy like I wanted."

"You got plenty of boys."

Daddy sucked snot and ended the conversation. He looked down at the baby in my lap, watching both of us with equal detachment. Carl Jr. said, "Her face is bright red, like Aunt Tula. Ain't it?"

"Tula do look like that, don't she?" Daddy grinned. His teeth were dark-edged. "We should have named her Tula."

SHE BURNED. I held her and she burned. I was hopelessly in love with this baby, I held her but she scorched me everywhere I touched her, her tiny mouth and hands, her damp cheeks. Mama held her to suck, Nora and I held her, she slept. Hardly more sound than a whimper, now and then.

I sat by her cradle. During the day the strong sun that fell through the front windows surrounded her in a haze of gold. She tossed her head back and forth in sleep. Mama hardly disturbed her, and Alma Laura ate less and less. Mama stared down at her, blinking and distracted. I held my breath. Mama's shadow passed away.

"We need a doctor," but Mama's voice was flat. "We need a doctor for that baby."

"If you're asking me for money for a doctor, I ain't got nothing to pay one with," Uncle Cope declared. We were sitting in the kitchen. Uncle Cope gouged a biscuit with his thumb, pouring syrup inside. "I ain't got nothing till the first of the month when I get my disability."

"That baby needs a doctor. That's all I know." Mama walked aimlessly back and forth, peering over the edge of the cradle.

Early in the morning we woke to Mama's wailing that the baby was cold, the baby was all cold, and I ran out there to see for myself. Alma Laura lay still and quiet, a small gray shadow in the light from the kerosene lamp, a gray lump of something twisted on itself, and I dropped my hands and refused to touch her, though I could not stop looking.

When she died, there was a lot of fuss, people running around. The deputy sheriff came to look at the body and make some papers. Then the man from the funeral home took away Alma Laura in a car.

She lived three months, three days.

We buried her deep in the ground. Daddy's family bought a small pine box and we took her to the same place where the baby boy was buried, the municipal cemetery in Kingston where Daddy's family owned space. I rode in the truck with Aunt Tula and Uncle Bray. At the graveyard was a big tent with chairs under it, beautiful folding chairs of deeply polished wood, and we sat on them in front of the box where Alma Laura would sleep. We buried the lump of her in the box, somewhere in that dark hole beneath. Men were preparing to lower Alma Laura into the ground as we walked away. Daddy and Carl Jr. carried Mama away from the grave, each taking her by one arm, as she moaned and hung her head.

At night, when I woke, Alma Laura floated beside me in the air. I was neither afraid of her lightness nor in doubt of her presence. I lay on my side and studied how she hung there, how light. I never tried to touch her, I had no need to do so. It was enough that she returned, that she floated in such a peaceful way.

I passed a birthday. Nora reminded me of the day when it came; no one said anything before. At supper, Mama patted me on the head and served me a syrup biscuit.

"I saw Alma Laura last night," I said.

"You what?"

"I saw Alma Laura. She came to my bedroom."

Mama's eyes focused to sharp points, and the fury of her hand crashed against my head. She grabbed me by the hair, slapped me across the face until I was dizzy and my nose ached, then threw me across the room like a sack of sugar. I landed with a bump against the sink, and froze there.

Mama blew out breath like a bellows. "You ain't seen a thing." The fierceness of her eyes withered me, and I shivered. "Say it again. Say it." She waited for a moment, and I shook my head to signify I would say nothing.

They left me alone and ate dinner. Because Daddy had not come home yet, the beating was not worse. When he came home, late, Mama served him pinto beans and biscuit, speaking in a sullen voice about Joe Robbie's doctor appointment.

I hid beyond the doorway till I was sure Mama would not tell. Then I withdrew to the bedroom and sat on the bed by the window.

AT NIGHT ALMA Laura continued to appear at my bedside, happy and gurgling, toes curling in the air. I told no one. I was old enough to have a secret now, and it made me more conscious of myself.

That she came to me made me feel special. I understood that she knew I always loved her best, better even than Mama who offered her tit.

That I had become more conscious of myself deepened everything, through every moment of the day. Everything I saw became clearer, and the days began to make a river of themselves, running under everything else. In my mind was a chain of memories, and I began to accumulate a past. I began to think, this week we have more food than last week. I began to think, I wonder if next winter we will be as cold as we were last winter.

Alma Laura grew, and I watched her progress when she was with me, and I never wondered how she could be here if she were really dead. I grew. I opened my eyes wide and studied my home. No one had to tell me, this time, when Mama became pregnant again.

THESE DAYS, WHEN I remember Alma Laura, I remember her the way she was when she finally stopped visiting me years later, after I had eloped with Bobjay. I was pregnant with my first child. She had been with me my whole life till then, always silent, sitting quietly beside me, as if her presence in my sight contented her. She grew as I grew, a little behind me. Sometimes, when she was not with me, I would see her walking in the distance, usually at the edge of woods or in some empty building near whatever house we lived in. She moved from house to house when we did, not like the ghost of the baby boy, who never found us again after we moved away from the Low Grounds. When I met Bobjay, at a fair in Onslow County, Alma Laura was silently walking beside me, faded in the yellow light of the midway. When I eloped, she watched from the edge of the yard as Bobjay carried me away. In my new house near Rocky Mount, she followed me from room to room. She shared early mornings, late afternoons, times when she could find me alone. Her presence was so familiar, by the last day I saw her, I hardly noticed her at all. I was pregnant, so swollen I could hardly move. Alma Laura sat with me in that little kitchen. She wore the same peach dress I was wearing, much thinner than me, and she smoothed down the skirt once. Then she walked to the door. She turned to me and smiled, and I knew she was leaving. The thought came very clearly in my head. She slid out the door and walked off through the yard into the woods. She stood at the edge of the woods for a while; I suppose she was looking back at me. She vanished into the woods and never came out. I never saw her again.

UNCLE COPE

UNCLE COPE LIVED with us, off and on, for as far back as I can remember, whenever the rest of his family had enough of him. Uncle Cope liked his liquor and, even on crutches, ran around with the Saturday night crowd of good old boys who hung around the pond. My daddy was famous among his kin for putting up with almost anything, and he appreciated Cope's mean streak, which was the reason Cope always left the metal frame bed he owned in our kitchen, no matter where he might be living himself for any given week of meals.

He had been crippled for as long as I could remember, from falling off the back of a truck and crushing one of his legs to splinters, a time when he was drinking moonshine with Roe Yates and his crowd, a story Uncle Cope loved to tell. "I like to scraped half my back off, sliding down that road," he would say, and then threaten to show the scars that covered his back. "If I hadn't been drunk, I'd have died. But I passed out before the shock could kill me."

Uncle Cope retained one remaining visible tooth on the

upper part of his mouth, at the front, hooked and long. He'd kept a few more of his lower teeth and several of his upper back teeth too. Like Daddy and Mama, he dipped snuff, Tube Rose or Black Mariah, which lent an orange cast to his teeth and tongue. Daddy chewed tobacco but Uncle Cope's teeth ached too much for that. He watched with envy whenever Daddy spat the dark tobacco juice.

We woke one Sunday morning to find the deputy sheriff in the kitchen doorway talking to Mama. It was early fall with the weather neither hot nor cold. Mama's thin nightgown hardly hid her large breasts but she had partly wrapped a blanket around herself, and faced him with her hair loose on her shoulders. I watched from the hall. To me she seemed suddenly very beautiful and young, standing in the shadow of the tall, broad man. The deputy took off his hat. His pistol hung from his hip. His pants were tight and his thighs were a funny shape, thin at the knee but fat at the hip.

He asked Mama a question. "I ain't seen Willie since last night," Mama answered, "and if Cope ain't here, I reckon he's with Willie."

"You sure you telling the truth? They ain't neither one of them in this house."

"I'll swear on the Bible if you get one."

"So if I was to come in that house, I ain't going to find Willie Carl laying up in that bed?"

"Lord, I wished he was. What you looking him for?"

"I ain't looking for Willie, I'm looking for Cope."

"What for?"

"I can't tell you."

"Why not?"

"Because I can't. Now look. If they ain't here, I got to go."

"Well, you better go on then. And you tell Willie to get back here when you see him."

"Yes, ma'am, Miss Louise."

I crept to the corner of the kitchen, quiet like an egg. Alma Laura was with me. She had begun to appear during the day now, mostly near me but sometimes not, mostly in corners or shadows but sometimes not. Madson tugged Mama's skirt and she lifted him to wave good-bye to the deputy, who made a lot of noise going down the steps. His handcuffs rattled, his keys jingled, and his holster flapped at his pocket. He was driving a black-and-white car with a light on the top, and he peeled out of the driveway in a cloud of dust. I was disappointed he never turned on the light.

As soon as his car was gone, Nora got busy in the kitchen, and she kept me busy with her.

Mama stalked back and forth across the kitchen, muttering. I had seen this look on her face before, when she threw me across the kitchen over mentioning Alma Laura, and other times, when she lost a child or had a fight with Daddy. "Wake me up so early in the morning," she spoke in a chain of words, low enough that I could hardly hear, "when I ain't been able to sleep for wondering where you are, you might be dead, and here comes the deputy sheriff, a-knocking on the door, and me so goddamn tired. I ain't been able to sleep. For all I know you laying in a ditch somewhere, you been out all night. Me and these goddamn stinking younguns with hardly a mouthful of food. You making biscuits, Nora?"

"Yes, ma'am." Nora scraped the dough carefully down each of her fingers.

"I'm helping," I said, "I'm putting the biscuits in the pan."

"Hush," Nora said, with a careful eye on Mama. "You should work, not talk."

"Make sure you rub aplenty lard on the bottom of that pan or else them biscuits will stick." Mama sighed, pushing hair back. A cloud of gentleness enshrouded her features for the moment. She lifted Madson, kissed his cheek. "My angel boy. Ain't you my angel boy?"

Madson gurgled and laughed. He planted his fat hands on her cheeks and leaned toward her. Now that he could take steps on those fat little legs of his, I hated him all the more.

WHEN DADDY CAME home, Mama met him at the screen door. "Deputy Floyd was here, looking for Cope."

"Shit," Daddy says, stomping through the door, "shit, shit, shit, shit, shit. When was he here?"

"Early this morning. He woke me up."

Daddy sat in the kitchen chair. "Make me a goddamn cup of coffee."

The fog of his anger settled over the kitchen. Moving without a sound, I withdrew into the other room, in the shadows. Alma Laura sat with me. We kept perfectly silent.

"Where were you all night?"

"Out. Don't ask me too many goddamn questions."

"Where is Cope?"

"How the fuck am I supposed to know where Cope is?"

"He's your brother."

"That don't mean a goddamn thing."

"Willie, what happened?"

"Louise, if you don't shut your goddamn mouth, I'm going to knock the shit out of you."

"Hush, Mama," Nora whispered.

"Deputy Floyd is coming back. You mark my words."

"Goddammit woman, you better leave me in peace, and I mean this minute. Get your fat ass in that other room before I slap the teeth out of your mouth."

"Go on, Mama," Nora whispered, the note of urgency increasing.

Mama shuffled into sight. I hid in the corner. Mama paced up and down. Daddy said, "Where the fuck is my coffee, girl?"

"I'm making it, Daddy. It has to make."

Silence. Followed by the sound of his spit dropping into the spit can.

"Is it any biscuit fit to eat? Or is it just them goddamn horse biscuits your mama makes?"

"There's some warm biscuit up here that I made. You want a piece?"

"Yes. To sop."

Nora brought the coffee and the biscuit. Daddy sopped the biscuit in the sweet coffee. I did not have to watch him to see him, I was learning to see him without my eyes. Alma Laura watched me. Mama watched me. I held myself completely still.

"The good Lord above help me," Mama said.

"You better shut your mouth."

"Hush, Mama," Nora said, or at least I heard it in my head. I was not sure whether Nora actually said anything with her voice. She had found herself a corner by now.

Silence. Mama rocked on her heels in front of the fireplace.

"Did you do something?" Mama asked.

"No. I done told you I did not do anything. Cope broke into a little grocery store near Smithfield. They seen him. You know Cope can't run worth a shit on them crutches."

"Was you with him?"

"No. Shut the shit up."

Silence. I edged away from Mama, toward the door that led to the bedrooms.

"Where are you going?" Mama hissed at me. "You keep your little ass right where you are."

It was as if she saw something ahead of us all. I held still again. As soon as I did, she forgot me. She paced again, hands on her belly. "Is they looking for you too? Is they?"

"Naw."

"Cripple goddamn son of a bitch," she hissed, "I hate that goddamn goose-legged bastard. He needs to take his ass to your daddy's."

"You shut up about my brother."

"Cripple bastard. Cripple son of a bitch. Walks on them crutches like some crawly bug. Sleeps in my kitchen like a white worm. I hate him."

"You better shut up, I said."

The raising of his voice brought quiet. Mama paced. She glared at me. "What are you looking at me for, you little strumpet?"

I studied the floor but listened for where she was. I could feel that she was watching me, I could hear her breathe. I slid along the wall toward the door but at once she said, "I told you to keep your ass right against that wall, and you better do like I say."

"Is that Ellen?" Nora called.

"Tend to your business," Mama said.

"Cope ain't bothering a goddamn soul," Daddy spat.

"The younguns is scared of him."

"They is not."

"They is. Nora is scared to get up in the morning, for fear he'll bother her. Ain't you? Them crutches scares her."

"He can't walk without them crutches," Daddy said.

"They still scares people. I don't want him in my house no more."

"This is my goddamn house."

"He ain't got no business scaring my younguns around here. And now the sheriff is after him. And you can't do nothing but sit there and take his side."

"I ain't taking nobody's side. You don't make a goddamn lick of sense."

"I make plenty of goddamn sense. I don't want that cripple bastard sleeping in my kitchen." She loomed over me now; I could bring myself to watch her face for only a moment. "I hate him. He ain't got the sense God gave a rat. And now the sheriff is looking for him."

"Louise. I have told you, you better shut your mouth, right now."

"Was you with him?"

He pushed back his chair, and stood. His footsteps echoed.

His silhouette in the doorway was taut like a wire. "Do you want me to take my goddamn belt off again? Or do you want me to get the buggy whip this time?"

I could feel the fierce heat of her glaring on the top of my head.

"You better answer me."

"I ain't going to say nothing else."

"Are you goddammit sure?"

She took short, sharp breaths, silent, except that her whole body heaved. "Yes."

"You better be. Because I don't want to hear another word."

As his footsteps receded, she made a sharp cry and turned to me with eyes like needles. She pinned me against the wall and kicked me, and her hands struck my face from both sides. I gasped and fought for breath. She slammed my head back against the plaster wall. Sharp pains succeeded one another like forks of lightning. I heard footsteps from somewhere but I was dazed. "I told you to set still." She kicked me again but not so hard.

"Leave her alone, Mama," Nora pleaded, I could not see where she was, "she didn't do nothing," and this distracted Mama long enough. I slid past her faded skirt and ran for the door.

I hid under the house, behind one of the outer pillars. Daddy kept dogs chained up further under, I could see their shadows moving. They were restless, thinking maybe I was bringing them biscuit crusts and fatback rind like Carl Jr. did. If Alma Laura had not been with me I might have been afraid of them, but she sat beyond the post, silent as always, a comforting shadow. The dog chains softly murmured. I kept between the dogs and the brick underpinning. I stayed in sight of Alma Laura. Upstairs, voices flowed and ebbed.

There was sunlight and heat in the yard, but where I waited I hardly felt those things.

SOON MANY MEN arrived at the house, including Uncle Cope, with blood in his hair. From under the house, where I remained, I studied the green truck, the blue car, in which the men raised clouds of dust on the road and in our yard. Uncle Cope struggled out of the back seat of the car, his loose leg dangling, him hopping on his good foot till he could get the crutches under his arms.

The dogs came alert and set to barking, straining at the chains. Upstairs Daddy's unmistakable footsteps crossed the porch. Voices greeted him and he shouted, "You sons of bitches is in trouble, the deputy's already been here."

Uncle Cope thwacked one crutch across the back of a cat that crossed the yard in front of him. I could see Cope's shoulders but not his head; he had come close to the porch now.

He lowered his voice. "You ran, you shit ass. Ain't nobody seen you, did they?"

"You know damn well I ran."

Uncle Cope hovered on the crutches. The limp foot dangled. "And now my ass is going to jail and you're going to sit right here."

"I can't help it, Cope."

"You son of a bitch."

"I ain't going in no jail just to please your ass."

Then, other footsteps from the house.

Mama's voice rose suddenly. "Is that Cope? You goddamn cripple son of a bitch."

"Louise, you better shut your mouth."

"Don't tell me what to do, you one-leg shit-ass. I wished you was dead. I wished the sheriff would shoot you when he catches you."

Uncle Cope swung round on the crutches.

"I hope they keep your cripple ass in jail till you rot." She must have been leaning forward, I could see her shadow. "I wished the deputy would find you right now. I wished he would drive up right now."

Uncle Cope and the others slid into the car. Other men were climbing onto the back of the truck. A line of dust rose as they fled along the road.

I CRAWLED OUT from under the house when things above were quiet. My belly was empty and groaning. Creeping up the steps, I entered through the door that led to the narrow hall.

From the bedrooms I heard no sound. Daddy sprawled across the bed, big boots pointed toward the ceiling, mouth slack, and eyes closed. The other room was empty.

In the kitchen Nora and Otis were sopping biscuit. Madson and Joe Robbie slept on a blanket by the stove. I rubbed my eyes and tiptoed to Nora. "You can have a biscuit too," she whispered.

Mama stood on the back porch. She had shoved her fists against the fabric of her skirt, the dress taut along her back. Soft hairs had come loose at the back of her neck, where the flesh was tender and smooth.

"Did she hurt you?"

I shook my head. I ate the biscuit to ease the pain in my belly.

"I'm keeping an eye on Mama, I think she's about to run off somewhere. Like the time she took us to the river."

I must have remembered. I guess I did, but I dreamed about the river too, her sliding down into it, and I could not always tell the difference between the dream and any memory there might have been. When Mama moved off the porch, Nora and I followed.

Mama muttered as she descended from the porch and crossed the yard. She headed into the woods behind the house.

She walked far enough to stand out of sight of the house, and we stopped short of her. She stood in a patch of sun falling down from on high, a dappling of her arms and of the dress she wore. Her hands rose up. It was as if they were separate things and they were rising away from her. She never made a sound.

Mama rises out of the river gasping, throwing water from her hair. Her breath rises up in trails of steam. The surprise of seeing her move so freely still echoes in me now. Her large, flat breasts lift, the yellowed bodice of the slip clinging to the high flesh. She says something, I can't remember what it is, something about the cold. But she addresses someone above my head, not me. Someone else is here, I can't remember who.

I was seeing this again in my vision as Nora and I shivered in the cold shadow of a tree. Mama stood in light, but it was as if she were drowning again, throwing up her arms as she sank into the golden sun.

She steps ashore. She is standing over me, shivering and dripping, and I can see the outline of her heavy belly, her rolling thighs. I am so in love with her, every part of me aches. She scoops me up, and her arms are strong but soft; I burrow into them. I weigh less than the wet slip.

But this time she does not set me onto the riverbank, gently, as before. She glares at me coldly, as if I am some fish she has dragged off the end of her line, and she takes me by the shoulder and flings me high, end over end, into the middle of the river, and I sink into the cold, and I am falling forever, and I never look down.

Mama made no sound in the sunny woods. Her hands sank slowly to cradle her belly. After a while she headed back to the house. When she passed Nora and me, hidden behind a tree trunk, she had no expression at all on her face.

DEPUTY FLOYD TALKED to Daddy for a long time, on the front porch, and Mama waited in the kitchen. She had paled and hardly moved. We waited in the kitchen with her. Daddy closed the door when he went outside and now spoke in hushed tones; we could hear his voice but not his words.

"He's going to jail," Mama said, and twisted her hands in her skirt.

But the sound of the voices remained cordial and clear. I retreated to the corner, out of sight. Joe Robbie sat with Alma Laura and me. I felt safe.

"I won't have anybody," Mama whispered.

"How are we going to eat?" Otis asked.

No answer followed. Mama touched the doorknob once, but Nora said not to open it. After a while Deputy Floyd drove away and Daddy came back inside. He fixed his eyes on

Mama, and they glittered. "Haden says they picked up Cope in Luma. Got him in the jail. He's headed there now to bring him back to Kingston. He says they ain't going to mess with me, so you can wipe that look off your face."

"Cripple bastard," Mama said, and a tear streaked her cheek.

He looked at her and blinked. They were looking each other eye to eye. For once they did not say anything.

WE VISITED UNCLE Cope in Johnston County prison. Mama refused to go. She was getting big with the new baby and swore it would be a hex to be in a prison.

I had gotten the prison confused with the war, somehow. I was certain that all the people I saw there were soldiers, that this was the army, these strangely dressed people behind the cage-shaped windows where we talked. Daddy sat with Cope and asked him what it was like in prison, and I wondered if Uncle Cope would go to the war with the rest. Daddy and Cope talked about the Japs, as they often did; but I was nervous because I feared the Japs might lurk somewhere very nearby.

Uncle Cope said the food was good and the people were nice. He was talking to his own daddy, my grandaddy Tote, and to my daddy, and to their sister Tula. They stood closest to the window and the rest of us were bunched behind, and because I was little, I could only glimpse a patch of the bald of Uncle Cope's scalp. But I could hear his voice, sometimes. "They treat us real good. They got us making things. I can read books if I want to, but I don't want to. I think I'm going to learn how to make license plates. You can pass the time right well. You-all don't worry about me."

I searched for the faces of the enemy, the slant eyes, the yellow skin, of which I had heard so much on the radio. But the sad faces in the room were all the same color as mine, some browner, some more freckled. When the time was up someone lifted the little ones to kiss Uncle Cope's cheek. I was barely old enough and large enough to escape brushing my lips against his pale cheek. I could almost taste the clammy skin.

WE RODE HOME in Uncle Bray's truck. Aunt Tula and Grandaddy Tote sat in the front, and Daddy declared he was stuck in the back with the rest of the niggers, and laughed at his own joke. I sat between his legs because he made me sit there, and dug his fingers into the space between my ribs. Nora stared at him and me. I felt a strange sickness in the pit of my stomach with him so close. The speed of the truck made a wind that whipped my hair across my eyes, but I sat perfectly still and never made a sound.

We ate at Grandaddy's house near Smithfield. Grandaddy lived with his oldest son Erbert, who hated Uncle Cope as much as Mama did and also refused to visit him in jail. Grandaddy's house was even dirtier than ours, and plainer, with chickens wandering in and out and dropping turds on the floors. But the kitchen overflowed with things to eat, everything from ham for the biscuit to canned vegetables from the summer garden. Nora drank bowl after bowl of clabbered milk and stuffed her face with cornbread. I ate my souse meat and biscuit with the same relish. Nothing had ever tasted so good.

Before we left, with Uncle Bray yawning and Aunt Tula

complaining about prison, Uncle Erbert slipped something into Daddy's hand. It was a paperback book, and I glimpsed a woman with naked titties on the cover before Daddy slid the smooth rectangle into his pocket. He caught me watching. His eyes sparkled.

"All right Willem," Aunt Tula said, "Get them younguns of yours in the truck and let's get headed home."

SOMETHING HAPPENED TO Uncle Cope while he stayed in prison. One morning Miss Ruby summoned Daddy to the Little Store to answer a phone call, and when he came back he told us the story. Grandaddy Tote had called him. Uncle Cope was cut up by a Mexican man, and he nearbout bled to death, according to Daddy, right in the prison yard. First the Mexican cornholed him, and then he cut him with a homemade knife. "He couldn't run, because he's crippled."

"Did they hurt him bad?" Mama asked.

"What does it sound like, Louise? Jesus. They cut him across the stomach. Nearbout spilled his guts out. You can kill a man like that."

"What is a cornhole?" Joe Robbie asked.

"It's when a man does it to another man in the ass," Otis explained.

We were in awe, Joe Robbie and I, and we watched one another.

"You younguns shut up asking them nasty questions," Mama ordered.

But Nora and Otis giggled, and Mama and Daddy hid smiles.

"I'd ruther die," Daddy said.

"But I'm sorry he got cut," Mama said, still snickering.

UNCLE COPE RETURNED to live with us when he had served his time. By then his stomach had healed up and his guts were back in place. I tried to see his behind where the cornhole was, because the word had stayed on my mind ever since I heard it, but nothing showed through his britches.

We had been told to keep our mouths shut about what we heard, but the very first night Otis got mad about Uncle Cope taking the bed in the kitchen again, and he called Uncle Cope a gimp-legged cornhole shit-ass. The whole story was out after that, and Uncle Cope, redfaced, screamed at all of us and waved his crutches till he collapsed on the bed. Because the bed was in the kitchen we could hardly leave him alone, so we blinked as he lay there in a spasm of fury. Otis laughed and Uncle Cope hurled a crutch at him.

Later we would tell the story this way: Mama laughed so hard she went into labor and had Corrine almost on the spot. The truth was close to that; Mama's labor did come on her during the laughter and at once the pains became clear and intense. She told us to find the colored midwife in Holberta and Otis headed toward the community of black people on an old, half-repaired bicycle he used to get back and forth from the Little Store. We still owed the white midwife for Alma Laura.

Uncle Cope's humiliation lay forgotten in the confusion of Corrine's birth. But I remember him, curled up like a ball of spite in his bed, red-faced, glaring at every shadow in the room.

I SAW THOSE eyes again, years later, when he caught me bathing when we had moved to another house down the road. Carl Jr. was working on an egg farm and we lived in the house rent free, in front of four long chicken houses full of white feathers and rivers of turd. Uncle Cope had a narrow bed in the back room with the boys, and one day instead of heading into that room to lie down he lumbered into the bedroom where we girls slept. I was naked except for my step-ins and socks, washing in the washpan. He shoved open the door and peeped in. He saw me and ducked his head. I laid down the white bar of Octagon soap and pulled the towel over my breasts, afraid. "Get away," I said, and Uncle Cope tottered a little on the crutches. His eyes were rimmed with red, a line of fire. He looked me all over with his tongue hanging onto his lower lip. I couldn't breathe. He hung on those crutches like he meant to come in the room. But I said, "You get out of here, Uncle Cope," and I held that towel against me. After a while, he backed out the door.

I told Mama that he had peeped at me while I was washing, and she slapped me sharp across the face and told me never to mess with that one-leg bastard again.

I had a dream about that look in his eyes. Mama was calling him a cripple cornhole bastard; they were in the kitchen and they were arguing, and she called him a hundred names I couldn't remember, and when I went in the room she was laughing at him and he was curled on the old, big bed, Uncle Cope curled up in a tight little knot with his eyes nearly swollen out of his head.

Later, I warned my own daughter never to be alone with him. I warned her right to his face.

UNCLE COPE VARIATIONS

SOMETIMES THE MEMORIES come even and pace themselves one by one, neatly. Sometimes there are harder places, like rapids in the river, where I am dashed from one side to the other in my little boat. Sometimes there is one thing that I fix on, that I see again and again.

Uncle Cope returned to live with us when he had served his time. By then his stomach had healed up and his guts were back in place. I tried to see his behind where the cornhole was but nothing showed through his britches.

This much is true, but there is more, rising from inside me, wherever it had been hidden. I can remember the day even more vividly, if I choose to release more of the pictures. He came home on a June Sunday when a storm blew in. He rode the Trailways bus to Kingston where there was a small station, and then he hitched a ride to the Jarman store, and hobbled on his crutches across the bridge. The truck driver threw his box off the back of the truck and it landed near one of the round-eyed gas pumps, propped against the thick gas hose. Uncle Cope reflected on it, then swung on the crutches up the dirt road.

The gash across his stomach had never been all that bad. The blade had failed to pierce the abdominal muscles, despite the stories, and his guts had always been right where they should be. The wound hurt him some, you could tell that much, as he crept up the road.

Otis and I saw him first. We were playing in the bushes near the road when he came swinging along in the dirt, his good leg pumping and his bad leg flopping. We knew there was a storm blowing, me and Otis were watching the clouds, and playing like we were hunting the Moss Pond monster. Otis had a piece of tobacco stick for a gun and I had a nice shaped branch I had found, which was, to my mind, a machine gun like in the war. The monster was mixed up with the Japanese and we were in the army as well as being expert monster trackers. So to have Uncle Cope appear like that was a natural part of the game, and we shot him several times.

Otis could be fun when he remembered I was half his size. He liked to hit too hard now and then, to remind me I was a girl and weak. He only hit me a couple of times that day. As we got older, he was acting more and more like Daddy and Carl Jr., and pretty soon that side of him would take over. We shot Uncle Cope and ducked down in the underbrush along the road, before he could see which ones we were. He poked that head this way and that, his neck stretching out like a goose. Then he swung down the road toward the house.

"That shit-ass is back," Otis whispered. "Mama will bust a gut."

"He's going to take your bed," I said, because Otis had been sleeping in the kitchen by himself while Uncle Cope was in jail.

"Naw he ain't. He can sleep in there with Carl Jr."

"That's his bed in the kitchen. Yes it is."

Otis puffed up and slammed his fist pretty hard into my shoulder. It was to warn me to shut up. I decided it was time to stop playing with him and ran to the house. The pain in my shoulder had nothing to do with it. But Otis said, "Where you going? You're mad at me now, like some sissy pants."

"No, I ain't," I shouted, but I kept running.

"Well, I know a secret about you."

I shook my head but stopped running for a moment. I could see he meant it, and I was suddenly afraid. "You don't know anything I want to know."

The wind was blowing as I went inside. We had eaten our Sunday dinner of greens and cornmeal dumplings. I had brought water for the dishes and Nora boiled it over the stove, herself drenched in the heat. The sound of a storm coming was welcome all through the house.

Inside everybody was saying hey to Uncle Cope.

Nora held Madson in her lap and played with his curls. Mama sat beside her in the rocking chair that was missing a slat at the back. She had a feather pillow under her. The baby she was now carrying lay low, and you could tell she was nearly done with this one. I missed the look on her face when Uncle Cope appeared in the door. But I remember the way she watched him as she rocked in the chair smelling the sudden cool edge to the afternoon. She narrowed her eyes like a sow when it wants to gnaw off your arm or your leg.

The expression remains so vivid as I remember it that I am seeing things new all the way back to then. How could she have hated him so much, just because he lived with us? What had he done to her in the long ago? I had no such curiosity then, but now that I have the luxury of reflection, of dwelling on her expression and remembering, I can see more. What did Uncle Cope do to Mama?

Daddy was saying, "Good God, Cope, I bet you're glad to have your scrawny ass out of that jail."

"You know it. You got something to eat, Louise?"

"It's some greens," Mama said, tucking the skirt down between her legs. Mama rarely wore step-ins, but remained as modest as her skirts allowed. "Help yourself, ain't nobody going to wait on you."

"Lord, I'm tired, that's a long walk from that highway on these crutches."

"When did you get out?"

"Yesterday. But I was with Bob Yates last night, you know him? He's Roe's oldest brother."

Daddy nodded his head.

"I was with him last night," he repeated, blowing and looking down at the grayed floorboards. "I went up there to see Daddy but he put me out. So I come on down here."

"Daddy put you out?"

"He damn sure did. It's that new girlfriend he's got. He's got a new one. And she put him up to it." Uncle Cope sighed.

"Well, you know you welcome to stay here."

Mama held still so that only her face twitched a little.

Otis came inside somewhere along in here. He nodded to Uncle Cope. Seeing him, Nora said, "Otis has been sleeping out here in your bed, Uncle Cope. He ain't going to be too glad to see you."

"What has this youngun been doing sleeping in my bed?"

Uncle Cope's tone was joking, but Mama took offense anyway. "The youngun ain't done nothing to your bed. It wasn't any harm in him sleeping on it."

"I ain't said nobody could use my bed. This is my goddamn bed."

"Shut your mouth," Mama said, though Daddy was laughing softly. This was the kind of a scene that always pleased Daddy.

Otis ducked his head a little but his face had turned red. "I ain't done nothing but sleep on it, and I like it, and I don't see why I can't keep sleeping on it and let you have my bed with Carl Jr."

"You white-ass son of a bitch, listen at you."

"Carl Jr. ain't sleeping with Uncle Cope," Nora said. "You can count on that."

"He kicks me all over the bed, and I'm tired of it," Otis said.

"Well your little ass is going to get kicked all over Carl Jr.'s bed again," Uncle Cope said, pointing at Otis with the crutch. He sat on the edge of his own bed, neatly made in the corner of the kitchen. "This one is mine."

"Nobody wants you here anyway."

"Hush that," Daddy warned Otis.

"I mean it. Mama don't want him here, and I don't."

"Well he's staying here, no matter what you or your mama want."

"You hear your daddy, don't you?"

Otis glared at him. "You ain't nothing but a goddamn gimp-legged cornhole shit-ass, I don't see why anybody has to put up with you."

Later we would tell the story this way: that Mama laughed so hard she went into labor and had Corrine almost on the spot. The truth was close to that; Mama's labor did come on her during the laughter. She told us to find the colored midwife in Holberta.

Uncle Cope went white, then red, then flung a crutch at Otis. He wanted to bellow, but Mama started to giggle with her hand over her mouth, and that stopped him short. When Mama started to laugh, so did Daddy. That gave Otis the courage to repeat, "A goddamn cornhole shit-ass."

Now the laughter became general, and even I joined in it, though I was not sure why the words were so funny or why they made Uncle Cope so angry. He was speechless and got crimson as the laughter continued, and tears sprang to his eyes, but he had only one crutch and was trapped on the bed. He rubbed his stomach like it was tender. He sat there like that, waiting for us to stop laughing.

Mama could hardly get her breath. When she did, the look in her eyes had turned inward and she made a sound like something deep opening up inside her. Like something waking up. There was a kind of convulsion across her, I saw it run through her like a ripple across a river. It was the first time I had ever seen her go through a contraction. The sound and the motion quieted everything else in the kitchen.

"My water broke," she said to Daddy. A wet patch was spreading down her skirt. "Carl Jr. is going to have to get the colored midwife, we ain't paid Miss Rilla yet for the last two times she come."

Uncle Cope's humiliation lay forgotten in the confusion of Corrine's birth. But I remember him, curled up like a ball of spite in his bed.

Nora handed Madson to me and I carried him like a sack of shit to his blanket. By then he was old enough to walk but he was lazy and liked to be toted and petted. I hated to hold him or to be near him, but I did what Nora said. Wanting to watch what was happening to Mama, I hurried the job, and Madson bumped his head on the stove and started crying just as the first clap of lightning lit over the woods. Otis rushed to get Carl Jr.'s bicycle from under the house, and Daddy gave him his logger's rain slicker to wear. Otis lit out for Holberta with the rain starting to spatter. He would be riding in the mud, which was what he liked best, whenever he could get the excuse to steal Carl Jr.'s bicycle.

Daddy helped Mama to their bedroom. The first pain passed and she could move on her own, but Daddy was feeling generous because of Uncle Cope's embarrassment. Nora set a pot of water on the stove in case it was needed, and I wiped Joe Robbie's mouth with his towel. That was when I looked at Uncle Cope. He was still sitting on the edge of his bed, twisted to a knot, with that useless leg dangling free. His whole body was quivering with fury, and nobody saw it but me. I was the one who finally thought to bring him the crutch he had thrown, that had not landed anywhere near Otis. When I handed it to him, he looked me in the eye and snatched it. His eyes were full of hate all the way out to the whites. His mouth was like a pale slash across his face. Now when I close my eyes I can recall it exactly, down to the fat mole on his chin that sprouted a cluster of gray hairs.

WHEN HE WALKED in on my bathing, it was not the first time he had spied on me. It would be hard to say when I first became aware that he lurked in the doorway or the window on afternoons when I could get the room alone to wash.

I had a fear of being naked in front of anyone, even my sisters. The fear came on me early. I would never take my dress off and let Nora see my dark nipples, I was ashamed of them. I would never take my drawers off in front of her. The same with Mama, only more so. Sometimes Nora would try to wash me but I would always squirm until she made me finish. This was all right when I was young and did not care to wash so much, but later I learned that people think you are trash if you go around dirty. So I got in the habit, in later years (in other houses) of washing every day, in the afternoon, alone. I would draw a washpan of water and carry it to the corner of the bedroom.

Carl Jr. was working on the egg farm, as I have said, and we lived in the house rent free. Uncle Cope had his narrow bed in the back room with the boys, and one day he lumbered into the bedroom where we girls slept.

The house on the egg farm was one of our nicer places, with electric lights and a hand pump in the kitchen. But we still used a johnny house in the back for our business. I could see it from our bedroom, blown with pages from old newspapers that we used to clean ourselves.

In the corner of that bedroom I could feel relatively safe. I had already moved to that corner, which was windowless, after Uncle Cope peeped at me through one of the windows. I set the washpan on the floor and took down my dress partway. I unhooked the bra I was wearing, one of Nora's old ones. I washed quickly without looking at myself.

Sometimes I would dry the top part of me, then dress it, before proceeding to wash the bottom. This was to keep me from getting too close to naked, because I especially did not like to be naked when I was alone. But that day I pulled off the dress.

I was naked except for my step-ins and socks, washing in the washpan. He shoved open the door and peeped in. He saw me and ducked his head. I laid down the white bar of Octagon soap and pulled the towel over my breasts, afraid. I said, "You get out of here, Uncle Cope," and I held that towel against me.

The difference was not that he came to peep, since he had often tried. The difference was that he walked into the room and wanted something else. I already knew what that was.

I told Mama that he had peeped at me while I was washing, and she slapped me sharp across the face.

Beyond my anger rose the image of Uncle Cope sprawled on the dirt with his belly cut open, and some man kneeling behind him, and putting inside him that thing that men have that they use that way. I thought I knew what the look on Uncle Cope's face had been when he first tumbled down into the dirt with the weight of the other man on top of him.

I had a dream about that look in his eyes.

Later, I warned my daughter never to be alone with him. I warned her right to his face.

This was when Mama lived in yet another house, near Wise Fork. By then I was married and no longer lived with Mama, but had brought my children there for a visit. When I said it, Uncle Cope nodded, as if he agreed with me, and turned on his crutches and left the room.

ONCE, WHEN I was very young, Otis and I were in my Grandaddy Tote's chicken yard, and we watched Uncle Cope beat a cat to death with one of his crutches. The cat had caught and killed an old hen. Uncle Cope's expression remained blank as he leaned on one crutch and flailed, methodically, with the other. He broke the cat's back with the first swipe and the creature howled pitifully until it could no longer make a sound. After a while the patch of reddened fur lay still. The chicken would be our supper, a rare feast. The cat was Grandaddy's and had to be killed, now that it had tasted chicken blood. The cat would be allowed to rot where it had fallen, unless the dogs found it. Uncle Cope looked down at both dead things as if they were fresh turds.

The memories mix together, as if they are rooms in a house and I am walking from one to the other, and in one room Uncle Cope is hanging over me on the crutches while I wipe Joe Robbie's mouth with the towel, and in the other I am wiping my own baby's behind clean while Uncle Cope lies passed out on the couch, half-snoring. In another room of memory is a picture of Uncle Cope standing without the crutches, beside Villa Ray Crawford, whom he used to date when he had two useful legs. After his accident she dropped him and married Jay Hawkins instead, and this was another reason Mama always had for hating Villa Ray, because if she had married Uncle Cope like she ought to, she would be the one having to take care of him, soaking the piss out of his sheets, and keeping him away from her daughters.

In one of these rooms, maybe, he is married to Villa Ray, and has two legs, and children.

We visited him in county prison only the one time. But later, when we were visiting my brother Madson in the state penitentiary, I remembered Uncle Cope in the jail.

By the time we visited Madson in the penitentiary in Raleigh, soldiers were fighting in Vietnam and I had all my children with me. We came specifically to bring Mama to visit her beloved son. Corrine and Delia came along too; we all squeezed into that '57 Plymouth with me driving. Walking into the visitor room to see my brother, seeing the guards and the barred windows, I remembered the county prison and Uncle Cope.

Uncle Cope said, "They treat us real good. They got us making things. You-all don't worry about me."

Madson said everything was real good in here, he was learning how to swim in these big bloomers, he like to drowned, but other than that everything was fine. They set you right down in with the Mexicans and the niggers, he said, and he grinned at me with the dark front tooth; he would have been handsome except for the tooth gone bad. "You got to watch out in here, not let anybody get behind you."

I was shy to kiss Madson's cheek, and I remembered, suddenly, the taste of Uncle Cope, the clammy skin on his cheek, and I thought, but I never kissed him that day, as I leaned toward Madson, as I brushed my dry lips softly along the smooth shaved cheek, and I could almost smell the rot underneath the aftershave, that my brother was rotting as he stood here, no matter how smooth or straight the part of his hair. I was the one who was remembering, I was the one who was tasting his skin, the texture of his shaven beard. I leaned forward and away.

It was like the kisses I would give Bobjay in the parking lot of the Walter B. Jones Alcohol Rehabilitation Center years later. Like the dry taste of Mama lying in her coffin, the heap of her suddenly shrunken, and the shadows of the sprays of flowers falling across her powdered nose. Like the brush bestowed on my cheek by Bobjay's daddy when I first walked into their kitchen as Bobjay's wife, the dry edge of his lips like a flake of something, sending a shiver through me, a warning. Like the last kiss I ever gave my daddy, one Sunday morning when he let me go to church before the breakfast dishes were done, him needing a shave and smelling of last night's whiskey. Like watching Mama press her lips against the cool of Madson's forehead as he lay in his own coffin, a few months before he would have been released from prison for the second time, had not another prisoner killed him in the exercise yard. All these memories knotted together, and I gained a sense of a kind of time where everything lies next to everything else and everything touches everything.

I hid under the house, behind one of the outer pillars. Daddy kept dogs chained further under, I could see their shadows moving. If Alma Laura had not been with me I might have been afraid, but she came to sit beyond the post, silent as always, a comforting shadow. The dog chains softly murmured.

I am there over and over again. There is a kind of cool and

safety, as if I have reached some final place. As if I have backed into a corner from which I cannot run. The choice is made. I am under the house.

Why does the memory of Uncle Cope's arrest bring out so much? Is it simply that I was older by then, or do I retain this many details from every moment, locked in the cells of my brain? Is there still so much left to mine?

Corrine was born sometime around the Battle of Midway in 1942, a definite event fixed in history. That would be when my Uncle Cope came home too, the same night Otis called him a cornhole shit-ass. While Mama was in labor in the house, Carl Jr. played the radio and we listened to the news in the yard. Our aircraft carriers were sending planes to bomb the Japanese, and the bombs hit practically every aircraft carrier the Japanese had. The ships sailed in the dark, away over there somewhere, beyond the trees, airplanes hurtling along huge curves, and big flat-topped ships tossed on waves of water. Carl Jr. held the radio close to both our ears. I had never seen an airplane, or a ship, or an ocean, but I made up pictures for the words. I was standing on the flight deck of the *Lexington*, sea spray in my hair, holding Carl Jr.'s hand. We searched the sky for Japanese planes. Somewhere belowdecks, Mama was having Corrine. The fantasy returns to me as real as the memory of any real event.

CORRINE

MY REACTION TO Corrine, when I first saw her sleeping in her cradle, was not like the feeling I had for Alma Laura or for Madson. I felt more of a practical affection. Corrine was born with swirls of black hair, and eyes with long curled lashes. She had a round red face and a way of squinting that made her look as old as Mama. She weighed five pounds when she was born, but she had the voice of God. When she cried, the cups rattled on the shelves.

We never had any doubt Corrine would live. When she was hungry, she roared. When she was wet or uncomfortable, she roared. When she wanted to be washed, she roared. When she needed any attention of any kind, she roared: she opened her mouth, her face flushed red, and a sound came out, like the whole fury of a storm wrapped up in a baby and stuffed into her lungs.

She was born on the lip of summer and when time came to work in the fields, we carried her with us. The job of watching her and tending Madson and her fell to Joe Robbie and me; we sat at the edge of the field, in shade if I could find it.

Mama, Otis, and Nora worked. Sometimes they worked in green tobacco and sometimes they picked cotton. A couple of times Mr. Allison called them for strawberry picking or whatnot. Mama hated to pick strawberries because squatting so far wore her out.

For picking cotton, Nora and Otis stayed home from school, and we all woke up before dawn. We ate cold biscuit from the night before, and drank sweet coffee. Carl Jr. and Daddy dressed for logging at the same time, so we were all shuffling around the house pulling on clothes and running fingers through the tangles in our hair. Mr. Allison picked us up in his truck. He drove us to the fields with the other white family that worked for him, the Hollands. They were not as low as we were, but they were pretty low, and their girl Nina, who was my age, had as few dresses as I did, all as thin and faded as mine. We went to work right away while Mr. Allison went to fetch the black families from Holberta.

It galled Mama that he picked us up first. She stayed mad all day, muttering as her hands darted among the cotton bolls.

Some days I watched the babies and Joe Robbie, and some days I picked cotton, when Nora wanted a rest. I picked in the row ahead of Mama so she could make sure I pulled only the bolls that were ready. The work came hard, and my body hurt from stooping down, from pulling the bolls, from the heat. Mostly the low of my back ached from the odd angle. I wanted to rest sometimes, but Mama drove me forward, telling me to get a move. I picked the cotton and dropped the bolls in my canvas sack that dragged the ground. I stooped slightly forward. The pain increased.

Once I said my back was hurting, and Mama answered, "You ain't even old enough to have a damn back."

Nora moved neatly along her row. Her body had rounded a little, I could see the difference when she leaned forward, when she planted a hand in the low of her back. Sometimes, when she straightened, the young black boys watched her. I could see the look in their eyes, one that reminded me of Uncle Cope, or even of Daddy.

I mimicked Nora in the fields. I pressed my hand into the low of my back and tilted my face up to the sun. I tied my straw hat below my chin with the same knot.

Every week, when the farmer paid us, Mama collected all the money we earned and kept it in the bosom of her dress. I think it was the only reason she wore a brassiere. It would be years before I thought of this as money I had earned.

At night, following the long day's baking in the field, Corrine continued as my burden. I changed her diapers and washed them in the pot. I bathed her and powdered her dimpled ass. I carried her to Mama for nursing and watched as Mama's expanding breast sank onto her face. I kept her baby dresses clean.

We didn't have much clothing for a girl, and most of that was what I had worn. When she heard about the new baby, Daddy's sister Addis gave us a box of stuff from her twins that died, and I was dressing Corrine in clothes from the box.

"Did you get that baby something to wear?" Mama asked, sitting on the porch in the cool of evening. "She ought not to go around so ragged."

"Yes, ma'am. I gave her a bath."

"Well, she needed it. Where did you get that little outfit on her?"

"Out of that box from Aunt Addis."

Mama shook her head so that her chin shook from side to side. "I hate we have to use that stuff."

"There's some good dresses," I said. "And the underwear is real clean and there's a lot of it, for later."

"You know them younguns died."

"Yes, ma'am."

"Your Daddy says Addis didn't have anything to do with it."

I waited. She reached for her snuff can and laid some of the fragrant stuff under her tongue. This gave her voice a slightly muffled sound.

"But Tula is her sister, and Tula told me she thinks Addis killed them babies. She thinks Addis smothered the both of them with a pillow. It was that Jenny woman put her up to it. And I think that's why she give us this whole box of stuff, because what she done worries her."

Lucky for us she had waited a couple of years to smother them, because now we had a lot of baby clothes.

"Your Aunt Addis is crazy. She never did get married to that man, the one that had them babies with her, and it broke her mind. Just like it was a watch and she wound it too tight. That's what Tula says. That's how Jenny got hold of her. Tula used to would tell me everything, when your daddy and me first got married. But now we don't hardly talk, because we don't live over on that side of the pond no more."

At night, I was the one who put Corrine to sleep in the cradle near Mama's bed. I never sang to her or told her stories; we are not like that, Corrine and I. For her I felt little of the devotion with which I might have tended Alma Laura, and, since I still had Alma Laura with me, I never changed that affection for something I might spend on Corrine. I tended Corrine because it was my work.

She thrived without anyone's particular affection, a fortunate trait. She drank Mama's titties dry. She basked in the summer heat, with flies walking on her eyelids, on the edges of her lips. On a blanket in the shade she kicked her legs and gooed. She laughed at thunder and lightning, she kicked at raindrops with her feet. I saw her upset only once, when a green tobacco worm crawled onto her foot. She frowned as if it stank and cried for a while, out of indignation, after I stripped it off. Mostly she lay on the blanket and took in everything, the hard work, the clatter of the mule harness, everybody's talk around the water truck. The hard months of summer passed easily for Corrine, because she grabbed for what she needed and grew on what she got. She passed scarcely even a day of sickness.

SOMETIMES ALMA LAURA watched us. I never saw any envy in her face, any sense that Corrine possessed something Alma Laura lacked. Once or twice I wondered if Alma Laura thought I might abandon her, now that I had a real baby to take care of. But I never detected such fear.

Alma Laura walked with me in the fields. She was no help with the cotton; my bag never filled a bit faster because of her. Her hand on my sore back muscles gave me no sensation at all. But she waited with me while I worked, sitting in the shade in the space between the cotton rows. About the only help she could be was to warn me about snakes and such.

She had kept growing as if she were still alive. She was always wearing the dresses I used to wear, and when she appeared in one, I used to wonder if it was also still hanging in the closet or folded in a box in the back room of the house. In the summer she went barefoot, like the rest of us. Wherever she was, she was always clean. I had a nice straw sunhat, though, and she never had one.

I practiced never to speak to Alma Laura, because Mama would look at me like I had head sickness. Mama told stories about a fever that would dry a man's brain inside his skull, which was how her daddy had died, she said. She checked me for signs of it, sometimes. Because I talked odd, when I talked, she explained to Nora. There was something about me that wasn't right.

I TALKED TO Corrine. I told her things she needed to know. First, that there are boys and there are girls, and she was a girl. I showed her the place between her legs and informed her that I also had a place like that. When I had to pee, that was what I used. But boys used something different, and because of it, everybody liked boys better in our family. Daddy especially liked boys better, but Mama liked them better too. Carl Jr. could come and go as he pleased, but Nora had to stay at home all the time. Nora and me were the only ones who had to tote the water and carry the dishes; nobody but us did both. Corrine would find out more about the differences with time, and so would I. Whatever I noticed, I promised to tell. Nora, for instance, was starting to get titties. I told her many other things, simple, to help her out around the house. I warned her you had to watch out for Uncle Cope's crutches because they were very hard, and if he put one on your foot he could break a bone. Joe Robbie found that out. She would also need to learn about Joe Robbie, because when she got older she would be the one to wipe his spit. Joe Robbie was bigger than me but folded up to where you could fit him in a wagon. The county woman promised us a wheelchair if the war ended, but the way things go for us, you never know. I told her you needed to get near the table come biscuit time, and when there are beans, you better grab a bowl and hide it somewhere before all the dishes get gone. You are the littlest one, and nobody will look out for you when everybody is the same hungry. Also, she couldn't expect this hot weather to keep up, because after it was hot it got cold, and after it was cold it got hot again, like that, in circles. So it would get cold soon and just wait. I explained about Uncle Cope and the cornhole, and about the county prison and the war. The war was hard, because of Europe and the Japs, but I got through the lecture. I told her there was extra meat in the beans when Daddy sold ration coupons and how Carl Jr. tried to enlist but he was barely sixteen. I told her Otis had a mean temper, worth watching out for, because one time he came after me with a shovel. I told her about the dead baby boy, but not about Alma Laura, who was my secret. I explained fatback and bacon and the difference. I explained getting credit at the Little Store. I explained that black women in Holberta made gardens for tomatoes but our mama didn't. There were more and more things as I talked, not less and less, the way you would think.

I told her to close the door when she took a bath. I told

her to keep a towel close by. When she was big she would need to be careful of these things. She would need to wait until the sisters were ready to go to bed to undress, and to keep close to me and Nora. If Mama had any dreams or talked in her sleep, it was best to cover your ears with the pillow. Sometimes Daddy gets mad when she wakes him up, or else he just wakes up mad himself, and then they fight in the wee hours. Then you have to sleep as best you can. Mama says never stare at a full moon. If you have to pee, nobody is going to walk out in the yard with you. We keep a slop pot on the porch, but it's always full.

I was conscious, the whole time, that years of telling her things were yet to come.

THE SNAKE'S TOOTH

WHEN WORD CAME a monster had been sighted in the woods around White Lake, about an hour's ride from us, Mama shook her head over the mess of snap beans Aunt Tula had brought from her garden. "Snake never bites you twice in the same place. But that monster is a-coming back here. You mark my words."

"I declare, woman." Aunt Tula fanned her face with a church fan showing angels leading children across a bridge. She fanned and snapped long green beans. Tips and middles. The sound was crisp and the motion clean. "Snap, don't twist, Nora. You waste, that way. And Louise, hush about that monster. Ain't nobody seen him since that colored woman."

"It eat her dog's head," Mama swore.

"Nobody seen it."

"Mr. Jarman seen it. He come up here and told us, didn't he, younguns?"

We nodded our heads. I was trying to snap a bean too, but my fingers lacked the schooling. I studied the bowl in Aunt

Tula's lap. I studied her slim fingers, Mama's fat one's. Don't twist.

"It's a snake I heared of," Mama nodded her head, "will bite you and latch on with its jaw, and won't let go of you till sundown."

"It ain't no such thing."

"A snake like that killed a man near Luma. They was talking about it at the Holiness. It latched onto his throat, and he coudn't draw one breath."

"You will tell a lie," Aunt Tula remarked.

"I believe it happened like they said at the Holiness."

"You don't even go to the Holiness."

We sat there in the late evening. We had worked a day, then Aunt Tula brought the sack of beans. If we helped her snap them we could have some, and new potatoes.

"Willie says you-all are moving again," Aunt Tula noted evenly.

"That's what he says." Mama sighed and studied the ends of snap beans in her lap. "It's a shame we can't keep this house."

This was news to the rest of us, except Nora, who never looked up from her work.

"Willie is having a hard time, ain't he?" Aunt Tula spoke as if Daddy were having it by himself. "But that's probably a sweet little house you'll be moving to."

"Ain't much to it from what I can tell."

"There's some pretty country around Holberta. That's a nice little piece of road down there, and you can see right to the pond."

Mama said, "These beans is a good size."

WE MOVED TO a shack near Holberta, where everything was worse. The house boasted no paint, only gray, weathered planks. Some of the windows had no glass and we nailed grease paper to keep out the rain. The back door hung on one hinge till Carl Jr. found an old hinge in the yard and nailed it in place. The stove flue was busted in the middle. We made brooms from broomstraw and swept, clouds of dust, but there was always more to sweep.

The well, in the backyard, had half a handle, with a tobacco stick tied on to make the rest. The well was hard to prime, and the walk to the kitchen and up the steps with a bucket of water could take your breath. We had another johnny house, this one a good ways down a path in the middle of some honeysuckle and blackberry bushes. The place reeked of snakes and mice.

Otis found a book in the johnny house the very first day. He never let me see it, and Daddy caught him with it and took it for himself. But I saw there was some man naked on the front, a drawing, showing everything the man had.

Across the road, around a curve and through some trees sat the houses of Holberta, a cluster of black families who grouped around Fork Road and Union Road at one end of Moss Pond. People walking to Holberta passed by our house. Seeing we were white, they turned their heads away.

An abandoned church lurked under trees at the bend in the road, and near it lay a cemetery. Them places were haunted, Mama said, because slaves were buried in the graves and they had slept so restless, they tossed the brick vaults out of the ground, you could walk and see it if you wanted. But it was best to visit over there in the daylight, because in the night it could be dangerous. Even in the day, you should be careful in the high grass, because of whip snakes that could whip around your legs and drag you down and choke you, or tree snakes that could drop down on you from a tree and bite you and kill you. Those were the main dangers, she said. Other than the ghosts.

Nora, Otis, and me walked to the cemetery near the falling-down church. Part of the steeple was hanging in the branches of a tree nearest the graves, and even though it looked like it had been steady for a while, we kept our distance. But you could see something had torn up the grass around the graves, and these brick boxes were shoved up from the ground. The stone crosses and headstones stood every which way. Deep shade from the oak tree, its branches no doubt full of tree snakes, flowed down to the graves.

Otis wanted to climb inside the church but Nora said no.

"Now we live in Holberta with the niggers," Nora said, "next to a nigger graveyard." After she said that, we went home.

Everything was harder there, too. The walk to the Little Store took twice as long, and my arms could hardly hold the boxes by the end; there was a black store in Holberta but we were not allowed to go there. In the mornings Mr. Allison picked us up for the fieldwork with the black families, and that left Mama muttering all over again. She herded us all to the front of the truck, and we sat there around her like a brood of chicks.

One day, though, she found out that two of the young boys on the truck, Cunning and Arthur, were the sons of

Annalea Bates, the woman who saw the monster and rescued her dog's body. All of a sudden she was all ears.

"It was a gray thing," Arthur said. "It had scales and a jaw."

"Mama ain't say nothing about no jaw."

"Hush, boy. Who telling this?"

"Misress Tote, it won't no jaw. Mama seen this gray thing, what was eating Raeford head."

"Raeford were our dog."

"And the monster ate his head."

"Mama run, but then she went back after the dog. Do you believe that?"

"Crazy fool," one of the other women said. "I would have left the dog where it was."

"What else did she seen?" Mama asked.

"Wasn't nothing much." Arthur shrugged. "She seen this gray thing. That was all."

"It was some tracks."

"That's right. It was some tracks."

"It was your Daddy's liquor, is was it was; that's what your mama seen," said the woman.

"Naw, it was a gray thing eating Raeford head."

We cropped tobacco through August, as far toward school as we could. Mama would work longer, if needed. I would certainly have gone to the fields with her to tend the smaller children. But this year I was starting school.

ONE DAY, WHEN we were waiting for the truck to take us home at the end of the day, Cunning Bates told Otis, "It was a witch hung in that tree behind your house. The Hawfords move because they found out."

"My daddy got us this house," Otis answered. "We use to live down the road towards the bridge."

"Your daddy is common. Ain't no white peoples want to live down here."

Otis flushed red and doubled his fists. "You hush."

Cunning shrugged. "You can live there if you want to. But it's not right." He paused for effect. "Sometime you can see that old witch under that tree, my mama seen it and her hair turn white."

Nora said, "You lie."

"It's the truth."

"I ain't seen nothing out there. It's no witch."

"You wait. When you see it, you wish you listen."

Cunning and Nora faced each other. "Who was the Hawfords?"

"It was people who live there who pick one season for Mr. James. They from Georgia, they real backwoods."

"They was colored."

"That's right. They went on back home."

Nora nudged clods of the black earth. Sweat had smudged her face, running in dark lines down her neck. The whole way home in the truck, she was quiet. When we got home, she sat on the bed for a long time.

ME AND OTIS went walking in the high grass sometimes, in the late sun after supper, trying to find a whip snake, until Mama said it was getting to be too late in the year to find them in this part of the country.

Daddy found the shed skin of a rattlesnake at the base of the tree where Cunning Bates said the witch was hung.

Daddy counted sixteen rattles, and Mama said to count one for each year the snake lived, but Daddy said that was a bunch of shit.

Daddy liked to chain the dogs under the elm in the front yard, because the pack of them had a vicious look and a hateful sound to their bark, and they made folks nervous. He had trained the dogs to hate everybody, even the rest of his family. But in Holberta everybody reckoned we had trained our dogs especially to eat black folks, and we became known as the trash with the ugly dogs in the yard.

Nora liked to sit with the dogs, she had no fear of them and even brought them the little we had to give them as food in those days, grease-soaked biscuit and wormy oatmeal. She and Carl Jr. were the only ones, other than Daddy, who dared go near their tree. When we lived in Holberta, Nora sat under the elm scratching their ears and brushing the knots out of their coats with half a brush she found under the porch. Whenever she was not working around the house, she sat dreaming with the dogs, their heads in her lap, flies buzzing around their ears. Mama fretted that her blood would come on her and the dogs would turn. "Dogs is wild like that, sometimes," Mama said, as Nora stretched, stood and walked toward us. "It was a man in my family who was eat by his own dog, one winter. They didn't have nothing else in the house to feed it."

"Oh, Mama, you make up a bunch of mess," Nora said, continuing to the bedroom we children all shared.

Mama tottered after her. "You better pick that dog hair out of that skirt else you won't be able to wear it to school."

"I'm quitting school."

"You hush that. You ain't no such thing."

"I ain't going to school."

"Well you ain't quitting, not unless I say so."

"You let Carl Jr. quit."

"Your Daddy did that."

A shiver was beginning to running through Nora's voice. "I hate school. I hate them other kids. I don't want to go back."

"Well, you're going back."

Nora reappeared in the door, her voice shaking and her eyes flooded with tears. "Then let me go to school with the niggers. We live in a nigger house. That's all anybody's going to talk about. So let me go to school with the niggers too."

Her words shocked Mama, who slapped Nora sharply, almost by instinct. A blank look on her face. She slapped Nora again, hard, with the flat of her hand, and all her weight behind it. Then, moving mechanically, she returned to the kitchen, sweetened herself a cup of coffee, took a biscuit off the plate and sat on the back porch, where two stray cats waited for a field mouse to die.

MAMA BOUGHT CLOTHES with some of the cotton money, and I got one dress for school. I got no shoes because some church lady had given us a pair from one of her daughters. We did all the school shopping in one day. Uncle Bray drove us to Smithfield, and Mama marched us from a shoe store to a dime store. I tried on the dress in the fitting room with the mirror. I was ashamed to undress at first because I was wearing only step-ins under the dress.

The new dress was green and blue plaid with buttons and

a smart collar. I looked at the dress and at me in the mirror. I could hardly breathe, my heart was pounding.

Nora knocked to find out what was taking so long, and she slid inside when she saw. She looked me up and down. "Show it to Mama," she said.

I held the bag in my fists all the way home, careful to keep the wind from snatching it out of my hands. Mama gave me a hanger at home, and I hung it on the tobacco pole in the corner that we used for our clothes, next to the blue-flowered dress that had been Nora's till she outgrew it.

THE DAY BEFORE school started, Otis found a piece of bone under the house and picked it up. When he had it in his hand, Mama warned gravely that he should have left it where it was because it was a rattlesnake's fang and it probably still had poison in it. If there was poison in it, it could kill anybody who touched it. But Otis had already touched it and, when Mama went back in the house, he wondered whether he was going to die.

"First you start to swell up, then you get numb," Nora had taken his plump white hand and began to stroke it with comforting gestures. "Then you get blue in the face and your heart stops and you choke to death. That's what Mama says."

"Daddy found a snake skin," Joe Robbie murmured. "If it was a fang I bet it was the same snake."

"How do you feel?" Nora asked Otis.

"I feel fine. I don't feel nothing."

"That could be a bad sign," Nora predicted.

We walked with Nora around the house. With the bright summer sun pouring across the road and dirt yard, we could almost see through the walls of the house to Mama's squat, round figure treading the rough floors of the kitchen. I was not thinking about the snake's bone or tooth or whatever it was, I was thinking about my new dress, and school to start, and the grandeur of things. But all of a sudden Otis started to cry and sat down and balled up his fists and shoved them against his eyes. "I feel funny," he wailed.

"Hush, Otis," Nora says. "You're being a crybaby."

"It'll be all right," Joe Robbie whispered. Nora carried Madson, who still refused to walk most of the time. I was dragging Joe Robbie in the wagon. We had worn a path around the yard, where the tree roots would not tip the wagon over.

"My shoulder stings. And my ears is popping. And I can't hardly breathe."

"That's because you're crying," Nora said.

"I ain't crying."

"You are too. Look at you."

"I can't help it, I'm scared."

We got him moving again and rounded the house to where Carl Jr. and Daddy were drinking. Daddy had started to drink with Carl Jr. pretty much every evening after they got home. They propped under the elm tree where a rusted-out icebox sat in the grass. Daddy was fussing with the snout of the bitch dog; he called her Patsy. "What's that fuss?" Daddy asked.

"Otis found a snake fang and it had poison on it."

"What snake fang?" Daddy drew one thin hand out of his overalls and reached. "Ain't no goddamn snake fang. Let me see."

Daddy always scared Otis, and Otis never would go near him. Otis was still carrying the fang in a rag, in case it was needed for the antidote. He gave the thing to Nora, who carried it to Daddy under the tree. Daddy took one look at it and spit. "Who told you this come out of a snake?"

"Mama. She said it was from a rattlesnake and if it was poison in it whoever touched it could die or get paralyzed." Nora reported the facts with the slightest smirk.

"Your Mama is full of shit about a snake. This ain't even no kind of a tooth, it's a goddamn fish bone." He scowled, gave Otis the once over, and curled his lip in disgust. "You sissy. Look at you, crying like some sugar-ass little darling. Ain't you got no better sense than to listen to your goddamn mama?"

He started laughing and passed the piece of bone to Carl Jr., who laughed too. Nora stood with them with her arms around Madson and one of the dogs licking a scab on her leg. Otis walked off, cussing. "Goddamn Mama," he said, and then added, "old fat-ass big-titty bitch," and he was headed in my direction and suddenly I couldn't get my breath. "She's an old goddamn fat-ass big-titty stupid bitch for lying to me." He swept by me still cussing, with tears stinging his face and his voice trembling, so angry that even when he had passed, the wave of him was still moving through me.

"He cussed Mama," Joe Robbie whispered.

I agreed that was what he had done.

WHEN YOU RIDE through Holberta nowadays, you find there are a few changes. The colored store is still there, painted fresh a few years ago and faded again. The houses have mostly improved, some of them pretty nice, bricked up, with fences and flower gardens. Yards decorated right up to the road with flamingos and cement art and whatnot. Not as many people live there as used to, that's true. But it's also true that most people, black and white, have moved away from Moss Pond.

The house where we had lived was a different case. I stopped there and walked a bit. The grayed siding had been replaced and the underpinning filled in, the whole thing painted a pretty pink with cream-colored trim on the windows and under the eaves. Smooth new double-glass windows replaced the grease paper and tacks. Best of all, a lawn was growing, with beds of impatiens, where only a dirt yard had lain before.

A sign out front read, "Mama Lisa's Homemade Mighty-Fine Quilts, All Patterns," then, underneath, the hours of the store. Closed now, but bright quilt squares peered through the windows. At the bottom, in small letters, was an addition, "See Where The Witch Was Hung."

But at the side of the pretty building, under the edges of the shade of that elm tree, the same junked icebox sat on the same patch of ground. The rust had eaten it to a lump of brown, and I stared right at it for a long time before I recognized it. The memory shot through me, Daddy and Carl Jr. propped there, the piece of bone passing from hand to hand. That happened lately, on one of my drives, that I visited Holberta and remembered about the rattlesnake and the tooth.

When I stopped at the Holberta store for a cold drink, paying in correct change, the owner, Mr. Detrice, shrunken as the Jarmans up the road, was explaining to another gentleman that a flying snake had killed a man near Luma, oh, a month ago, swooped down out of the trees and latched onto his shoulder, and the man couldn't draw one breath, the snake gripped him so tight. "You don't see them kind of snakes around here like you used to," the other man added at the end of the story. "Used to find aplenty of them."

"It's that new road," Mr. Detrice swore, "the pond half dried up after they put that road in, you can't even fish," and nodded to me as I was leaving, a nice white lady stopping at his store. I stood there in the middle of Holberta sipping my Nehi. I could not remember that I had ever stood there before.

JOE ROBBIE

WHEN THE DAY came that I started school, Joe Robbie finally understood he would never do the same. I got home from the first day and found him in the corner of the bedroom with his eyes red and swollen. "Hey," he said. "I was by myself all day. I didn't play with Madson."

"You can play with him. It's okay."

He shook his head. His lip was trembling and he scowled. "Did you like it?"

"It was okay."

"Who is the teacher?"

"Miss Sterndale. She's fatter than Mama."

He nodded his head. "Did you learn to read books?"

I sighed. "Not yet."

We sat quietly together. His eyes were wet, but he kept himself rigid. "Do you know why I can't go?"

Because he kept watching me, I shrugged, and waited beside him. "You can look at my books," I said.

He shook his head. I wiped the spit from his mouth and then wiped the rest of his face with a wet rag.

HE SPENT THE days alone after that, not by his own choice but because Madson lacked the patience to sit with him and Corrine was too tiny to be much company. I wished I could have shared Alma Laura with him, but he had never seen her, not even once, despite all the times she kept us company.

Maybe he could have functioned in the schoolroom, but he could never have made the trip. To catch the school bus, we had to walk the mile and a half to the end of the dirt road, to the Little Store. The bus refused to drive into Holberta because, other than us, only black kids lived there. Every morning, while we walked along the road toward the pond, the colored school bus passed us, throwing up dust, the driver smiling and lifting a pink-palmed hand.

We might have dragged Joe Robbie to the end of the road in the wagon and then toted him onto the bus and hauled him into a seat and out of the seat and off the bus and then into the school building. But even then we would not have any wagon and would have to drag him to his desk too.

Mama said it worried her that he sat there all day, doing nothing except looking at the pictures in comic books that the county woman brought to him, paid for by donations made by the Junior League of Luma. Studying them superhero books, she said, and gaping off into the sky like he was out yonder somewhere. She had no understanding when he cried because he could not go to school; she herself had survived with nearly no schooling and figured that he would survive too. He had his family, she always said. God had given him that.

He told me the stories of the comic books. Superman was out flying in the galaxy, he said, where he run into the Green

Bad Guy near outer space. The Green Bad Guy had a black mask and this green outfit and big muscles, like Joe Robbie showed me in the pictures. But Superman looked like himself and had big muscles too, along with super strength. At first the Green Bad Guy was winning and then Superman was winning, they went back and forth like that. Then the Green Bad Guy chained Superman with the green glowing chains that circled Superman's legs and arms. He beat up Superman real bad, to the point that Superman was injured and stuff. He even tore Superman's costume, and Superman almost didn't have any shirt at the end. The green glowing chains kept him imprisoned and weak until the Batman rescued him. The Batman searched and found him, then took off the chains. The Batman traveled through space in a spaceship that he made himself in his basement. Superman and the Batman teamed up to defeat the Green Bad Guy, and they killed him and exploded him, and then they went home. They lived together, according to Joe Robbie. Since neither of us could read the words then, his accounts remained definitive.

Sometimes he looked at the ads in the back of the comics, the Charles Atlas ads that promised a muscular body through dynamic tension in a few minutes a day. "I wish I could get some muscles," he would say, "then I could walk." Almost like a litany.

ABOUT THIS TIME Mama took Joe Robbie for a doctor check and announced afterward that the doctor had told her Joe Robbie had a new muscle disorder. But when we asked her what kind, she had no idea. So for a long time we told everybody that Joe Robbie had a new muscle disorder but we didn't know what kind, and we supposed that the doctor was planning to tell us as soon as he knew.

The doctor had been trying to tell Mama that Joe Robbie had a neuromuscular disorder, and we learned that when Aunt Addis took Mama and Joe Robbie to the doctor, one day when Uncle Bray couldn't make the trip. Aunt Addis brought them home and told us what the doctor had said. It was really just another way of telling us what we already knew, but Mama had thought he had given her a new name.

One time, Joe Robbie told me, pointing to the color-filled frames of the comic book, the Flash and the Atom went on this voyage through inner space into the inside of secret buildings, and they made the Flash as small as the Atom through a super discombobulator that shrank him to tiny size. They were saving the world through searching for a secret for weapons, and the secret was hidden in the laboratory of Dr. Einstein, who was the blue-haired man with the big muscles inside his white lab coat. Dr. Einstein planned to rule the world through bombs and guns such as those nobody else had. But the Atom got inside the laboratory because he could get tiny enough to go anywhere, and the Flash was faster than Dr. Einstein, and they all fought in the lab at the end until the Atom and the Flash had the secret to the guns and the bombs. After that, everybody was arrested. Neither the Flash nor the Atom pulled off their shirts, but they were always wearing tights and performing feats of strength with bulging chests and arms.

When he told me the story of a comic book, he went into a kind of trance. I turned from page to page, and he gave me the particular scenario for each panel on each page when I pointed to it, sometimes in a sentence and sometimes in a miniature story. He described all the objects in the panel and made something of them. He rushed from one panel to the next.

"This is you," he would say, when I pointed to the beautiful brunette. "This is you when you get big and meet the Batman."

"But I don't want to meet him."

"Yes, you do. He's a superhero. He's real good."

"I don't care. I'd be scared of him. You want to meet him, I don't."

My indifference to the Batman displeased him, but he rose above it by ignoring it. "Anyway, this is you. And you're with the Batman and he's got to save you from the bad guy, the Yellow Pearl." We had been hearing about the yellow peril on the radio, and the villain in this comic book had a yellow costume.

"What is he going to do to me?"

"He's going to make you do it and then hit you," Joe Robbie decided. "But the Batman won't let him."

"If he does let him, I won't like it."

"But he won't, because he lets good things happen, not bad ones. Then he rescues you, see. You're swinging with him on the strong rope that he keeps in his belt. It has these hooks. You see?"

"Hurry up and get to the end, I'm tired."

"We can't skip any."

"Just leave stuff out."

He always remained patient. "Okay. So you and him swing

on the rope back to the place where he has a motorcycle hidden and he even has a helmet for you. And then you ride over the long roads home, only the Yellow Pearl still wants to find you and hurt you."

"But he can't."

"No. Because the Batman protects you."

"He can't protect me. I can protect myself. Because I have my own house and I have a job."

"Not in this comic book you don't."

"Well that's what I have."

I told him about school, to the degree that I understood anything about it, having only started. At school we sat in seats side by side, and my partner was Nina Holland. We had a bench near the back. I liked to sit with Nina because sometimes she didn't bring a lunch either, and it was easier to sit beside somebody who wasn't eating, during the lunch break.

We took naps in the afternoon, and I explained that meant that you laid your head sideways on your desk and you rested on your ear like that till it ached, or else you crooked your arm and it fell asleep, and you closed your eyes, and you did like that until the teacher said it was time to learn letters.

Joe Robbie was curious about everything and asked questions. He wanted to know about the other kids and what they looked like, and the teacher and how she acted. I described some of the kids, including the ones who had expensive clothes and clean hair and faces. Some of their mothers and fathers came with them on the first day, and I told Joe Robbie about it then, after he stopped being upset and started asking questions. The parents were all kinds, but some of the women even wore hats.

We talked most often in the kitchen when I did chores, like stacking firewood or drying dishes or cleaning the slop pot. Joe Robbie sat on his stool with the pillow for a seat cushion, always near the stove. He liked to sit there because he was usually cold, and there was a fire in the stove even in the hottest of summer. He had a murmuring, whispering, soft kind of voice, and he slurred a bit so you had to listen very close.

I told him the teacher, Miss Sterndale, could ask you all kinds of questions, like, one morning, she asked us all what we had for breakfast. It turned out that me and Nina Holland had the same thing, biscuit and sweet coffee, which we both called coffee soup, and she dipped her biscuit like I did. She asked what our fathers did for a living, and I said mine worked in the woods logging, but he only worked when he felt like it. Everybody laughed and I blushed and knew I had said something stupid, so after that when she said anything to me I kept it short. "I hate to talk in the class," I told Joe Robbie.

When I was at home, Corrine became my baby, but sometimes Joe Robbie could help with her. He was strong enough to hold her while she was small and could warn me when she messed herself. Most of the time Nora was with us, but some of the time she was working in dry tobacco with Mama, at Mr. Allison's farm. Even then Nora had the harder chores for herself, making supper being the worst of them, and doing the heavy dishes, and carting most of the water. She had time for her own homework—she stayed in school—after supper when the dishes were done.

Once Joe Robbie asked her could she teach him how to read, and she looked at him like he was a stump.

When Daddy and Carl Jr. came home, Joe Robbie sat quietly in the kitchen, shy of them but wanting to listen to their talk. He liked their dirty jokes that made them stomp the floor laughing, and he liked the rough gossip about the other loggers. "I can't understand a goddamn word Tyrone says, can you?"

"No, I tell you what, Daddy, when he opens his mouth I just stand there."

"He was trying to tell me something today, and he was talking like he had some goddamn shit in his mouth, and I told him not to fuck with me any more if he can't talk English. I be goddamn if I have to listen."

"Shit-ass don't do a lick of work because he's always acting like he don't understand what he's supposed to do. I hope a log falls on his ass."

Daddy pulled his coffee toward him, "I need me a drink of liquor, but they ain't nothing but this shit-ass coffee."

"I need me a drink too, it'll take this taste out my mouth."

"We ought to walk up the road and see what old Roe Yates got."

"That son of a bitch will steal from you." Carl Jr. tilted the hat down over his eyes. "Last time I bought a jar from him he didn't give me the right money back. You ready to go?"

"You got any money? I don't."

Carl Jr. shook his head. "Yeah, I got some. Come on."

They walked together out the door. Joe Robbie watched them like a light had faded inside him.

Usually they stayed away for a while on a trip like that, drinking with the Yates boys or with whomever was down at the Little Store, but that time they brought home some of the stuff Roe Yates made. Carl Jr. and Daddy laid out under the tree drinking while the rest of us did laundry in the yard. Otis puffed with the ax, splitting logs for the washpot fire. Nora and me stirred the clothes boiling in the pot. The babies were crawling in the grass near Mama, who worked the clothes in the rinse water.

Joe Robbie sat with Daddy and Carl Jr. under the elm tree, Joe Robbie in the wagon beyond reach of the dog chains. We heard Daddy laughing, and I saw Carl Jr. taking the jar down from Joe Robbie's lips. He wiped Joe Robbie's mouth and slapped him on the back.

"What are you giving that youngun?" Mama wrung the water out of one of Daddy's shirts.

"I thought he ought to try something new."

"You letting him drink that liquor?"

"Louise, the youngun never has any fun."

"That ain't the kind of fun he ought to have."

"You got plenty to do around that fire, you don't need to be worrying about me and Joe Robbie."

"You'll be sorry if we have to take him to the doctor because you mess up his brain."

"It ain't going to hurt him, Mama," Carl Jr. swore, "he ain't had but a taste."

"I want some," Otis said.

"Shut up, Otis."

"If Joe Robbie can have some, why can't I?"

Joe Robbie was smiling. One hand fluttered up, soft and

white, to brush his throat. "It's hot, all down in here." The usually slurred voice was even softer. "It's all right Mama, I like it."

Daddy and Carl Jr. laughed, and even Mama smiled a little. Carl Jr. held the bottle to his mouth again. He swallowed, eyes fixed inside the jar. The stuff ran down his chin, and Carl Jr. wiped his mouth again. He reached his hands to the jar vaguely, as if he would take it, and Carl Jr. laughed in a gentle way. "That's enough, sport. You don't want to go getting the big head and thinking you can handle it like I can."

"You ain't neither one of you worth a shit," Mama said. "Neither one of the three of you. You mark my word, Joe Robbie, you better not turn into no drunk."

"I ain't no drunk." He leaned his head to the side, as if it had become heavy. Pillows propped up his back or else he would have slid out of the wagon. "This is funny, Mama."

"Your mama got drunk one time," Daddy said.

"Lord, Willie, don't tell that."

"She did. She got drunk. We was drinking out of a jar about the size of this one, ain't that right, Louise?"

"Lord," Mama dipped her hands into the rinse water, a blush rising along her neck.

"That's right. It was a right good-size jar. And me and her, we sat right at the table and we drank it. Carl Jr. won't nothing but a rat running round between our legs, the rest of you hadn't even been thought about. And then we got hot and we sat on the porch, and your mama hiked her dress up, and she won't wearing any drawers. I swear. You Uncle Cope got him a good look."

"I wished you wouldn't tell these younguns that story."

"I done told it."

"I wished you wouldn't."

"If your ass weren't so big and you could get drawers around it, and you might not embarrass yourself."

"There you go."

"Go what?" He had passed the bottle back to Carl Jr. "I ain't doing nothing but talking."

"I forgot about I hiked my dress up that high," Mama held up a pair of Daddy's drawers, yellow at the front, "I was hot."

"Carl Jr. got him a look too. I bet you don't remember it."

"No, I don't remember it."

"I wished you would shut up," Mama repeated, but then pressed her lips together. Her eyes, full of vague hurt one moment, mildened the next. "Anyway, I never drank another drop of that mess."

"What shit you speak."

"It's the truth."

"You tell a lie and you know it. And I could prove it, but I ain't going to give away everything I know."

"I appreciate that," Mama said.

MAMA KEPT A soft spot for Joe Robbie even after Madson was born, and while she was nursing Corrine she found time to feel sorry for Joe Robbie and to pamper him. She made him syrup biscuits and fed them to him with her fingers. When the others were at school, she would walk to buy him a cold drink at the Jarman store, a concession she made for nobody else. She used money she saved to buy extra batteries for the radio, so he could listen even when Carl Jr. was logging. So Joe Robbie told me about bombing in London and submarines near Raleigh, and about Mr. Roosevelt, the president. He also learned to sing Grandpa Jones and Mother Maebelle Carter by heart, in a voice you could barely hear, with his eyes rolled back in his head.

His trips to the doctor ate up a lot of the money we made working in the fields. He was the reason I got only the one new dress the year I started school, to add to the one faded hand-me-down dress I owned, provided by Aunt Tula. He worsened and improved, as he always had. On some days, though, he became too weak to leave his bed. With me in school, Mama tended him herself, or else kept Nora home to help with him.

"He's got worse since your daddy give him that liquor," Mama swore.

"He was already getting bad like this, Mama, that stuff ain't hurt him, I don't think."

"Well, I know." Mama sighed, and tucked her chin down in a way that made her skin fan out like a collar. "That liquor changed this youngun."

"The doctor ain't said so."

"I ain't told him your daddy got him drunk."

"Well, you ought to tell him then."

"I ain't. They might put your daddy in jail."

"Oh, Mama, this is some more mess you're making up."

"They put you in jail when you manslaughter somebody the same way they do when you murder. I know. They put my brother in prison when he manslaughtered somebody with a tractor."

"Daddy hasn't manslaughtered nobody."

Mama sighed. The argument had become too complicated. Whenever that happened, she started from the beginning again. "That liquor messed up this youngun's brain. Your daddy done that. When he dies, it won't be on my conscience."

Soon after that, Joe Robbie told me, "Mama says my brain has swollen up, and that's why I lay in the bed all the time."

"Does it hurt?"

"I don't feel anything."

"Maybe you're tired," I said.

He shrugged, a hardly perceptible movement. "I don't do anything but look at comic books all the time. Ain't nobody to ride me around in the wagon."

"If you would get out of bed, I could ride you around."

"You're in school."

"I know. But I could do it now."

Instead, he told me another story from the new comic book they gave him at the doctor's office, where, Mama swore, the nurses loved him to death. This comic book was thicker than most, and I sighed. "But this time I get to say what the girls did."

"Okay. But if I don't like it, I can change it."

"That's not fair."

"It's my book."

I crossed my arms and set my mouth. He opened the cover and started.

Superman had flown off into space again and headed back from this faraway mission past Jupiter away off, and all of a sudden he saw this explosion like the wreck of a spaceship, and sure enough, it was. Superman flew to it and found nothing but flaming balls of wreckage and dead parents and their little boy, who was a orphan, and because the parents were dead, Superman took the boy with him to the nearest planet, and he doctored him, because the boy was injured and couldn't even walk. It took the boy a long time to wake up and Superman was very worried and wouldn't move him and kept bringing oxygen and stuff. But finally the kid got better and Superman asked him who he was and told him his parents were dead, and then he took him back to Earth. And by then Superman wanted to be the boy's new daddy. And he taught the boy to read like all the other kids. But the boy stayed really sick from the injuries he had gotten in the space wreck, and no matter what Superman did, he couldn't cure him. He worked and worked but he couldn't. They went to doctors together, until it made Superman too sad. Then the boy got so sick he stayed in bed all the time and he laid there and he couldn't even move his head, and then his brain swelled up in his skull and he died. Even Superman couldn't do anything about it. Then he described the child's funeral, and all the relatives who came and cried, and the long-lost brothers and sisters, and the aunts and the uncles, and everybody was sad because the child had died.

HOLBERTA WINTER

THAT SEASON PASSED as the hardest of our winters. We lived barely better than animals in a barn, trying to burn enough wood in that iron stove to heat a house with cracks in the walls and floors and nothing but grease paper in many of the windows. Daddy swore he never intended for us to live in that shack through the hard weather. He had wanted to move by Thanksgiving. But come December, with a hard frost on the ground, we were still walking the mile and a half from Holberta to the main road to catch the school bus. Daddy had stopped talking about moving us to a new house at all.

I have no clear recollection as to why those times became so particularly difficult, but I suppose it must have been money, because that winter after Corrine was born, we had less than usual in every way. My winter coat rode halfway to my elbows and barely covered the bottom of my butt. Nora had no coat at all, and wore something Daddy used to wear in the fields when he farmed. We stretched biscuit and fatback as far as biscuit and fatback would go. We took no lunch to school and we ate little afterward. For breakfast we had coffee soup.

On weekends, to save on firewood and to keep us from working up appetite, Mama made the smallest children stay in bed all day. Otis, Nora, and I spent our day gathering firewood from the surrounding woods, not an easy task since all the folks in Holberta scoured for wood in the same place, and knew the country better. Mama shivered in the house, wearing both her dresses and wrapping herself in a worn quilt. Uncle Cope, whose bed occupied one corner of the main room of the house, sat watching her, the covers wrapped around his bloated stomach.

When not gathering wood to burn, we lay in our beds in the bedroom listening to the whistling man in the trees outside the house. Wind made the noise, but we spoke of the man the sound resembled, someone high in the tops of the pines, walking and whistling from limb to branch. Probably in a hurry because of the cold, according to Joe Robbie, probably hurrying home to get to his own fireplace.

I was glad, in those days, to go to school, because at school we had a coal-burning furnace that heated every room. Though I found it hard, every day in the middle of the day, to watch the other children pull out their wrapped sandwiches and parcels of cold fried chicken.

Christmas break interrupted even the warmth I enjoyed while learning the alphabet under the supervision of Miss Sterndale. We stayed at home for the two furious, frozen weeks near Christmas.

Mama said the winter might be so cold because of the war. The Japs and the Germans might have drawn off all the heat, they had blown up so many bombs. The weather was different now than when she was a girl, and Uncle Cope agreed with that. Wasn't so cold in the old days, he said. Sure wasn't, Mama chimed.

For Christmas we had a basket of oranges, and Daddy and Carl Jr. split a quart jar of Roe Yates's best blend. Daddy fought with Mama and at one point shoved her against the stove. She burned her arm and knocked down the flue, and the house quickly filled with smoke while Carl Jr. and Otis hurried to fix the flue and Nora held Mama's burned arm under the spigot and pumped water nearly cold enough to freeze over the angry patch of skin, Mama and Nora shivering outside in the frigid Christmas wind. When they came inside, Mama smeared lard on the burn and Carl Jr. finished fastening the flue back into place, retwisting the strips of tin that had provided its support in the first place. The smoke cleared out of the house.

Daddy, passed out facedown on the bed, slept till sundown.

By then I was old enough to know what Christmas provided for other people, like the children at school, who talked of nothing else for weeks. In those days even a wealthy family rarely gave as much as children are given now, but we were given nothing, like always. Going to school, I knew the difference.

Mama made black-eyed peas for New Year's Day and told us that for every pea you ate you would get a dollar for the new year. We ate ourselves sick.

It was my job to carry the slop pot through the cold, up the slight grade along the path that led to our johnny house.

Winter-dead honeysuckle overflowed the roof. The planks of the walls and the floor were none too sturdy, and each step was accompanied by a sickening spring. I dumped the pot without looking, from as far away as possible, and tried not to hear the horrible sick wet sound. I ran to the pump and rinsed out the pot, no matter how cold it was. Inside, I stowed the pot in the corner and closed the lid tight.

To do our business during the cold, we carried the pot into Mama and Daddy's bedroom, closing the door for privacy. When Daddy was in the room, I took the pot in the other bedroom, and so did Nora. It was cold and nobody lingered. Something always struck me as odd about stripping down my step-ins, squatting and cleaning myself afterward in Mama and Daddy's empty bedroom, a place where I had never spent much time at all. Their bed seemed much higher off the floor than our beds, and bigger, in some way. The emptiness echoed.

At night, we lit the rooms with kerosene lanterns. Otis carried the five-gallon can to the Little Store whenever it emptied, and filled it, and bought wick or begged credit for what he bought, and came home. When school was in session, Nora did homework by the dim light; but she worked at it fitfully, without much hope. At thirteen, she was in fourth grade for the second year. Otis never studied or did homework at all. Being only in the first grade, I hadn't much homework yet. But I was beginning to notice what was what about books and paper.

For days that winter we hardly ate. On the coldest days we stayed absent from school, and I, who had already learned to love the whole going away it involved, sulked in the corners.

I had to hide my unhappiness from Mama, who had no tolerance for my pouty moods, as she termed them. "I never seen a child love school before, not in my life."

She had caught me, crouched against a wall near the stove, a sour look on my face. I whispered, "It's not that cold, I could've walked."

"No, you couldn't, missy, you shut your mouth."

"You would freeze your hind end out there, Miss Smarty." Nora opened the iron grate of the stove to poke the burning log. Bright embers shot high.

"You goddamn right you would." Daddy's voice resounded. "You set your ass right where it is like your mama told you."

Daddy and Carl Jr. were home a lot in those days; it was too cold for logging crews to form. Daddy was sober out of necessity: there was no money even for drinking.

Soon after New Year's the yard covered with snow. Joe Robbie and I were delighted to see it, since we had never seen snow before. A softness, like white chicken feathers, only finer and stranger. Mama watched with a sour face as it blanketed the yard. Bitter wind blew up through the floorboards and streamed around the loose window frames. We stuffed summer clothes in all the cracks and wore everything else we had; we huddled near the stove, almost close enough to scorch ourselves. The wood burned faster than anybody could imagine, and we wondered if the fire would last till morning.

Nora and I went to bed wearing our clothes. We took the baby with us, because Daddy said him and Mama needed the bedroom to themselves. Corrine made soft noises and pedaled the air until the quilts and blankets settled over her.

"Keep her head above them covers," Nora commanded.

"She's fine," I said.

"It was a baby in Smithfield smothered to death in the bed with his sister, and he died, and now his little sister hears him crying all the time."

"Corrine can breathe, can't you, Corrine?"

"But what about in the night when she gets twisted up in the covers?"

"She won't."

"Shut up," Carl Jr. muttered from the other bed, "people trying to sleep."

We kept Corrine between us and tucked ourselves around her. The three of us rested in our warm nest, listening to the wind howl through the house. Soon came the regular creaking of Daddy and Mama's bed, across the thin wall, behind a door that barely closed.

What they did there was called fucking or screwing, and Otis knew a lot about it. One cold night, when the rhythm made noise, Otis said, "Goddamn, the whole house is rocking," and Carl Jr. laughed.

Joe Robbie asked, "What is it?"

"Nothing, Joe Robbie. Go back to sleep."

"No, tell me."

"Ain't no use to tell you, honey," Otis said, "you ain't got no peter no way."

Carl Jr. said, "Hush that."

From Otis's descriptions, I understood that when Mama

and Daddy were fucking, Daddy liked to lay on top of Mama and do it. "He lays all over top of her," Otis revealed, "and then he does it and he does it till he goes real fast and then he can't do it no more."

"He don't," Joe Robbie whispered, because Otis made everything sound nasty.

"He does. I seen it. He lays all over top of her and he sticks his thing into her and he does it."

"That's not nice."

"You don't know what's nice or not."

"Hush," Nora said, "don't none of you have no business talking about it."

"Mama loves to fuck him," Otis said, red-faced, and Nora stood in front of him, squinted her eyes, and struck the palm of her hand across his face as hard as she could.

The fat in Otis's face flushed bright red in the shape of her slap, and he shoved her hard, backward, across the bed.

"You goddamn bitch," Otis said.

"Call me another bitch and I'll slap the shit out of you again."

From the bedroom, Daddy called, "You younguns better hush that fuss before I have to come out there."

"Nora slapped the shit out of me," Otis shouted.

"If I have to come out there to you, I'll slap more than shit out of you, you little son of a bitch."

Silence followed. The creaking of the bed began again.

We listened sometimes. All of us. The sounds took on an eerie edge, with us hearing and knowing, together. When Mama and Daddy reached their high peak of breathing and the creaks of the mattress ran together like a voice, we watched each other and, usually, someone laughed. The laughing choked us all, because we could not let Daddy hear us, at such a crucial moment. "You don't want to mess him up at the end," Carl Jr. noted, and Otis snorted, and Nora blushed.

Even Joe Robbie understood the joke, some. He laughed, and refused to look me in the eye.

Once the topic lodged in my mind, I learned about sex everywhere. One cold evening in the bedroom, Otis asked Carl Jr., "How does a snake fuck?"

"I don't know. I never heard anybody who seen it."

"A mama snake lays eggs," Nora added, chipping the ice that formed over a bucket of water during the night. "A mama snake can crawl right over your face and lay a egg in your mouth, and then the egg will hatch and next thing you know you've shit a snake."

"It's a lie," Otis says.

"Gramama Baker says it's so."

"You haven't talked to Gramama Baker."

"Yes, I have. Aunt Lucy wrote me." Aunt Lucy was the only one of Mama's sisters who could read or write.

"Did she tell you how they fuck?"

"No."

"The man snake can't crawl on top like a dog does," Otis explained.

"Why not?" Carl Jr. asked.

"Cause it ain't nothing on top of a snake."

"How do you know? You ever been on top of a snake?" Carl Jr. and Nora laughed, and Otis blushed to his collar.

"No I haven't. Smart-ass. But I know it's no pussy on top of a snake."

"You talk so nasty."

"A snake got a pussy somewheres."

"Well, Otis, you sure talk like you want to find it." Carl Jr. reared back in the chair when everybody laughed, and I startled myself by laughing too, because I suddenly understood the joke was funny. That pussy word was nasty, and Otis was nasty for wondering about how to find one on a snake. Then I remembered that I too had a pussy, and I felt suddenly confused, as if I should sneer at the thought, the way Otis did when he said the word. As if I should sneer whenever I thought about my pussy.

One day Daddy said to Uncle Cope, while they were drinking sweet coffee and watching another snowfall, "Norbit Holland would stick his peter in a knothole if he wasn't afraid of splinters."

They were discussing a man who had recently broken a leg in a logging accident, working with one of the few crews that was trying to clear timber during the snow. Norbit Holland was Nina Holland's daddy, and Nina was the only other girl in my class who came to school in dresses as faded as mine. I paid attention to the part about Norbit Holland's peter, because of the way Daddy said the word. A slight curl to his lip, and a sharp glint in his eye. He sometimes said the word "dick" the same way, and it had begun to occur to me that peter and dick meant the same thing. The little baby peter I had watched flopping uselessly on Madson's stomach was the same dick that Norbit Holland was willing to stick into a tree.

"Norbit wouldn't know if he got splinters in that ratty dick of his, he ain't got enough feeling left in it."

"I seen that boy fuck a goat one time."

"You full of shit."

"No, I seen it, I swear."

Uncle Cope wrapped a quilt tight around his shoulders and shoved his feet closer to the stove. "Well, I reckon I'd as soon fuck a goat as fuck his wife."

"That's a fact." Daddy's eyes lighted on me and moved away, as if I had suddenly become invisible. I was scrubbing the biscuit pan with a cloth, because Nora said it was not clean enough. I had tucked myself, with the pan in my lap, into the corner behind the stove, a warm spot, but closer to Daddy than I liked to be. "That woman has got a dog pussy hung on her. I swear."

"You ain't seen it."

"The hell I ain't. It looked like a pussy you would see on a wolf. I swear before God, that woman had fur."

"Shit you say, Willie Tote, you ain't seen no such of a thing."

"Hell, Cope, she'll probably show it to you if you ask her to."

Between my legs was smooth and dry. Even without my hand there, I could feel it. But when my daddy talked about Nina Holland's mother, I felt a strange thing. I felt the nastiness of myself.

Mama sat with Daddy sometimes, wrapped in a quilt of her own. She rarely spoke, except to laugh at Uncle Cope's and Daddy's dirty jokes. Once in a while she would say something, like telling Nora not to sweep over Otis's feet with the broom or else he would never get married, or asking Daddy what day the ration coupons came. We listened to the radio, about Eisenhower, the yellow devil, the Hun, and Roosevelt. At night we heard Little Jimmy Dickens and Grandpa and Grandma Jones, as long as the batteries lasted. Otherwise we sat in the echo that formed around our voices. We fought the cold, ate what we had, and waited.

WHEN I LOOK back there, turning over and over the memory of that hard winter in a house not fit for people, I amaze myself that my hatred does not burn me crisp. Even then, I must have begun to understand. Other children had already begun to teach me about living. Other children lived differently than we did; they did not have to gather wood in a picked-over forest in shoes too tight, with socks for gloves. Other families had sausage with the biscuit in the morning and meat in the beans at night. I could not have said these things, but I was beginning to know. I followed Nora through the dark rooms of the shack, through the barren woods with my arms full of branches, or to the cemetery at the edge of the churchyard. I followed Nora and carried Corrine and began to know.

MAMA SAID

MAMA SAID YOU should be careful when washing dishes to keep the front of your blouse dry, or else you would probably marry a drunk.

Nora washed dishes carefully, holding the flat low part of her stomach away from the wash pan. Sometimes she took a towel and tied it around her waist. She washed each glass, each dish, with careful, deliberate movements. Water rarely overlapped the edges.

When I began to wash dishes, with Nora as my teacher, I was careful as I could be, but sometimes I splashed water on my blouse.

Ellen will marry a drunk for sure, Mama said. Ellen can't stay dry at the front to save her life. You'll marry a drunk, Mama said, and blinked, and looked at Daddy who had fallen asleep with his feet near the stove.

Mama said if you drop the rag while you're doing dishes, and the rag hits the floor before you catch it, you'll have company before the floor dries. Mama said, I know we're going to have company today, and I looked at the wet rag on the gray floor boards. This was the next house, Piney Grove, after we finally moved away from Holberta. Nora glared down at me as I picked up the rag. "I ought to slap you," Nora said. "Get me a clean rag."

Nora was angry at me, and I would marry a drunk. I was still staring at the wet spot on the floor when Aunt Tula knocked at the door with a bushel of butter beans.

"I brought the younguns something to shell," Aunt Tula announced. "You can eat these. My beans is coming off good this year."

When you go into a house, use the same door you came out of the last time, or else you'll have bad luck the whole day. Mama said, "Tula, you can't come in that door."

"Hush, Louise, this is the right door."

"No, you left by the front door last time."

"I did not."

"Yes, you did. You was talking to Cope about something anothers, and you dropped your pocketbook on his foot. His good one. You remember."

"Lord have mercy."

"You got to come in the front door. You don't need no bad luck." Aunt Tula remembered all of that and walked around the house to the front door. She thanked Mama, afterward, for her prudence.

We shelled the beans. All day we had been chopping cotton; it was easy work to sit on the porch and slide my thumbs along the edge of the pod, splitting it open to reveal the easy bean inside. Nora and I did the shelling. Corrine stood near Mama's skirt with a fist full of biscuit, gnawing it slowly.

Mama, swollen with another child, sat near us, chewing from the same bread.

Never sew on a Sunday, because for every stitch you make, you'll shed a tear within a year. This was Aunt Addis's house, and I was sitting on the brocade couch; Aunt Addis had handed me needle and thread, but I was watching for the cat. Aunt Addis kept a cat, mostly in the yard, and I was terrified of it; my hands trembled as I threaded the needle with a blue thread I had never seen before, both bright and dark at the same time. We were sewing on a Saturday but Aunt Addis repeated the wisdom she had learned. I never sew on a Sunday anymore, she said. Do, you'll cry the whole year through. I sewed one time on a Sunday, she continued. It was the year my babies died.

I visited Aunt Addis because she was taking care of Daddy's mother, Nana Rose. Nana Rose had shriveled to the size of a big spider and sat in Aunt Addis's dark front bedroom, propped on pillows nearly bolt upright in the bed, wearing a checked bonnet, as if the sun were very bright. She chewed the inside of her lip and glared out the window, the curtains of which were kept open so she could watch the path at the side of the house. I helped Aunt Addis with Nana Rose's bedpan, helped with the wash, changed the linen, helped Nana Rose in and out of bed. Now and then Nana Rose fixed on me with her eyes and knew me. Aunt Addis told her my name many times.

"Your daddy is a sorry son of a bitch." Her thin, long hand with the sharp fingertips dug into my shoulder. She had slid out of bed and decided to speak according to whatever laws were at work inside her head. "I know. He's my son. And he's as sorry as that goddamn daddy of his."

"Hush, Mama," said Aunt Addis.

"Don't tell me what to do." Nana Rose arced a hand weakly toward Aunt Addis and caught her across the cheek with the softest of slaps. Nana Rose often slapped Aunt Addis like this, and sometimes she could manage a pretty good lick; Aunt Addis blinked, her jaw working. One day she would slap Nana Rose back, I thought.

When you have a bad dream, make sure you eat something before you tell the dream to anybody, or else it will come true; Mama said this too. Like the bad dream where Alma Laura was drowning and could not reach the top of the water. Or the dream I had so often, where Mama stepped down into the river, the skirt of her slip floating up around her legs, and the cold like a sharpness in the air. When you had a bad dream, you were supposed to eat something before you told the dream. But when you have a good dream, you should tell it before you eat anything. Then it will come true. Mama took me to the porch, early in the morning. The sun had begun to color the edge of the horizon; we stepped onto the porch that faced the chicken yard. This was years later, after Nora married and left the house. I was the oldest daughter now. Mama whispered, "I dreamed Carl Jr. was alive."

Or the dream I had, later, that I was Frog Taylor's daughter and June Frances's sister; or the dream that Bobjay drowned in a flood; or the dream I still have sometimes, that I hear a knock on the door and open it and there is Alma Laura, prim and neat in a sweet conservative dress, almost as old and stooped as I am. She holds the end of her string of pearls the way I do my diamond brooch. She grins as big as the full moon, and I invite her into the house. We have fresh sweet tea with lemon and I show her my garden. As usual, Alma Laura never speaks. She has grown to a handsome old age, her skin still strong and clear, her lids not quite as drooped as mine. But my hair is darker, she has more gray. We tour the garden and return to the kitchen. There, we step back and study each other. We are prosperous. We have lived to be old and comfortable. Alma Laura smiles with serene satisfaction. Vanishing then, always, after that moment of perfect contentment. Sometimes the dream continues past that point, and I am looking everywhere to see where Alma Laura has gone.

Or a hundred other dreams I could think of, that I would have wanted to come true, at least in bits and pieces, if I could have found someone to listen before I ate.

Mama said, when you see a blue bird make a wish, and if you see a red bird next, your wish will come true.

We were walking in the woods along the shore of the pond or the bank of the river. I heard the hollow echo of birdcalls over water. We were following Mama, and she walked faster than we. She carried a bamboo fishing pole over one shoulder. We were small, Nora and Carl Jr. and Otis and me. Carl Jr. carried me part of the way. We were headed to go fishing with Mama, who was hungry for fried perch. We walked so fast the branches whipped back at our faces.

Mama came to the riverbank and stripped her cotton dress over her head. When I remember this, it is suddenly too much like my dream. She wore the white cotton slip and in the heat the sides of the slip clung to her damp thighs.

She laid down the bamboo pole and reached into the can of worms she carried, that Nora and Carl Jr. had picked out of earth they had spaded in the backyard. Mama pulled out a fishing worm that stretched and popped in half. Over her head, a whir of wings, flew a blue bird that flashed through the clearing. See a blue bird, make a wish, Mama said, and closed her eyes.

When she opened her eyes, she glanced hopefully around, not at the river where the fish swam but at the branches of the trees. She jammed the steel fishhook through the fleshy part of the worm, and the worm curled and writhed along its free end. See a blue bird, she said, and kept glancing at the trees, and then glided toward the edge of the river in her battered, black shoes. She arced the bamboo pole and the worm in its agony soared through the air with a plop into the dark river. See a blue bird, Mama said, but I don't remember whether she did. She stood shadow-dappled in her soft slip, cool in the summer afternoon, fishing in what must have been the river and not the pond. Somewhere, I think, she is still there.

Years later my daughter dropped a comb and reached for it, and I said, without even stopping to think, "Step on it." My daughter looked up at me but her hand had not yet touched the comb, so I said, quickly, nudging her foot with mine, "If you drop a comb you have to step on it before you pick it up, or else somebody will lie about you before the day is done."

She smiled at me as if this pleased her somehow, and

stepped on the comb. An image of my mother flashed across her face, as if all the similarities of their facial bones were suddenly lighted. She faced the mirror and combed her carefully tended bangs.

Never hang a calendar before the new year begins, or else the family will have a bad year. I never remember a calendar in our house, though Mama repeated the saying to anyone who would listen in the days before a new year dawned.

When you rode in a car and you saw a black cat run across the road, you drew a cross on the window to send away the bad luck. Mama applied the rule to every cat, not only to black ones. She licked the tip of her finger and drew on the window, leaving a smear that she could see.

If you dreamed someone died, then pretty soon there was bound to be a wedding close by, but if you dreamed about somebody who was already dead, it was sure to rain.

We were visiting Uncle Bray and Aunt Tula; they had come to fetch us in Uncle Bray's truck. We would sleep at their house tonight, and tomorrow we would take Grandaddy Tote to his brother's funeral. We had eaten chocolate cake, fresh tomatoes, butterbeans that I helped to shell, potatoes mashed smooth with a fork. Uncle Bray had a son named Reno but he was not Aunt Tula's boy, and when they were all in the room, they hardly looked at one another. Reno slept in a room in the barn, and that night he took Carl Jr. with him to sit up drinking. The rest of us were sleeping all over the house, some in the living room on the rug, and extra bodies in all the bedrooms. Nora, Corrine, and I had a pallet of our very own, at the foot of Aunt Tula's bed, where Aunt Tula, Mama, and Madson also slept. We were excited that we could sleep in our clothes and that we could see right under Aunt Tula's bed to the enamel slop pot she stored there, for when she had to pee in the middle of the night. When I took off my shoes I set them on the pedal of the sewing machine and Aunt Tula saw me and frowned and moved them, and I thought she was angry because I was not supposed to touch the sewing machine, but she only said, "You shouldn't lay your shoes where they're higher than your head, or else you won't be able to sleep."

If you stepped over somebody, you had to step back over them right away, or else they'd die soon. I stepped over Otis, and Mama made me step back. Nora stepped over Carl Jr., and Mama smacked her across the legs with the fly swat and pushed her over Carl Jr. from the other side. Corrine stepped over Delia, and Mama led her across the baby again, holding her chubby hand.

Once one of my sons stepped over another, and the saying ran through my head, a crazy sound, if you step over somebody they'll die soon, but I said nothing to my son.

But with my daughter I would have spoken the words, I thought. I would say the words my mama said to me, no matter how stupid they sounded. It would not have been that I meant to say anything, the words would have flown out of my mouth. Like the thought of my drunken husband when I am standing at the kitchen sink now, damp on the front of my blouse.

I loved my mother with all my heart and soul. In the years that followed the winter in Holberta, I loved her with an intensity like nothing else I had ever known.

By the time we moved to the house in Piney Grove, where we would live until the war ended and Nora eloped, Mama had borne eleven children, nine alive and two either stillborn or dead soon after birth; and Joe Robbie died before his eighth year. Mama had worked in the fields every spring, summer, and autumn I could remember, and the labor and the birthing of children stooped her, drew deep lines in her face, caused her eyelids to droop. She had grown larger with the years, and now the fat of her calves hung down over her ankles. Weathered skin swelled over her cheeks.

Alma Laura and I watched her. It was Alma Laura who told me when Mama was pregnant again.

Once I had walked past Mama and Daddy's room on a Sunday afternoon, and as I stepped on the creaking floor-board at their door the jarring sent the door open a crack. I could see Daddy's pale hairy butt flailing up and down and round and round, and Mama laying there with her nightgown pulled up, lolling in the bed like a lake of herself, tongue flickering against her lower lip. I heard a step behind me and ran out the front door quickly. But the image of Daddy somewhere inside Mama stayed with me.

I knew from the pig harvest and the seasons of pigs' lives that if a pig mounts a sow you get baby pigs. It was easy to learn the rest from Daddy's talk. Now I had seen them through a crack in the door.

Daddy talked about Mama sometimes, him and Uncle Cope or Carl Jr., or sometimes even Otis. "I like it with some rhythm to it, and Louise rolls like a pond, she does," Daddy told Uncle Cope.

"You shouldn't talk to your brother about me."

"You don't worry about how I talk, you take care of frying that fatback."

"It's some cold biscuit, Daddy," Nora said.

"But it ain't no fatback till your fat-ass Mama fries it."

"You just got finished telling me how much you like that big ass of hers," Uncle Cope grinned.

"I don't like to look at it. I just like to lay all over it."

"Mama's crying," Nora said, and that only made Daddy and Uncle Cope laugh the harder.

"Your mama is as weak as water," said Aunt Addis, when we were sitting beside the bed where Nana Rose slept. "Your daddy is common even if he is my brother, and your mama is sorry and don't lift a finger to goad him. You don't want to be poor and sorry and common like the rest." Then she sent me to the kitchen to mix up a pan of biscuit.

"Too much water," she said, looking down into the biscuit pan, "that's your mama's biscuits you're making, not mine. I want mine," and snatched the flour sifter out of my hand, tugging my hair in the back so I would remember.

"Mama's going to have a baby again," I said; but these days I would have to think about it to remember which baby it was. Aunt Addis looked at me, scowling. "Again?"

"Yes ma'am."

"Lord God. That man is going to kill her. And her sorry enough to lay right down flat of her back and let him do it."

AUNT ADDIS

DURING THE SUMMER when Mama had sent me to stay with Aunt Addis to help with Nana Rose, I turned nine. At the news that Aunt Addis had asked for me, Nora puffed up jealous like a mad animal. She banged the water dipper on the side of the bucket and flung a handful of biscuit dough onto the pan, raising a cloud of white flour.

"I need you to stay here with me," Mama told Nora, and what she meant was, Daddy liked Nora's biscuits better than Mama's, and Mama wanted Nora there to cook.

Nora shot me a look of pure hate, and later she threw the cat on me again.

I had grown to have a terror of the cats that lived in the woods, under the house, or in the neighbors' yards. Whenever one of the mother cats had kittens, Nora would find the kittens and throw them on me, on my legs at first, then aiming at my face. I had scratches on my calves and forearms and, once, on the bridge of my nose.

"You go ahead, drag your skinny self to wipe Nana Rose's

ass, see who cares," she said. "Here, say good-bye to this little kitten before you go."

The screeching thing flew toward me through the air, calico, red, tabby, spotted, black, yellow eyes with slit pupils that terrified me, and with a yowl it smacked into my tender forearms where I had thrown them up over my face, and the claws like needles raked my skin, and Nora laughed. The kitten landed with its four legs splayed out reaching for anything solid. I screamed and knocked it away from me and felt my new scratches and looked at Nora.

We hated each other keenly and simply for a moment. Then I turned and ran.

Once she had tried to throw the mother cat, but it twisted in her hands and gave her a gash of her own, wicked and bloody, along the cheekbone.

I put my clothes in a bag, including my only shoes that I was saving for school and my blue skirt that I liked, and I sat on the edge of the front porch till Uncle Bray came to pick me up in his truck. Behind me I could hear Nora crying and Mama cursing and Corrine screaming about something I couldn't understand. I was going to stay with Aunt Addis. The thought made me breathless.

When Uncle Bray pulled into the yard, I ran to get in the truck with my bag in hand, and I sat there while he visited with Mama a minute before driving me away.

Aunt Addis and Aunt Tula lived close enough to each other that it was easy to walk from one house to the other, at least in daylight, but also far enough to keep them separated. The path from Aunt Tula's ran along the north end of Moss Pond for a little while, then meandered toward Spike's Creek

Road where Aunt Tula lived. You could walk the distance from one house to the other in half an hour. Whenever I went there, Uncle Bray would take me home to his house, and Aunt Tula would fill me up with bacon biscuits and homemade cornbread and then set me walking on the path. Watching me eat, Aunt Tula would shake her head and say, "Look at this poor youngun eat. You know she doesn't get nothing to eat at her house."

"It's a wonder she's got a scrap of meat on her bones," Uncle Bray agreed.

"My brother is as sorry as there is. Drink you some more tea, honey. It's sweet, ain't it?"

"She loves that tea."

"I can't get enough sugar to make it like I really like," Aunt Tula patted her hair, "because of the war."

The walk through the woods frightened me sometimes, because I traveled alone and usually carried a bag of something or a jar of something from Aunt Tula to Aunt Addis, plus the sack of my clothes. The woods had an eerie quiet; one hardly hears a quiet like that any more. "Did you like your walk?" Aunt Addis would ask, laughing when I hurried across the yard to the back door.

"There was something following me at the last part," I panted.

"Hush that mess. There's nothing out there to follow you."

"Aunt Addis, I swear there was. I could hear it coming behind me."

"The only thing you heard was yourself, all worked up to a pitch. Now come on in the house."

"I was scared that monster came back and was going to get me."

"Lord have mercy. You listen to that mama of yours too much. There's nothing got nobody in these woods since I don't know when. Now come on in the house, I said. Your Nana Rose was asking about you. And I got a peck of things for you to do around here. What's wrong with your leg?"

"Otis chopped it with the hoe."

"Well, mercy. Let me see."

A long dark scab traced the side of my kneecap and along the bone the skin was red and flamed. "Your brother did that?"

"Yes, ma'am. Him and I were fighting and he got the hoe after me. And I busted him on the head with a rock." I sighed. "He called Mama a fat sow and I told him he ought not to talk about Mama like that, and we was at one another pretty quick after that."

"You and Otis are always fighting."

"He ought not to call Mama names. I can't stand it."

For a moment she stood looking at the knee, hand soft on the top of my head, a warm pressure, one of the few times I can remember being touched.

She fed me a slab of cornbread smeared with white lard and a cold cornmeal dumpling in pot liquor, delicacies such as I only dreamed of in my mother's kitchen. I wolfed down whatever she set in front of me, and she watched with her mouth set to a thin line. "Don't your mama feed you, child?"

"We ain't eat nothing but biscuit with meat grease since Monday."

"Watch how you talk."

"There hasn't been any food since Monday."

"That's better. Why not?"

"Daddy can't work because he hurt his back."

Aunt Addis sputtered. "The only way your daddy hurt that back was hunched over your mama." She glared at me and said, "Now, you get to scrubbing the baseboards in your Nana Rose's room. Get right down on your hands and knees."

I swallowed the last of the buttermilk that cooled my belly and gave me such a warm feeling underneath my ribs. It was the most delicious buttermilk and cornbread and at the end of the few minutes I had eaten enough food to make me swoon. I stood up burping and headed for the back porch to find the white enamel pan for baseboard washing. The burp brought the slightest smile out of Aunt Addis.

I scrubbed till my elbow ached sore, bending down as best I could with my bad knee. I wore out one cloth and Aunt Addis fetched me another. "There's germs all over this room." She watched me at my work for a minute, tying an old rag around her hair. "If we don't keep it clean, a sickness will come on Mama that will take her for good."

"I ain't dead, girl," Nana Rose croaked. "I ain't sleep either."

"No, ma'am. You aren't."

"Goddammit, I know I ain't."

A moment later Nana Rose started snoring again, and Aunt Addis left to take down the blinds in the front room. Pretty soon I could see her in the backyard. The blinds hung from the clothesline, as Aunt Addis furiously scrubbed and rinsed.

"It's a goddamn shame I stayed so long with that son of a bitch," Nana Rose mumbled when she woke again, spit draining from the side of her mouth, eyes closed but fluttering, as if the lids could not get fixed and still.

My knee ached, and pretty soon bending down opened the cut again and I was bleeding, oozing a little. I ignored it until Nana Rose sat up straight in the bed, glared at me, and pointed one long thin crooked bony finger. "That youngun is bleeding."

"Shew," Aunt Addis said. She had entered the door with clean towels and set them in the wardrobe, puffing as she stood. Her eyes came to focus on me. "Ellen. Oh Lord, look at you. I reckon I ought not to have you bending down like this. Stand up and show me your knee again."

I raised the edge of my skirt.

She took me to the back porch and washed it clean with Octagon soap that stung. "Has there been flies in it?"

"They fly around, but I swoosh and don't let them crawl on it."

"Because they can lay eggs right in the wound," pinching up her nose, "I seen a man with a leg like that, before they cut it off. Maggots crawling around in the leg." She spoke practically, without a whiff of pity. "So you keep flies out of it unless you want to end up without a leg."

"No, ma'am, I don't," I said, wincing when she spread Merthiolate on it, and thanked her when she cut a clean white sheet-piece from the rag bag and folded it up in a pad to cover the cut.

At the end, patting her own hair back into place, she admired her handiwork, the pad tied to my knee with a clean strip of Nana Rose's old yellow housedress that she would never again rise out of bed to wear.

"Can you work?" Aunt Addis asked.

In the bedroom, as I sat on the floor by the baseboard, bending my good knee, Nana Rose asked, in her powdery husk of a voice, "When did you put my good dress in that bag of yours? It won't near ready for rag picking."

"Mama, that dress was so thin you could poke a finger through it. When I laid it in the rag bag it fell to pieces by itself."

"That friend of yours makes the soap so strong it rots cloth."

Aunt Addis tucked her lips together in a tight line. "That friend of mine has a name. You know it as good as I do."

"I might know her name and I might not like to say it."

"Jenny," Aunt Addis said to Nana Rose. "There, see? I said it for you, so now you don't have to."

Nana Rose pursed her lips together and then shot a wad of tobacco juice into the spittoon on the floor beside the bed. By then, I had knelt over the baseboards and begun to scrub again.

Later I scrubbed the wall behind Nana Rose's night table and the night table itself, both stained with tobacco juice that had missed the spittoon. Nana Rose slept peacefully through the trickling of water into the bucket, the rasp of the cloth on the wall. With one hand she clutched the top of the quilt that warmed her, a grip so tight she might have feared someone would come along to snatch down the covers at any moment. Her skin lay fine as tissue along the bones and veins.

After Aunt Addis checked the wall, the table, and the baseboards, I helped her hang the blinds in the front room, where they made the light cool and pale. Aunt Addis had a couch and two chairs in the front room, and a rag rug and two tables, not the same but similar, with a picture of Nana Rose in a frame on one of the tables. I considered this a lot of furniture, and Aunt Addis spent the rest of the day dusting and polishing it, with me to help.

When we were nearly done, Miss Jenny, tall and lean, appeared in the doorway. "You still want me to wring that chicken's neck?"

Aunt Addis gave me a sharp look. "This youngun needs some meat on her bones, that's what it looks like to me. Do you think you can eat a piece of fried chicken, Ellen?"

"Oh, yes, ma'am," I said, and my stomach started to dance.

"Then I'll kill that yellow-looking one," Miss Jenny said, "she hasn't given an egg in two weeks."

"I don't know how you think you know which chicken lays which egg."

"I know," Miss Jenny said, and turned, and vanished, her long shadow trailing behind her.

Out the window, while rinsing my saucer in the pan of cold water, I studied Miss Jenny as she grasped the yellow-feathered chicken by the neck and twisted the body through the air. Through the window I heard the crack of bone and then the chicken's garbled cries as it circled the yard in a final run, head flopped over to one side. I had never watched a chicken die.

Miss Jenny scalded the chicken and plucked it clean, so fast it was hard to believe, the smell of wet feathers clinging to her hands and filling the porch. Aunt Addis gutted it and cut it up for the frying pan. For Nana Rose she boiled a short thigh till the meat was nearly falling off the bone, adding a dumpling to the thin broth, and when she had cooked this bland stuff, a good while ahead of our supper, she set me on a tall chair to feed the old woman. Mostly Nana Rose lay back on the pillow, wheezing for breath and accepting the food I offered into her mouth when she felt it against her lips. When she chewed the dumpling, a line of meal strained through her lips and down her chin. I wiped this away, and she opened her eyes. Glaring like a hoot owl, she said, "I guess Miss Princess couldn't be bothered to feed me herself."

"I wanted to do it," I lied, and this answer confused her to the point that she closed her eyes again, and reclined on the pillow.

"I wish the Good Lord would go on and call me," she murmured, as I settled the spoonful of chicken meat and broth to her lips. She sucked greedily and gummed the food.

When she had eaten and drifted someplace between sleeping and waking, her breath moved haltingly in and out with a sound like the rasp of my washrag on the plaster walls beside her bed.

I brought firewood for the cookstove and buckets of water from the pump outside, while Aunt Addis cooked our supper. The smell of frying chicken made my mouth water, impossible to think of anything but the food to come. Miss Jenny hefted the ax by the woodpile and split kindling with strokes as strong as Otis's. Her arms, relaxed, hung veiny and thin, but when she swung the ax, firm muscles tensed. She caught me watching and I turned away.

At supper I ate the drumstick, handed onto my plate by

Aunt Addis, her mouth set into its thin line. We ate in the kitchen with Miss Jenny, listening to Nana Rose's snores. Aunt Addis, watching me eat from beneath partly lowered lids, paused to listen to the sound. "She's resting good today. She's had her three little naps."

"Her breathing sounds better," Miss Jenny agreed.

"It's some more potatoes if you're still hungry." Aunt Addis turned to me as if by accident.

"Yes, ma'am," I said, and she dished them out, listening to Nana Rose again.

Miss Jenny said, "It's not every day we fry a chicken. You better eat good."

"I didn't have fried chicken in a long time. Mine is good."

"Here's you the neck to gnaw on," Aunt Addis speaking gruffly, but with the tiniest smile at the corners of her mouth. "Then you can boil the water to wash these dishes."

I sucked at that chicken neck till the bones were as clean as Aunt Addis's kitchen windows. Then I stoked the fire and boiled the water for dishes, as I had been told.

Aunt Addis had a particular way of washing dishes, beginning with the glasses, then the plates and saucers, then the spoons and forks and such, then the pots and pans. Always do them the last, she said, because they dirty the water. She stood near me while I washed to teach me what I should do, like scrubbing between each fork prong and cleaning the backs of the plates as well as the fronts. Sharp-tongued as she was, she kept her patience when she was teaching me; not like Nora, who criticized the least thing I did. At the last I scalded the clean dishes with more boiling water from the kettle, pouring the water carefully over each plate, to kill the filth, as Aunt Addis described it. Boiling water kills all kind of filth, she said.

Nana Rose woke with a fever, and we piled blankets on her till it broke. Aunt Addis sat by her bedside with a lapful of cross-stitch, and when she caught me watching she gave me a swatch of cloth and set about teaching me the simple stitches. Always run the front stitches one way and the back the other, she said, to keep it neat. At first I worked clumsily with the needle and almost jabbed it in my nose trying to thread it, but later, mimicking the precise movements of Aunt Addis's deft fingertips, I got better. I practiced in the light from the kerosene lamp at Nana Rose's bedside.

As miraculous as the cross-stitch and the housecleaning was the fact that Aunt Addis troubled to teach me anything. Adults hardly ever paid attention. Aunt Addis spoke in the same rough tones and harsh words as Mama and Daddy. But underneath was something else, some part of her that watched me as if I were a tender shoot pushing up through the ground in springtime.

I practiced until time for bed, when Miss Jenny entered Nana Rose's bedroom for the first time, bringing quilts and a feather pillow for my pallet. I slept on the floor in Nana Rose's room, by the side of the bed where she could see me, in case she needed help to pee in the night. That first night she never waked to ask for help, but all night murmured in dreams about her children, Sudie, Tula, Wainright, Alice, Cope, and Willem Carl, my Daddy. Those were the names I knew, but there were more. At dawn she called me out of sleep, "Girl, get up here and help me out of this bed before I bust."

After I helped her back in bed I carried the slop pot carefully out the back door and picked a path through patches of gray dirt, avoiding the dewy grass. I dumped Nana Rose's pale piss into the sitting hole and returned to the house. Nana Rose had begun to snore again, but in the doorway stood Aunt Addis, watching in her housecoat.

I WALKED WITH Miss Jenny through the woods to Aunt Tula's house, to help carry fig preserves that Aunt Addis sent. The jars made a pleasant rattle in the potato sack bundled in my arms. I had drunk a glass of buttermilk and eaten half a hoecake for the walk, since Miss Jenny said I looked too scrawny to carry much. We walked through the woods along what Aunt Addis and Miss Jenny called the Dry Path. When I asked, Miss Jenny allowed there was a path called the Wet Path, too, shorter but crossing the wetlands where Miss Jenny preferred not to walk. We picked our way carefully so as not to jostle the jars of preserves.

Aunt Tula received us on the back porch as if she had been expecting us. She sniffed each jar of the sweet figs as if she could determine the quality of the contents using only her nose. "It's got a pretty color this year."

"It come out pretty good."

"Uncle Bray loves his fig preserve," Aunt Tula said to me, "I can't keep enough in the house."

"Addis done real good this year. He'll like these."

"Well, it's a good thing. Mine didn't come out worth a hoot."

She packed us up with a whole pound cake, a mess of collards, and jars of sweet pickle to take to Aunt Addis. She had plenty of eggs she could have given us, the hens were laying good, but we thanked her and said no. We had enough to carry. So Aunt Tula made us each three fried eggs, for lunch. She fried my eggs exactly like I wanted, with the yolk a little runny but thick at the bottom, and I sopped the yolk with cornbread.

"You never seen such a mess of eggs from such a pinched-up bunch of chickens." Aunt Tula dipped her fork into her own solid yolks. "The roosters is going around all puffed up about it."

"We're getting about the same eggs as ever," Miss Jenny said.

"Addis's chickens is some good layers," and I noted that Aunt Tula laid a slight stress on the word "Addis's." Aunt Tula sighed, the bottom of her chin quivering. "How is my mama?"

"She's right quiet this last couple of days."

"She still running fevers?"

"Twice, three times, lately. She don't seem so bad to me, even when she's hot, though."

"She eating?"

"We get something down her every now and again."

"You ought to see to it that she eats. Keep up her strength."

This had the effect of quietening Miss Jenny, and pretty soon after that she rinsed her plate in the pan of water by the window, and I did the same with mine. Aunt Tula rose from her own seat.

"Bray would sure love to visit with you-all, if he was here."

"You tell him I said hey. All right?"

"I'll tell him."

Aunt Tula looked me up and down. "Ellen, you never had so much meat on you. Addis feeds you pretty good, don't she?" Again, stressing the word "Addis" for effect.

"Yes, ma'am, Aunt Addis is a good cook."

"That sorry mama of yours can't hardly keep food in the house. It's a good thing you come up here to see us, ain't it?" She studied me while I blushed.

Miss Jenny tugged me by the collar toward the door. "We got to go, girl."

"Yes, ma'am."

"You stay with your Aunt Addis for a while, you'll get fat as your mama," Aunt Tula, fixing her eyes on me again, said sharply.

"We work Ellen too good for her to get fat," Miss Jenny announced, very loudly. "Ellen is a good worker, too. Come on, girl. We got to tote these sacks down that path."

"Don't you break one of these jars." Aunt Tula gave my ear a tug to help me remember.

"She didn't break one coming, and she won't break one going," Miss Jenny declared, and eased me away from Aunt Tula's outstretched hand.

NANA ROSE'S DREAMS

AS NANA ROSE sickened more, a change came to Aunt Addis's house, a cloud of tension filling the rooms. Aunt Addis moved cautiously in the vicinity of the sickroom, and Miss Jenny stayed out of the house whenever she could. Nana Rose perched clawlike in the bed, her body decaying, exuding a sweet smell. But from her eyes and from her clenched jaw radiated the fiercest strength and sharpest hatred. Most of the time she hardly understood where she was or who we were, except that about half the time she recognized Aunt Addis and tried to slap her across the jaw. Now and then, on seeing my face in the lamplight while I was putting lotion on her dry arms, she said, "Your daddy is a goddamn rat-ass son of a bitch. Do you know it?"

"Yes, ma'am."

"Don't let that man mess with you."

"No, ma'am."

"Don't let any man mess with you. Do, you'll be a whore."

"No, ma'am, Nana Rose, I won't."

Once she grabbed me by the hair at the back of the head. She was suddenly as strong as a girl and pulled my face to hers. "You lay down with your grandaddy, don't you?"

"Nana Rose, let me go, that hurts."

"You answer me, girl. You lay down with your grandaddy, don't you? Nasty little thing."

With her free hand she tugged at my ears, and I squealed and pulled back. She gripped my head tighter and glared at me.

Aunt Addis heard her shouting and found us, but she had to call Miss Jenny to help her pry Nana Rose's hands out of my hair. Tears of fright ran down my face.

"All you young girls are bitches," Nana Rose shrieked, and she repeated the words for an hour or more while Aunt Addis, Miss Jenny, and I huddled in the front room listening to her hawk-call voice. "My husband took up with bitches all his sorry life."

I HELD THE pan full of warm water while Aunt Addis washed Nana Rose's yellowed hair. Limp strands flecked with suds draped Aunt Addis's fingers, while Nana Rose, head bowed, stared fixedly into the flower pattern of the rug.

"I feel old," Nana Rose muttered.

Aunt Addis laughed. "You are old, Mama."

"I ought not to be."

"Well, why not?"

Nana Rose swung her bony head up and looked Aunt Addis square in the face. "You think it's funny to make fun of your mammy, don't you, you dried-up bitch."

Aunt Addis swallowed. She rinsed the suds from her fingers and, using a washcloth, dripped rinsewater through Nana Rose's hair.

"I hope you get miserable and old like I am."

"I'm sure I will, Mama."

"With nothing to take care of you except some bony dried-up bitch and her stringbean friend."

Aunt Addis carefully dried the strands of hair with a small towel, squeezing out the water. "You ought not to talk so ugly, Mama. I do the best I can."

Nana Rose's voice rose in pitch. "A dog wouldn't do what you do. That's why God took your babies."

Aunt Addis froze. Long seconds trickled past.

She finished drying Nana Rose's hair, then carried away the pan of water. When she was gone, Nana Rose clamped her mouth shut on her mostly toothless gums, glaring straight ahead at the gap between the curtains, the last bit of outside left to her.

"Open them curtains some, and quit gaping at me, you skinny biddy," Nana Rose snapped, and she scarcely bothered to glance at me as I raced to the window.

AT NIGHT, WHEN the house was dark and everyone slept, I lay awake tossing and turning on the pallet, listening to Nana Rose's dreams.

"Cope," she began, "don't hang off the back of the truck like that, fast as your daddy goes, he'll sling you out. Cope. Don't lay all over the truck like that." Then followed the sound of her lips smacking, a moistness that sounded like a dryness. Light of the full moon spilled across her face. She turned on her side, hair matted on the pillow, and smacked her lips again. The sound of her breathing followed, a bellows, a breeze, and a frightened, strangling sound. "Get him off the road. No, you left some of him. Get all of him. Get all of him off the road. I can't stand to see him lying there like that."

"Paulie," she called, "Paulie," and later I learned Paulie was her sister, dead for years.

Lips clicking again, parched as paper. The sound continued, until I finally stood from the warm pallet. We kept a glass of water by her bed. I held the glass to her mouth and dropped a thin trace of water across her lips. She swallowed greedily and her knobby-jointed hands reached vaguely upward toward my hand. She almost woke, almost slept. She drank the water and rested more deeply for a while.

While we both waited for sleep her words kept running through my head, a thread of connection through all my dreams. Paulie, she said, come close to my bed. You can sleep with me. Crawl under the covers, all right sweetheart? We can eat some chicken liver all mashed up. I killed three chickens for the chicken salad for the Easter supper, there's three livers. We can boil some rice till it sticks. You can scrape it out of the pot with your spoon and I can eat mine off a saucer, like I like. I want to eat my chicken down by the creek. Paulie, we can go down there together. There's a good place to hang your feet in the water. I'll take my children down there one morning. I'd like to drown every one of them. You don't know I have children, well, I do. I had me eight that lived and four that died, and I am wore out. I can't chase after butterflies and such today. I can't run around after dragonflies today. So let's just sit here cool by the creek. And we did, Nana Rose and I, we sat there beside whatever creek flowed in her mind, and I was aware that I was Paulie to her, that this old woman in the room with me was Nana Rose, in her dream or mine. We sat underneath the shade of a summer day at the riverbank with our feet in the cool water, and I worried that there lurked something under the water to bite my feet, and I suddenly could not breathe, and Nana Rose's voice went on carrying words into my head, Paulie, sit still, and if you be quiet the fish will come up and kiss your toes. They're tasting you to see whether they can eat you. But it feels like a kiss and anyway, they can't eat you, they can't even bite you good. While the children are off in the woods to play. Willem and Addis and Tula is buck naked. When we come fishing they run around in the woods, and Willem plays just as sweet as the rest. Nana Rose spoke as if we were merely young girls. We sat by the river in her mind. I was aware that I was asleep and lying on the pallet on the hard floor at the foot of Nana Rose's bed. But while she talked in her sleep, the dream drifted like a water of her through my head; we were both dipping our feet into the dark water.

Finally, her eyes glazed over and she lay back into bed. The rasp of her breathing marked the passing moments, the arc of moonlight across my face on the pillow. I settled down on my pallet, and she did the same on her bed.

"Someone is here to kill me," she said later, as I was at the edge of sleep again.

IN CHURCH, WHICH I had begun to attend with Aunt Addis, we prayed for Nana Rose's health, including the preacher from the pulpit, at the request of Aunt Addis. Bless this woman with an abundant old age and fullness of health to taste of her sunset years, the preacher said, and this was about the prettiest thing I had ever heard. The prayer left me with a feeling of benevolence, as if I myself had prayed each word, and I was certain that I would not, for instance, draw up all shivery the next time Aunt Addis and I helped Nana Rose onto the bedpan. I dreaded the sight of Nana Rose's shrunken butt cheeks. The process of tending her had become a kind of torture for me, because my images of her mixed with dream images and grew powerful. The flat flaps of her breasts frightened me, so stretched and wrinkled and laced with dark blue veins. I looked elsewhere. I concentrated on Aunt Addis's careful hands as she lifted Nana Rose off the bedpan and cleaned her and pulled down the nightgown around her pale, stringy legs. They had given up on underwear because Nana Rose always grabbed Aunt Addis's hair and pulled it when Aunt Addis helped her into or out of her drawers, and if Aunt Addis complained about it, Nana Rose slapped her across the face again. Even to the last, Nana Rose had enough strength to give some sting to a slap, if she put her weight behind it. She jarred Addis's jaw a couple of times when I was there to see.

WINTER CAME AND the bedroom was cold. We moved Nana Rose into the living room where there was a wood heater, and I slept between the heater and the foot of her bed again, tending the fire through the night. Aunt Addis sent me to school as many days as she could spare me. Sleeping in the front room gave me eerie chills. Firelight moved shadows on the walls and in the room, across the living-room furniture that had been shoved to one corner. Out of familiar surroundings, I would wake in that room with the still-delicious feeling that I was sleeping somewhere I oughtn't, like falling asleep in a car that was moving, and waking, and wondering where I was.

Her sickness came and went like a tide. But she, being stubborn and strong even at her age, recovered after every stretch of fever.

But I was telling about Nana Rose's dreams, and I recall a lot about them. I have been remembering those nights, my long dreamy sleeping in that room, where the dreams continued, waking and shoving logs into the wood stove, waking exactly enough to do so, twisting my hair over one shoulder to keep it out of the upward shower of sparks. Out of balmy darkness I rose from my pillow, opened the grate and checked the fire, golden embers dancing, a shimmering terrain beyond the hot flames, and Nana Rose asleep on the bed with her mouth hanging open and her jowls drooping down. I jammed another split log through the mouth of the grate, it barely fitting, and flames poured upward around the new log, visible till I closed the grate and settled down again. I could not tell if I was waking or sleeping. I lay with the roar of the embers in my ear, and then her voice as she began again, always again: Get me a bucket of water. I want to soak my feet in cool water. My feet is hot. It's hot up under this house. I don't know if I ought to tell you anything about myself. I already told Jesus yesterday. Jesus come by and sit on the edge of the bed. And I says Jesus, I says, you sitting there like some kind of a spook. And Jesus was looking at me and all. He got this twitchy smile. Rose, he says, I want to tell you something. Where I go, you coming after me. And then he got on up and went on out.

She quieted, and I pictured Jesus on the edge of the bed, more substantial because her description of him was clouded. His weight bowed down that side of the bed and Nana Rose hung toward him with her jowls, chins, the loose skin on her arms all descending toward Jesus. We were all in the room, and Jesus said he was cold, would I tend the fire? So I got up and tended it as he asked. I was so tired, my arms hung heavy and I couldn't lift the wood, and after a while I couldn't breathe, and the light was hurting my eyes. I shoved a log into the fire. Then it seemed like I hadn't and I shoved another one. Then I woke up with Nana Rose standing over me.

"Jesus is changing everything in me," she said.

I blinked my eyes and tried to wake up. After a while I whispered, "I'm asleep."

"Shut up, heifer. Ain't a drop of water in my glass. Go dip me a cup of water out of that bucket."

She kicked me with her bare foot and I stood. My feet nearly froze to the floor.

"Jesus is changing things," she said as I was leaving, in a voice that made me look back at her, at the way she moved her head when she talked, pecking emphatically, like a preacher-chicken. "Jesus is changing things in this house."

When I returned with the water she looked at me with her buzzard eyes and said, "I'm ready for the kingdom. Are you?"

"No, ma'am, I'm not ready yet."

"Jesus is changing things in you too."

I held the cup for her to drink.

"You go to that church with Addis. Don't you?"

"Yes, ma'am."

"You like them church people?"

"I do."

"You pray for your gramama in that church?"

"Yes, ma'am. The preacher, he prays aloud, and I pray along silently."

"Well, it's working, because Jesus is changing things in me tonight. Jesus is getting me ready for the kingdom. Glory hallelujah. Add a log to that fire." She kicked at my feet to move me toward the firebox. "It's cold."

"There's no room for another log in there," I said. "I just added one. I'm sleepy."

"You can't be asleep when the Lord is working."

"I got to go to school."

"You can't be sitting up in school when the Lord is working."

"Yes, I can. Jesus can work on me right in the school."

When I turned around her hand was already there and fell across my face, with a weight behind it that seemed awesome since the hand itself appeared frail and fluttering. "Sass," she hissed, "Jesus don't need no sass out of your lips, heifer. Put another log in that goddamn fire like I told you, and then crawl your scrawny ass into a corner where you can watch Jesus work. We're bound to be up all night."

I found a small length of wood and made a show of doing like she said. Seated at her bedside, she fumbled with the matches to light her kerosene lantern. She had forgotten the electricity again; the electric lamp was already burning right beside her but her eyes had got so dim she couldn't tell. After a while she gave up with the matches because she failed to open the box.

"Heal my hands, Lord."

Silence.

"Heal my hands. Show me, Lord."

Followed by the fumbling sound of the tips of her fingers on the matchbox.

She sat down. I closed the grate. One moment the fire was dancing in reflection on her throat, on her cheeks, the next the room dimmed as the fire lowered. I stood up from the pallet. I turned off the lamp. Now we rested in the dark except for the bit of light from the stove grate. She sat on the edge of the bed.

"Turn that light back on."

"Jesus wants it off, Nana Rose."

"He don't want no such. You don't know what he wants."

"Well, he was right here when I was turning off the light and he didn't stop me."

She had begun to sober up from her drunken awakening, her certainty that the time for the transformation of all things had finally come. Awake, she understood the world was not changing so fast after all. Her voice quavered with a tentative warble. "Jesus is still working in me tonight. Amen."

"Amen. Good night, Nana Rose."

"Go to sleep then, goddammit."

She stayed on the edge of the bed for a long time, and I watched her in the dark. When she began to shove her feet under the covers, I slipped over to her and helped her, bracing her back against the pillows, then lifting her legs the way Aunt Addis did, wrapping my arms around both. I settled the covers around her, and she lay back, and the rim of her eyelid caught firelight as if she were crying. Or else her eyes were tired and watery. I went back to bed.

"Goddamn whore hound," she hissed. Then we slept.

We dreamed together again. Her voice carved a channel through my head.

Night merged into night. We were always waking in the wee hours of the same morning, visiting the same moment, Nana Rose rising over me, kicking my shoulder, spilling the water or drinking it so I would have to rise to fetch more.

She dreamed with the voice of Paulie, and I heard the rhythm of it like a current in the midst of a river, Paulie speaking about herself. You're not right. Your head's not right. You know it? Paulie don't read and write. Sister learned how, but Paulie is stupid. Uncle Mack rides me on the mule when we come back from Kingston. My bottom is red. I got welts on my bottom, my dress is stuck. Paulie down in the woods. Down yonder. I can see the mule, and Uncle Mack on the back. Uncle Mack on the mule. Paulie in the dust, following in the dust.

SOMETIMES AUNT ADDIS heard the commotion and stood out of bed. She might come in the room where Nana could see her, but often she stood in the shadow. She watched and listened as Nana told about Jesus, about Paulie's walks, about Willem and the girls. Sometimes she covered her ears as if the words hurt going in, but she never stopped listening. As if she were waiting for a sign.

"I hate you," Nana declared, trying to spit at Addis during a bath. "I hate you, lousy bitch whore," but she was bone dry, she failed to collect even a drop of spit, and so she was making the dry spit sound and hunching forward pathetically, and this enraged her, as Addis scrubbed her face with a wet cloth. She balled up her fists and struck Addis in the eyes, and Addis dropped the cloth and backed away, momentarily blinded. She knelt on the floor with her hands on her eyes, and Miss Jenny came to fetch her without a word. Nana Rose sat stubborn and half-bathed on her pillow till Addis could see again and came to finish the bath.

She had blacked both Addis's eyes, and we watched the purple bruises spread over the next few days. You never saw such black eyes in your life, the color of glistening violet tar. It was as if Aunt Addis were making the bruises spread by an act of her own will, to purple and darken out of spite. I caught her studying them in the mirror in the front room. Touching the dark edges tenderly with her fingertips.

"I had me a bruise or two in my life," Nana shrieked. "There's not a woman alive hadn't had a bruise or two. You needed your share, that's what."

NANA ROSE BELIEVED she was broadcasting on the radio. The wind howled that night and stirred all the curtains in spite of the fact that the windows were closed, in spite of the rags we stuffed in the cracks. Close to Christmas but not Christmas yet. My mother had said I must go home for Christmas Day and besides, Nana had recovered from another fever and looked fit to live to a hundred or more. She sat higher on the pillows as if she were rising over the bed. She believed she was the voice on the radio, "Coming to you live from Goldsboro," she muttered, "spacious skies and apple pies. It's a war on honey, that's what. Coming to you over the air waves from Goldsboro, North Carolina, what more could you want than music?"

Whenever she saw Addis she began to shriek, "Whore strumpet, dog pussy strumpet," in a piercing voice that left her gasping and red-faced. More and more of her care fell on me, especially during the holidays; the last time Addis tried to feed her, Nana stabbed at the back of her hand with a fork and almost broke the skin.

But on Christmas Eve night she sat up on the pillows and forgot the radio, forgot Jesus on the side of the bed, and called for a bowl of chicken and rice. Addis brought it to her and Nana Rose stroked her still-dark hair with a gnarled hand, till Addis moved away.

When I die you don't even have to bury me, you can just haul me to a ditch. Do you hear me? I got a hold of some liquor tonight, and I can feel it in my blood. Did you know I had me a drink of liquor? I can see my time coming, and nothing but a common whore to bury me. You heard what I said. Don't look at me like that. You are a whore. You are common. You and that friend of yours, laying up in that room wrapped up in Satan. You have Satan to thank for what you do. When my heart stops beating I hope you can hear it. I know you got that skinny youngun listening. That runt sitting up all night listening to my heart fluttering, waiting for it to stop so she can run wake you and you and that friend of yours can have a party because I'm dead. I know you. I know what you goddamn want. Whore hound. Sneaking around this house like you're somebody. When I die you can drag my body to the ditch. You can throw me in the pond, you can drive me down to the bridge and throw me in the water right there. Nobody cares what happens to me when I die. I won't be buried in no church like decent folk. You can save yourself the trouble of a funeral. You can haul me down to the river and throw me in.

THE DAY AFTER Christmas Miss Jenny stripped all the beds, including the one Nana Rose was lying in, and she boiled all the sheets in the washpot, and rinsed them, and wrung them out, and hung them on the line. She started at dawn and worked through to dusk.

"I know what she's trying to do," Nana hollered, trembling with a new fury.

Aunt Addis stood perfectly still with her arms folded against her stomach, looking out the window near the bucket of water in the kitchen, listening to Nana's voice reverberate on the plaster walls.

"She's trying to kill me."

Outside, sheets unfolded like sails on the line.

Someone must have seen, because the story spread around. Everybody knew what would happen if you changed the sheets between New Christmas and Old Christmas. We had no neighbors within sight of the house, but someone must have seen. Because soon the story reached every lip of the pond that Jenny and Addis put a hex on the old woman by changing the linen.

"My own baby girl, she wants me dead." Nana sat weakly

against those pillows with her tongue hanging partly out, as if she had lost control of it, and she took desperate, gulping breaths, each labored as though it might be her last. "Whore hound. Strumpet. What are you looking at?"

But when the women lifted Rose out of the bed, when they changed the very sheets beneath her, she never made a sound. She sat in the chair tight-fisted with fury, but she never said anything, as if she knew she had better start saving her breath. They changed the sheets and made the bed and lifted her tenderly into the nest of it. Her mouth worked as if she wanted to spit again, but she knew it useless to try.

They moved through the house with the clean sheets cold from the winter line. Nana chewed the inside of her lips with her gums and stumps of teeth.

I fed her. I bathed her. Addis no longer dared. I spooned soup into her mouth and wiped it. I lifted her head and sponged her face with a cool cloth. I listened to the rasp of her breathing day and night, while she fell slowly back against the pillows.

No longer waking in the night, we slept, like shipmates riding a river, buddies on a raft. She no longer called me names or spoke to me at all. I had dissolved into her notion of herself, somehow. The hand that held the soup spoon was as good as her own.

When she died, late one night, I was holding her hand and then, the next moment, she was no longer where she had been. Her hand became a weight, and I lay it onto the quilt.

As if she knew the very moment, Addis came into the room and pulled me back, away from the bed, and then she walked up to the edge of it, alone.

Then Miss Jenny came in and stood at the other side of the bed, and I knew with certainty then that Nana Rose was dead, because she would never have let Miss Jenny stare at her like that.

IN THOSE DAYS you hardly ever saw the flowers at a funeral that you would expect today. For Nana, I hardly remember a bloom, though surely there was a spray of something, lilies maybe, or something else from the season. Something for the top of the casket.

We buried her in the blustery winter. It was one time I can remember I ever saw my daddy sober, and so early in the morning, too. The Bakers, my mother's half of the family, wanted to get an early start for Zebulon and had crowded all on one side of the grave. We said a prayer, and I held onto Carl Jr.'s belt.

Some of the women from church had come; but not many. Mr. Jarman had come but not Miss Ruby. The preacher's wife had not come. Not all of Nana Rose's children came either, but Aunt Tula wheeled Grandaddy Benjamin to the foot of a tree and parked him there. She claimed he cried, but I never saw a tear.

My daddy came, pasty-faced and wire-jawed, having scraped the beard off his face but with a wad of tissue stuck next to his Adam's apple, held in place by a spot of blood. He stood beside my mama, who hardly came up to his shoulder, standing with her legs thrown wide as if she were in the middle of a field. I remember being embarrassed by the sight of my mother standing with her legs wide open like that, with light pouring through her legs in such a way that it was apparent she wore no slip. Standing flat-footed in worn shoes.

THE LAST NIGHT I slept in that room, toward the end of January after Addis and Jenny changed the sheets, the reason I was holding Nana Rose's hand at the last is this. She dreamed my dream, right before she died. I had been dreaming about Mama walking along in the marsh, heading away from the Wet Path toward a part of the woods where I'd never seen anybody walk before, toward the old mill above the Little Store. Mama waved good-bye and then she was heading down into the water, as if there were steps beneath the surface and she were walking down them. As in the dream same as before, Mama vanished into dark water. "I'll see you come sunrise," Mama said, "don't forget to make the biscuit."

She said the words and I popped awake. Nana Rose was making the tiniest breathing noise, an easy sound, like waves, and then she said, plain as day, "Don't forget to make the biscuit."

The words rang out. Her voice seemed full and young. For some reason I understood what that meant, and I climbed out of the pallet and walked to the bed. I took her hand like holding it was the most natural thing. When she looked at me she died, I saw it, like something going out of her eyes, and that was that.

A MAN'S MAMA

DADDY SHAVED WOOD with his pocket knife beside the stove. Carving toothpicks, he said. He had been sitting there the whole of February. He refused to get in the truck and go to work in the morning when Mr. Jarman came. Carl Jr. went, but Daddy refused to get out of the chair. We had eaten the last biscuit from the night before. I put sugar in the coffee till it made me sick to drink. Before I walked to meet the school bus I heard Mama and Daddy arguing again. "These younguns has got to eat a mouthful every now and then," Mama said. "You need to get up from there and go to work."

"A man's mama don't die every day," Daddy answered.

"A man's younguns get hungry every day."

He never answered, when any other time he would have slapped her across the room for talking to him like that.

I could look him in the face for once, and did. I was hardly afraid at all, only curious about his face, because it softened when Nana died. Maybe I had the instinct he would harden again and I wanted to study him in this state. He reared back in the chair once Mama left him alone, and chips of wood floated to the floor from the tip of his knife. His hair was thinning along the top, more so than I had noticed, and the lines across his forehead had deepened in the thick, weathered skin. He was looking down at nothing, the knife and block of wood working in his hands. He pouted, his lips pursed. His teeth were dark and stained, his beard heavy, the flesh of his neck beginning to go stringy. He was tired. He was lonely. I had never seen Daddy this way.

Aunt Tula once told me Daddy used to be a sweet little boy. This is something people will almost always say about a hell-raiser, that he was sweet as a child, but Aunt Tula's face changed when she said it, and I got the whiff of a girl inside her, stirring restlessly. Your daddy was the darlingest little boy. He was the best-tempered baby, I know, because I had to take care of him. We were standing at the side of Nana Rose's grave I think, and I had seen Daddy in tears, while Aunt Addis comforted him. Aunt Tula whispered in my ear, patting my shoulder. Your daddy wasn't always like he is. He had a goodness to him, one time. While he sobbed in a deep, wrenching way over the grave of his mother.

"When a man's mama dies, he's all alone," said Daddy, drunk, beside the stove.

Mama slammed the empty flour tin across the room. "I haven't eaten a mouthful this morning. Not even one biscuit."

"Get my sister to pray for you," Daddy whispered.

"You got to get some money."

"Get some money your own self."

"You done spent all mine. I give it to you and you spent it. I know what you bought too."

"You best hush."

"I don't want to hush. I want you to get up from there."

Daddy took a deep breath and leaned back against the wall again. Mama wheeled and backed away, the thin dress clinging to her hips and buttocks. She walked with a rolling motion, on the sides of her feet. Her toenails glittered a scaly yellow, the feet swollen and freckled. I stared at her feet as she passed me.

Calm settled onto Daddy when Mama retreated and the room settled into temporary peace. In my imagination I was peeling potatoes. In my lap lay a bowl with potatoes freshly scrubbed, and me peeling them one at a time, the brown peel unraveling and dangling to the floor, the white potato gleaming in the bowl. For supper. Boiled potatoes. The smell would fill the house.

Aunt Tula said, Your daddy had a peaceful nature when he was a boy. I mean a real little one. He wasn't one of those would tear off the wings of flies or the legs off spiders or anything like that, he wasn't the kind to drown kittens. Not when he was a boy. But a change came on him. I don't know why. He started carrying around the playing cards with the pictures of the naked women on the back. I saw the pack of them one time, on his dresser, and I looked. Your daddy fouled his mind with that kind of nasty stuff when he was a teenager and it warped him from the sweet-natured boy he had been. When your daddy was a teenager, he started to run with the lowest kind of drunk trash. All the boys in our family ran with trash.

"Make me a cup of coffee," Daddy spoke the order in a flat voice and looked at me. He offered his white mug toward me, gripped in his hairy red knuckles.

Coffee boiled on the stove. Nora had gone to school today, so it was my turn to stay home. I took the best potholder and folded it twice. I poured coffee carefully because Daddy got mad if I spilled. The thought of his yelling voice raised the hairs on the backs of my arms. Spooning sugar, I stirred.

"I loved my mama," Daddy declared, as I carried the cup to him.

He splashed coffee on my hand, taking the cup. I kept quiet about it because Daddy hated it if you complained. One of his pet peeves with Mama remained that she complained so much. I tried to back away but he looked me up and down. "Get me a biscuit."

"There's no biscuit," I said.

He cuffed me sharp across the jaw. It didn't hurt much, it was for show. "I said get me a biscuit, girl."

"It ain't no biscuit in the house," Mama screamed, and I ran off before Daddy could swat me again. "It's no biscuit because it's no money. We got not one cent. And the Jarmans froze us on credit. Pretty soon it won't be no coffee and no sugar, neither one. So you set there and holler at the younguns like a jackass."

At Joe Robbie's funeral, two years before Nana Rose's, Daddy had stood like a creosoted post in his dark hat and borrowed suit, and gazed at the husk of Joe Robbie in the casket as if he were vapor or a passing breeze. He had shaved but not neatly and from where I was standing a patch of beard was visible beneath his chin. Beside him, clinging to his arm, Mama heaved and sobbed.

At Nana Rose's funeral, I scarcely remember my daddy at all, until the end, when Aunt Tula whispered in my ear that he was crying. I remember Uncle Bray's hand, his two nub-fingers bright pink at the ends. He kept me by him and Aunt Tula, and I pretended I was their daughter as Nana Rose's casket hovered over the open grave. The coffin hung as if floating in the air. Later, at home, I would hear Mama say to Aunt Tula, "Willie was all tore up. He was sobbing like a baby, he wet my dress across the shoulder, and he was shaking. I never seen him like it."

"He did love his mama," Aunt Tula echoed in a hollow voice. "Where is he?"

"Over to Roe Yates's house, buying liquor."

"I guess he's going to have to drink him a bit to get over the funeral."

"I guess he is."

But even Aunt Tula kept quiet when she heard Daddy's heavy footfalls across the porch. Aunt Tula without Uncle Bray was a tad more timid than with him. "Evening, Willie."

"Evening, Tula. You come over here to check up on me?"

"No, Willie, I come to see how Velma Louise and the younguns is doing."

"Well, you better not be checking on me. I don't need no biddies messing in my life."

"Me and Tula was having a cup of coffee and talking about your mama's funeral."

After a while, Daddy said, "I had me a drink of liquor."

"Did you?" Tula asked cleverly.

"I might have me another one." He slurred, blinking slow like a lizard on a rock.

"I don't doubt it," Tula said.

"Get me some coffee," Daddy said to Mama, who sighed and stroked the hair along the back of her neck as she rose.

"Sit down," Tula said, and Daddy, who was weaving badly in the air and changing the position of his feet abruptly from time to time, dropped his weight into a nearby seat. He blinked again, as if the change in perspective surprised him. Now he and Tula were on a level.

"Mama's dead."

Tula's chin quivered. "I know."

"You remember when we was little, how good Mama was?"

"Yes, I do."

They looked at each other. I froze in my spot and watched. Something incandescent passed between them, as if time were dissolving on them before my eyes, and for a moment the brother and sister lit up from inside, the boy and girl who had begun inside these two. I can see their faces now as clearly as I see the veins on the back of my hands. I am glad I was old enough to remember.

"We ain't got nobody," Daddy said.

"We got Daddy."

"He ain't no good."

"Hush, Willie."

"I miss Mama."

"Well, you never came to see her."

"I still miss her."

"Well, you should've came to see her. She would have liked it."

Tula's admonition died on the air, and Mama moved toward the table. The moment faded. Tula looked at her hands and Daddy wiped his eyes. "My mama's dead," he stated in a flat, dull tone. "I miss my mama."

"Well, you wouldn't feel so bad about it if you had come to see her before she died."

IN THE PRESENT

ONE SUNDAY I woke early and hoped Mama would let me go to church. It was April, after the war was over, and we had been working in Mr. Taylor's tobacco beds, leaving Mama so tired she would want to stay in the bed till way past dawn.

I woke before Nora, rising to stir the ashes in the stove, kindling a small fire that would make a bigger one, then hurrying outside with the water bucket. The well stood at the side of the house, where I primed it and pumped it while the sky washed lighter. The wind cut through me, so early. Across the fields it lashed, stirring up dust.

Sunday morning had a special feeling, even at this hour. For me, the feeling grew out of the possibility that Mama might let me out of the house today, that I might be able to put on my good green check dress or even my new blue skirt and white blouse, and attend church. When Mama gave permission, I left as soon as breakfast dishes had been done, or mostly done. Daddy never said no, only Mama.

In the remaining dark I carried the slop bucket off the back porch and down the path to the outhouse. Careful that the bucket not splash its muck on me, I pressed the lid firmly and tried to ignore the tendrils of stink that drifted upward from it. Each step I placed carefully, feeling the ground with the bottoms of my feet. The smell of the blooming honeysuckle along the path clouded thick in the air, densely swollen, a smell I would always remember from that path, because of the way it mixed with the mess in the pot and the odor of the outhouse. I heaved the slops into the outhouse pit, the sound framed with someone's rooster crowing, from a shack further back in the woods where colored folks lived.

I washed my hands by the pump and headed indoors.

Nora had heard me and stood in the kitchen tugging at her dress where it bound her across the ribs. Her breasts were slightly flattened. "You get a bucket of water?"

I nodded and drew a second bucket without being asked. Nora stoked the stove.

"You're all on fire to get to that church this morning, ain't you?" Nora asked.

I AM REMEMBERING that morning as if it were the present, even though I am years past any such morning, even though I no longer have a wood-burning stove to stoke or a hand pump to raise the water from the well. I am stepping on the path to the outhouse carrying the slop bucket, I am ten years old, Nana Rose has died, and I have to live at home again, but on Sunday morning if I am good I can leave the house in my nicest clothes and sit in the clean room on the painted pews among quiet, contemplative people who regularly sing songs and pray together. The memory spins through me again: I am breathless during the walk to the outhouse and trying to hold my breath at the same time so I can avoid the smell of the bucket; I am wary of the path, the tricky places where the tree roots raise up without warning like snakes at my feet. I am remembering as if I could walk outside my house now and find the path to the outhouse waiting for me again.

I have been standing at this window with a hand across my chest, squeezing. Suddenly I remember making biscuits that spring morning, wanting so much to get the job done, standing and squeezing out biscuit dough with Nora whispering in my ear, "All you study is that church. I hope you sit in those pews till you rot." In the present I am only making my own coffee and a slice of toast for my breakfast but my wrists are heavy and I can hardly move for the remembered smell of the biscuit dough, the sweet lard coating my fingers.

"IF YOU WOULDN'T get in such a hurry you could do something right," Nora said, "but all you study is that church. I hope you sit in those pews till you rot. That place is all you can think about."

"You hate my biscuits no matter what I do," I said.

"Well, you won't change my mind with that bowl of mess you're working on right now."

"You could come to church too."

It must have taken her a moment to understand what I meant. She glanced at me and then back at the bowl. "What do I want to go to any church for? It's nothing but a bunch of old biddies who don't do anything but make fun of you if you can't dress as good as they do."

"They're not all like that," I said. "They sing hymns and tell the stories of Jesus. You should try it."

"I been to church, I know what it is."

"Well, you could try it one more time and you might like it."

She took the bowl of biscuit dough from me and shook more flour into it. She studied the dough as if it were rising before her eyes. I knew she wanted to go. I knew she would refuse. "These biscuits look like mush, Ellen, you need more flour in this dough. I can't see why I have to tell you that every time."

I stood there blinking.

"Go wash your hands and wipe off that syrup bucket so Mama can have a sop with her biscuit."

"You ought not to be so bossy," I said, but I wet a cloth and wiped off the syrup bucket and then my own sticky fingers.

After that I spared no more time to try to talk Nora into coming to church with me. I concentrated on doing all the work I had to do before Mama woke up. When the water on the stove boiled hot, I used some of it to wash the dishes we had left soaking the night before, and then I filled the bucket again, hauling the water with the handle banging against my thighs as I walked.

IN MY KITCHEN, now, a rage comes on me, a quiet one, but strong enough to bind me across the ribs and rob my breath. As if someone is waiting for me to cook for him, to bring him something, as if one of my brothers or husbands or uncles or my daddy or my grandaddy or the sheriff or some other man has asked me to bring him something that he is probably sitting in plain sight of. Bring me a cup of coffee. Get me a biscuit. Find my suspenders, these pants are baggy. You need to do some laundry so I have some clean clothes to wear. The voices wait at the ready. I have heard them all my life.

I go outside, I shake my head to clear it. I have a little yard and I walk in it, I admire the bloom of my azaleas and scoop up the petals that have fallen to the ground and put them in a plastic bag. My neighbor thinks me crazy for doing this but I hate the sight of flower petals decaying on the ground underneath the flowers that are still alive. I dump the petals behind the shed where there are also piles of decaying roses, dogwood blossoms and even the remains of a few camellias. The smell of the roses overpowers everything, even the honeysuckle. I take a deep breath of it. But still in my mind's eye I see Nora's hands working the biscuit dough, a morning so long ago.

WHEN MAMA LUMBERED barefoot into the kitchen, her housedress already hanging limp on her shoulders, I asked her if I could go to church. Right away, Nora chimed in, "There's still a whole lot of your work you haven't done, missy."

"I know I have to do everything before I go." I turned to Mama with an expression I imagined as earnest and appealing. "I promise I'll do my work."

"I don't need you worrying me about no church this morning."

"Please, Mama, let me, I want to go so bad."

"I said, don't bother me youngun, else I'll take this firewood after you." She waved a split log at me, standing with the stove grate open and studying the fire. I stepped back by instinct; she had clubbed me on the head with firewood often enough. "I waked up with a headache this morning."

Nora added, smiling at me, "There's a whole pot of beans for you to wash up here on the counter. You need to get your ass to work."

When I neglected to move to the beans quickly enough, Mama cuffed me across the face, a warning sting. The movement startled me and I backed up, blinking, toward the pot of beans.

I washed the beans, swollen from their soaking overnight, and then lifted them out a handful at a time, cleaning out the husks, the dark beans and the ones that were deformed. Nora could not abide a deformed bean in her pot and she was sure to find the very one I let get past me. While I was working she fixed on me like a hawk.

NOW IN MY own home, as I stand over the sink pouring water over a pot of dry white limas, I am thinking, almost out loud, I should not cook the beans because they will give me gas. Anyway, I have much better food than beans these days. I have fluffy clean white bread in loaves, some stacked in the freezer from the recent sale at Food Lion, I have pork chop thawing and sandwich meat, ham and turkey. Not one ounce of fatback or bologna resides in my house. I have frozen vegetables from my garden, and jars of canned tomatoes in the pantry. I have learned to make a pickle or two. Nowadays I can eat beans because I have a taste for them, and today I do. So here I am standing over the mouth of the drain sifting my hands through the heaviness of white beans in water.

I scoop off the husks, the dark ones, the ones that are deformed. I will not abide a deformed bean in my pot. I must sift and sort till I have found every last one.

But the memory of that Sunday morning hangs me up: the drifting nature of the memory, like smoke, so fragrant when you catch it. I stand in my clean white kitchen. I step to the back door, I wipe my hands on a towel and pause where I can see the blooming of the roses beside the shed. I have the smell of beans and water on my hands, and the heady drift of the honeysuckle from the fence. The vivid present brings up the vivid past, and for a moment I am standing again in that dingy kitchen so long ago, my hands in the pot, the pile of beans shimmering in the cracked bowl, the water cloudy.

But I shake my head and I am watching my roses, years later, and I wonder what connects the two times when at the same moment floods me the fact that I already know. The smell of honeysuckle. Through my backyard, as through that dark kitchen on a long-ago Sunday, flows the smell of honeysuckle in full bloom, the heady thick odor drifting through the kitchen, overpowering even the smell of the half-rancid sausage Nora has begun to fry.

Again I shake my head and this time I have moved toward the roses, I am walking, startled as if I do not know how I could have gotten here.

I am thinking, I want to go to church. I want to sit in the pews with a clean dress. I don't care if somebody has to go with me. We will sing the songs of church and we will think of the Lord on high and we will pray some prayers. Maybe I will see Aunt Addis and she will sit with me. Maybe Carl Jr. will come with me; he can sleep on the back pew like always. All the while I sort and grade the beans I am thinking about the holy face of Christ that I see in church sometimes. Alma Laura has also seen the face of Christ. His glory hangs over us like a big balloon. Alma Laura will go without me if Mama won't let me go. I don't think it's fair for Alma Laura to be so free when I am not. But Alma Laura would probably see things differently.

"I'm always cold of a morning," Mama muttered, standing so near the stove she is apt to cook herself.

"I'm done with the kettle," I said, "you want me to rinse that biscuit pan?"

"I barely got the biscuits made," Nora said, glancing sideways at me. "You tame your little ass down. Breakfast won't go any faster because you're jumping up and down to get to that church."

Carl Jr. shuffled in, scratching his head. "What's wrong with Ellen wanting to go to church? I'll go with her, you know Daddy won't let her go by herself. If I can get a clean shirt."

"You ain't got but one clean shirt and it ain't ironed."

"Then Ellen can iron it and I can go," Carl Jr. said, and I was already reaching for the flatirons to warm them on the stove.

"Look at her move now," said Nora with a sneer.

I was transfixed by her expression for a moment, the meanness of that look, and at the same time I grew aware that her body had become different than it was, more curved. The cotton dress clung to her breasts and thighs. I studied Nora in her meanness, a memory as vivid as the scent of the drooping arm of this rosebush covered with blossom, so thick with smell I am almost drunk.

I have buried my sister Nora, in the present. She died of kidney disease some months ago. All her children came to her funeral and cried, and in spite of the fact that my sister lay dead, I thought it was a fine sight. I thought my sister had done well for herself, to have so many children willing to cry at her funeral. Since then I have visited her grave and I know she waits in it, her body anticipating resurrection in her dry vault.

But the Nora I cannot escape is the one who rises out of me, the one who turns to me when I am setting the pot of beans on the stove. "You let them beans alone now, you'll ruin them if you put in the salt. You let me season them beans."

I IRONED CARL JR.'s shirt and Mama refused to say a word, though she glared at me now and again. I checked the biscuits in the oven and told Nora when the tops toasted brown. I boiled the grits and kept them stirred, in between resting the flatirons on the hot stove, and ironing the shirt, and carrying Carl Jr. his coffee with three spoons of sugar. I moved from one task to another like a good girl without complaining. I thought about my blue skirt and white blouse that were nearly new given to me by Mama's sister Lucy Baker as hand-me-down from her daughter my age. I had only worn this outfit to church twice before and now I could space it with the green check dress Mama had bought me out of my money from working in cotton and tobacco over the summer. I had begun to think of that money as my money now, even though she still collected it, kept it and spent it as she pleased. I could wear one outfit one week and one outfit the next. This made church easier to deal with than school, where two outfits did not last so long.

When Daddy shuffled into the kitchen scratching his behind through his overalls, I brought him a hot biscuit and he tossed it from one hand to the other while I rinsed out his coffee cup and wiped it dry.

"You make me sick." Nora glared at me as I moved back and forth.

"She twists that little ass around here like she's going somewhere. I ain't said she could go nowhere." When I approached the stove, Mama cuffed me again to warn me, not much harder than before, but I still backed out of range. "That goddamn church will fill your head with a bunch of mess. I know all about Jesus. Jesus can wipe my goddamn ass, that's what Jesus can do."

Nora pouted over the kettle of hot water, the plate of sausage dripping with grease, the pot of grits. I fed Madson and the baby, then I ate, but by then the grits were mostly cold.

When I had eaten the last mouthful of grits, Carl Jr. said, "Get your dress on. It's a long walk to that church and I don't want to bust in on them people when they're ringing that bell."

No one else said anything, except Daddy, who muttered, "That girl is crazy for a church, ain't she?" I slipped quickly away from the table and hurried to the bedroom where I splashed water on my face and searched for a clean slip.

I had no Bible to carry but I pretended, as we walked, that I had a black leather Bible with the words of Jesus printed in red letters, as well as a hat and white gloves, wrist-length, as fine as any rich man's daughter. We took a cut through the woods back of a couple of shacks where the colored people lived, a teeny naked boychild creeping through the yard in a tee shirt but no pants, carrying the slop bucket toward the johnny house, his miniscule wee wee jiggling at every step. His round black bottom glistened with dew. I was embarrassed to look, but Carl Jr. hooted at him to make sure he knew he had been seen.

Miss Ruby Jarman was out walking in the tiny yard at the back of the store, where it butts up against a clay bank, but when she saw us out so early headed for church, she ducked back behind the building, curlers clutched at her stringy gray hair. Spread over her bare white calves like spiderweb lay nets and vines of blue vein, like something that had ruptured.

We could hear the welcoming music flood down the hill from the church while cars turned into the driveway and people climbed the steep bank.

"We're going into the house of God," I reminded Carl Jr. as we began to trudge up the driveway.

"You betcha," he agreed, and we walked right in.

For the introductory service before the Sunday School session we sat at the back of the sanctuary, farther than which Carl Jr. refused to go. Usually he would stretch out on the back pew to sleep during the Sunday School class. Carl Jr. was a thoughtful sleeper and never snored.

As for me, I sat politely and anxiously among the other Sunday School children, keeping my back straight and sitting with my hands in my lap in such a picture-perfect way that I could continue to imagine myself as having gloves on my hands and a Bible in them.

Today I managed to get a seat next to June Frances Taylor in the Sunday School class, and she smiled at me and passed me a note. It was a real note; I had half expected it, tangibly white and crispy, and I could hardly wait to sneak to open it at my side, where I read, with a thrill down my spine, "My Ma says you can have Sunday dinner with us today. Say yes or no, your friend, June Frances Taylor." She had even made narrow "yes or no" blanks so I could check one or the other, though I had brought no pencil.

I blushed and raised my eyes shyly.

June Frances watched me cautiously out of the corner of her eyes, and I blushed more and nodded.

Behind her head, Alma Laura appeared and sat demurely with her hands in her lap.

The window hung open, and with every passing breeze the room washed with waves of honeysuckle, a huge old vine that ran along the fence at the back of the church.

IT IS AS if she is with me now, here, in the present. As if I will find her somewhere working the soil of my yard. I have lived with the dead so long, it's hard to tell who's who sometimes.

I am smelling the roses in my own yard to block out the scent of the honeysuckle from long ago.

I am lost in that Sunday in the past, and I have no idea whether Mama will allow me to go to the Taylors' for dinner. We work for the Taylors in their fields. I have chopped many a row of Mr. Albert Taylor's cotton since I grew old enough to wield a hoe. I have handed many a truck of green tobacco to the loopers, and I have picked my share of cotton. Mr. Taylor is a placid man who never raises his voice, who always shaves clean and behaves circumspectly. June Taylor stands like him, with her shoulders slightly slumped, and she stares at the ground when she walks, as if checking for potholes and such.

June Taylor is in my grade at school, but I have never visited her at home. Maybe that explains why this memory clings to me vividly. Sometimes she brings two cheese sandwiches for lunch, and when she does, I can have one; I can still taste it. She sits next to me and speaks to me in a quiet voice as if we have always been friends, and offers me the cheese sandwich without a word, without even asking, so that I do not have to say, yes, I want the sandwich. The weight of it rests in my lap. I unwrap the wax paper, inhaling the fresh bread, the scent of yeast. Smooth and white, the mayonnaise. My stomach is gurgling, and I already wish for something to drink with my sandwich.

I wish I could see her now. I heard years ago she ran a diner down the highway from here, maybe in Smithfield or Luma, I can hardly remember. I wonder whether she still owns it; I hope she is still alive. She would have aged straight and tall, I think. Hair pulled back neatly off her face and no bangs. The skin of her forehead always shone very clear and white.

She was never very much for the outdoors. I can picture her standing with me, inhaling the scent of these tea roses and these evening damasks; she would be wearing a hat and scarf, maybe even sunglasses, and she would be squinting behind the sunglasses, and sniffing delicately at the roses, as if too much of the scent would make her drunk.

We had known each other all our lives, or at least for most of our lives, but when I was ten years old and going to church we became friends. At first she watched me in the Sunday

School class with a special suspicion; I would catch her at it and she would look away. Then she started to stand beside me during recess on the school playground. We simply stood together and glanced at each other. I noticed her clothes had worn thin, though not as thin as mine, her shoes were scuffed, her socks were darned. For some reason this realization relaxed me and suddenly the idea of being close to her became easy.

Then one day at lunch she said, "I brought two sandwiches."

In the classroom everyone was opening the tops of desks, unfolding lunchpails or unwrapping cloth-covered bundles. My empty stomach growled.

June spoke in a whisper. "I can't eat but one."

When I unwrapped the sandwich, June refused even to glance at me or to acknowledge my actions in any way, until I had finally stuffed the corner of it into my mouth and took out a bite. That first day June Frances brought two sandwiches, she looked at me, dark-eyed and sad. We chewed our lunches together. I avoided disturbing June's somber mood, but for myself, I was almost delirious. I had never eaten lunch at school before, and my belly was turning flip-flops to have so much in it so early in the day.

At the end of the meal June broke her pickle in half and gave me one end. I chewed, savoring the fine quality of the pickle brine that streaked my chin, all but smacking. June chewed her pickle in small bites, holding it delicately with the tips of her fingers. The white skin of her face and neck nearly glowed in the light from the window, and a smattering of tiny moles mottled her throat to behind one ear. The tracery of moles fascinated me, some no larger than pinheads, some the size of peppercorns.

Depending on the dress she wore, some days you could see more of the moles and some days you could see less. I wondered, in a formless way, how far the dark spots reached along the slender part of her back. I wondered if all her skin were as pasty and white as the mild flesh under her chin and along her throat.

"I want you to come to my house," she said one day, and my heart stopped, and the whole universe wrapped itself in this one moment. I had waited for her to look at me with exactly this serious expression, to make exactly this request. She had the troubled blinking gaze of the gospel soloist from Goldsboro who sang at church some Sunday mornings. June Taylor carried an air as if she saw all in the faces of the people around her, every imperfection in every soul. I myself did not see so much but I was willing to learn.

"I have to ask my mama," I answered.

"You can come Sunday after church."

"I have to ask." I sighed, trying for an effect of melancholy like hers. "But I guess it will be all right."

BUT I HAD never asked, and now it was Sunday.

All during the church service I sat with the folded note in my hand, the heat and sweat of my hand softening the paper, till by the end of the service it was moulded to the shape of my palm. June Frances sat with her parents and Piggy, her older brother, swollen to the size of a black bear in his suit. I sat by myself a few rows behind them, studying the backs of their heads, Mrs. Taylor's tattered hat, Mr. Taylor's cowlick and sprinkle of peppery hair.

No other earthly human being distracted me, except Johnny Holland with his slick hair and square, thick shoulders, passing the collection plate and flirting silently with all the women of the congregation.

When the sermon was over and the preacher had prayed his last prayer, I filed out of the church with all the rest, stopping to find Carl Jr. who sat up and rubbed his eyes on the back pew. He had put so much hair grease on his head the hair was all stuck together smooth in the back. But he still thought he was cute, and so did Jeanie Foy and Carol Askew at the end of the pew, giggling with their hands over their mouths.

While Carl Jr. and I walked down the aisle I said, like it was nothing, "June Taylor says her mama wants me to come to Sunday dinner at her house."

Carl Jr. blinked slowly, but made no reply.

"Did you hear me?"

"I heard you." He paused. "I never heard you say anything to Mama about going to the Taylors for dinner."

"I didn't say nothing to her because I didn't know."

Carl Jr. eyed me sideways, then began to smile. The smile was telling me something about freedom, but years would pass before I understood.

"I don't know why you're grinning at me all stupid like that."

"Mama will tear your tail up when you get home."

Mrs. Frog Taylor walked up just then, clutching that hat to the top of her head, with June Frances trailing her like a pale moon. "Tell Mama I'll be home after a while," I said, in something of a hush, and ran to the Taylors' wood-paneled station wagon with the chrome stripe dangling off the side. June stood in the shadow of the car and waited for me, one moon-colored arm thrust forward into the sunlight, pale skin alive with white light. She was so happy I was coming, she clamped her lips tight together and stared straight ahead as her father, Mr. Albert Taylor, slid his broad shoulders behind the steering wheel and started the car. He rolled down the window and hollered to his wife, "Come on, Frog."

"I told you, don't call me Frog at church." She walked tottering on her spike heels, turning to wave to Mrs. Rilla Spokes, the midwife, "I can't stand you using that name in the churchyard."

"Whatever you say, darling." He swung open the door for her, she shoved her wide butt through the door and onto the seat, and beyond her head stood Carl Jr. at the edge of the churchyard, grinning and waving.

I waved feebly to Carl Jr.

"This here is Ellen Tote," Frog Taylor said, by way of introduction, while arranging her faded skirt on the car seat. "We are taking her home to Sunday dinner with us."

"I know who it is," said Mr. Albert, chewing the wide edge of a blade of grass. "She's been picking in my fields since she was knee high to nothing."

The daring of what I had chosen came to me fully when Mr. Albert slipped the car into gear, pumped the clutch, and coaxed us forward. Carl Jr.'s figure dwindled in the rear window. Side by side, squeezed against each other by the bulk of Piggy Taylor, June and I waited for the car trip to end. We sat circumspectly, our eyes fixed straight ahead, neither daring to look at the other. I could smell the trace of molasses on her breath.

I AM FEELING the constriction happiness brings to the chest; I stand beside the fence at the back where I have trained the honeysuckle to climb and knot. The memory continues rippling through me. I saw the Taylors' farmhouse in a whole new light, now that I could expect to walk inside it. The house sat prim and quiet in its Sunday repose, and the clouds lowered over it, the tops of the pin and water oaks moving. Beyond the fields, against a backdrop of pines, stood a lone sycamore, the outer bark stripped away to reveal chalky whiteness. Beneath the tree a cemetery stood, in the middle of the field. I noted details I had never before considered about the Taylor house and its surrounding fields and farm buildings. I could smell the hogs in the pens, out of sight. I stepped out of the car onto a dry mud rut where the tractor had crossed the yard.

The house, up close, had a dilapidated look. My heart flooded with sympathy when I comprehended the look of it. A rusted-out washtub sat indistinctly in high brown weeds. An old washboard lay flat in the grass, June showed me the corrugated tin washplate but refused to lift it out of the grass, because of snakes. An old rusted pump and well stood at the side of the house, but the well must have dried because spiderwebs filled the spout. The wooden lid that covered the well had rotten boards and we were not supposed to climb there, according to June Frances. A colored boy drowned in that well once, June informed me, before her daddy rented the farm and moved the family into the house. But you could hear the boy whimpering, sometimes, of an evening.

When she spoke like this, the strange spirit of her drifted very far away. We stood over the dangerous well and stared down into the dark spaces. June stared at the well with longing, as if she might ease into the mouth of it herself.

The new pump stood inside Mrs. Taylor's kitchen, and before we changed clothes I primed it and pumped a bucket of water for the cornmeal Mrs. Taylor was mixing, and some to heat to wash the early dishes, the ones that were already stacked at the sink under the window. A pot of cactus sat in the windowsill, furry and prickly, and I studied it because I had never seen cactus, while I waited for the water to heat.

Because she was busy, I had time to look around. The kitchen was very plain, its walls dingy with soot, as if the chimney flues needed repair, or as if there had been a fire. I had always thought the Taylors rich because we worked for them, and I pictured Mrs. Taylor as having every convenience, like the women in the radio dramas that Carl Jr. played for me in the evenings. But the kitchen table was battered wood that had been painted over many times, the washbasin nicked and scarred, the water dipper bent and beaten back into shape. Mrs. Taylor changed from her Sunday dress into a cotton dress with a stained collar and mended pockets at the waist. She had patched June Frances's jeans. Mr. Taylor's overalls showed wear at the knee and his boots needed new soles. Everywhere I turned I found more evidence.

Yet there was some difference I could not yet define. Something having to do with the neatness of things, the clean quiet of the house.

Piggy, gross and white, walked through the living room with no shirt, the bib of his overalls hanging in front of him, hollering at his mama to find him a shirt, and he just stood there like that, a round, bulbous, slick white thing with a head stuck on one end of it, and small dark nipples marking off the upper part of him, and a navel drooping and smiling across his lower gut.

"You giving them hogs some feed?" Mr. Taylor asked, peering over the top of his *Farmer's Almanac*.

"Yes, sir," Piggy sighed, "soon as I get me a shirt."

"You're getting to be big enough you can lay down in the mud with them." Mr. Taylor shook the almanac and raised it in front of his face again.

"Hush, Daddy," Piggy said.

THE SUN HAS given me a headache again, so I sit in the cool house to sip a cup of water. I am not one of those who will waste a slice of lemon on a glass of water; I drink mine plain from the tap. My children buy their water bottled from the grocery store but I fail to see the sense in that. My water comes from a well drilled in the backyard, same as when I was a girl, only now an electric pump raises it out of the ground and sends it cascading through my pipes and spigots.

I have a clean white kitchen, with wood cabinets for my china along one wall. I have a side-by-side refrigerator-freezer in the kitchen as well as an upright freezer in the utility room, visible from where I stand. From my garden I have frozen enough corn and peas to last through the winter, eating no more than I do. Pots and pans of every description line my shelves, and three sets of dishes, water glasses, tea glasses, juice glasses and even, tucked away at the back, a pair of wine glasses and a shot glass for whiskey. Food cools in the refrigerator, enough to last for weeks. My own little Saturn sits in the yard, in case I need to shop for more. In my closet are dresses, blouses, coats, shoes, skirts, pantsuits, nylons, a box of jewelry to which I occasionally add new necklaces, bracelets, or brooches. I bought a separate box for my rings. I have a dishwasher, a washer-dryer, a humidifier. Carefully placed furniture fills every room and carpet warms the floor wherever I want it. All these things belong to me. I have collected them through my whole life, helped by my second husband, Ray. My first husband, Bobjay, I forget whenever I can.

I go through the whole litany, sitting at the kitchen table sipping the water. The pounding in my head subsides.

BEFORE WE CHANGED clothes, June Frances showed me her treasures. She had a ring from the fair given her by her father, the gold band tarnished and flaking, but you could see how bright it used to be, the band, and the heart-shaped setting with its real diamond points, as June described them. "The purple stone is an amethyst," she said, "but not a real one." She had a locket of hair from her Grandmother Beatleburg, the best I could make the name out, tucked inside a tarnished locket that opened when she pressed a clasp at the top. The tiny bundle of hair was the same color as June's, which was to say, it hardly had any color at all, it was the color of mud or dirt, a kind of dingy brown. The hair had a surprising weight when June let me hold it. She kept back the locket itself, which might be damaged. I soon surrendered the hair, tied with its bit of blue ribbon. She hid the locket carefully under the rest of her treasures, the seashell from Morehead City, the rock from Cherokee in the mountains, the fool's gold from Asheboro, the clay doll from Williamsburg. "We never went to Williamsburg," June sighed. "My cousin sent me that. It is in Virginia."

June spoke exactly and precisely, and I imitated her. "Did you go to all these other places?"

"Well," she considered, "not exactly, but my parents went to Morehead City and Piggy went to Cherokee on a church trip." The fool's gold had been given to her father by his brother Alvin, a tramp and a bum, according to June's mother, a man who showed up now and then with his pockets full of useless junk, to beg another handout, to eat all the food in the house and take up space sleeping on the couch.

"That must be worth something, if it's gold."

She shook her head, pursing her lips together. "It's not worth a thing. That's why they gave it to me."

Her bedroom had plain white walls, plaster with cracks running all through it and raw wire where the electricity had been added through the house. Someone had painted the wires once but the paint had flaked in places. The ceiling had shadowed from smoke, but the room was clean, the floors had been swept, the mess shoved as far into June's room as it would go.

From the open door drifted the sound of Frog Taylor at

the bottom of the steps. "You girls get down here and help me. I'm tired after all that sitting around in church."

I giggled and June gave me a rolling-eyed look. "She is so corny."

I zipped up my borrowed overalls, which fit pretty good except for the thick roll of extra length around my ankles. June packed her treasures carefully into their secret hiding places, and changed clothes herself, taking her own sweet time, I thought. But I feared to go downstairs without her, so I waited.

"June Frances, I'm not going to call you down here again."

"We're coming, Mama," June singsonged at the doorway. Sighing, she slumped to the bed and pulled socks over her bare feet. She went downstairs like that, in her socks, but I went barefoot, as usual.

WHEN I AM in the kitchen in the morning, sliding the milk out of the refrigerator, taking it by the handle, thinking about the weight, who am I doing this for? I must be doing this for somebody, I cannot possibly be lifting this milk out of the refrigerator for myself. Because I have been serving people out of one kitchen or another all my life, I stop and think. Because I am alone now. I am the one who wanted milk, though later it will upset my stomach, like beans do. I want the soothing silky taste, but not poured into a glass and drunk, no. Poured into a white cup with a smooth handle. The white milk in the white cup. I lift it to my lips.

I am barefoot, but now it is because I like to be, and sometimes I wear only socks, scrubbing the sock bottoms happily across the linoleum, and sometimes I wear socks and slippers, and sometimes I wear slippers but no socks. Freedom is a great thing, and consists of a thousand insignificant details.

All night I have been remembering. The memories have torn loose and float free in my head. I am entering Frog Taylor's kitchen. June Frances stomps down the stairs behind me, deliberately making the biggest noise possible. A cloud of good smells surround me and my flip-flop stomach. Mrs. Frog is standing with a wooden spoon dipped into some delicious-looking gravy and she offers me a lick. June pushes me forward toward it, landing in the room with her own peculiar heavy bang.

"June Frances, what have I told you?"

"Not to jump in the kitchen because I might break something."

"And what else?"

"To be like a lady and not make so much noise when I come down the steps."

"I wish you could do those two things for me." She spoke in a listless way, and heaved her chest a bit with the languor of her breath. She moved her arms in the same weighted way, from breadboard to sink, carrying a bowl of raw turnip greens. "It would make your daddy and me the most happiest people in the world."

"There is no such word as 'most happiest,'" June sniffed.

"Be that as it may," Frog said, and turned to the sink again. "June, you need to dice those potatoes. It took you so long to change clothes, I had plenty time to finish peeling them. And Ellen, sweetheart, I wish you would take the tops off those strawberries, all right? Us women always have to work."

A bowl of strawberries sat by the pump. Red and ripe, they gave off scent even before I pinched out the tops. I could smell them halfway across the room. I washed my hands carefully and set to work. The smell rose to cloud my head; I had never inhaled any odor as tempting as that. The only time I could remember eating strawberries was on a cake at Nana Rose's funeral.

"When you get the tops off, you should wash them under the pump and then slice them in half." This was not Frog, but June herself, who had suddenly become bossy. "I like my strawberries sliced in half like that."

"Well," considered Frog, "Ellen can wash them. Then we'll see."

"Yes, ma'am."

"Ellen might not like her strawberries sliced like that," Frog reminded somebody, but it was hard to tell who.

"These come out of our strawberry patch," June informed me. "I picked them."

"June, honey, you need to be working and not talking. Your daddy and your brother are hungry."

"Then they can come in here and cut up these potatoes."

"You watch your mouth, young lady, before I knock a knot on you." But the threat was voiced aimlessly as Frog stirred the gravy.

"I do not see why we have to wait on them all the time," speaking in that clipped way again, as if she were reciting a line from a radio show.

"Hush, June. I bet Ellen has to help with the cooking at her house too, don't you, honey?"

"Yes, ma'am. My daddy and my brothers, they don't

hardly do anything." I blushed, conscious that I might have said too much. The ends of my fingers stuck together with red from the strawberry tops. I held them to my nose and took a deep breath.

"Do you complain about it all the time to your mama, like my June Frances does to me?"

"No," I said, though it was not really true; in my head I did complain, all the time. But I would never have said anything, or else Mama would have knocked me with the firewood again.

The dinner was ready, and the men came in, and suddenly the kitchen seemed crowded and small, with Piggy's rounded shoulders hunched forward over the table and Mr. Albert's bony elbows and big hands and feet tucked into as small a package as he could make. Everybody passed everything politely, and I listened to them all and asked for things like they did. June, for instance, said, "Please for some biscuit," to her mama, and her mama passed her the plate, and June reached for one. Or she said, "Please for some sweet tea," or, "Please for some more gravy." So I did the same, though I was shy to speak the first time and missed the squash when it came by.

"Ellen needs to try some of this squash." Frog had been watching and lifted the bowl over my plate, allowing me to dish out as much as I wanted.

We ate. I had never eaten so much in my life, so many bowls of steaming food, the roast pork so tender it melted beneath the smooth gravy, the potatoes carefully mashed, mustard greens cooked with bits of ham and flavored with pepper vinegar on my plate, fresh biscuits fluffy and smooth, squash fried with onions. We ate from blue willow plates and drank from tea glasses into which ice had been chipped to keep our drinks cool. I shoveled food into my mouth like someone drunk and giddy, tasting everything. Only now and then, watching the others, I got cautious, afraid I was making a fool of myself.

"This girl can eat," Mr. Albert said.

"You want some more potatoes, honey? And have you more of this gravy. It's not even worth saving, as little as it is."

"Please for some," I replied, holding my plate.

When dinner ended, my belly was smooth and round as a stone.

I KNOW THE Taylors pitied me during that meal. I believe, looking back, that I knew it even then. I could feel their pity like moistness in the air. This sympathy made itself evident in the words Mr. and Mrs. Taylor said, half-joking, before and after we ate. Lordy, would you look at this child put away the food. I have never seen a girl eat so much. Are you sure you aren't a little boy? She's so skinny you could poke a thread right through her. They must not feed her at home. We need to keep her on the farm where we can fatten her up.

"Does your mama cook good food like my mama does?" June asked.

"Me and Nora cook, mostly," I answered. "Mama don't like to."

"You must be two good girls to do all that work for your mama," Frog pointed out.

"You're probably lucky Velma Louise stays out of the kitchen, is what I figure," said Mr. Albert.

"Hush that," Frog said.

I had never heard anybody use my mama's name like that, so casually, right out loud, as if there were nothing special about her at all. This was not like when Daddy said her name, even when he was angry; when Mr. Albert said, "Velma Louise," it was as if my mama were not there, but instead some stranger had taken her place, someone Mr. Albert could recognize but I could not.

"My mama cooks real good," I said in a small, shy voice.

They were spooning strawberries into their mouths but stopped. "Well, honey," said Frog, "I'm sure she does."

"She just don't like to."

The words trailed off into nothing.

MEMORIES OF MY mother drift in and out, mingling with images of June Frances, of her family, of my visits to her house, both that very first Sunday and all the times later. Mama drifts across the bare gray planks of our kitchen, dressed in a loose, faded housedress; but it is as if this happens again now, in my kitchen. She has pinned back her hair and rolled the sleeves of the dress onto her shoulders, exposing dimpled flesh. She is wearing no underwear, I can tell by the sag of her breasts and the way the back of the dress outlines her buttocks. She is angry with me, the expression on her face sullen as a boy's. "You spend too goddamn much time with them Taylorses," she mutters. "You need to stay home and help your mama like you ought to."

"I can do my chores before I go. I made the beds and I ironed the sheets and the pillowcases and I got the beans to soaking."

"You don't care about your mama half as much as you care

about them Taylorses." She looks at me directly, her eyes large and mournful. "I know you don't. It's because you think they're better than we are."

"Mama, don't be like that."

"I know how you are. You set up there with that Frog Taylor, and you talk about me." She stands facing me with her hands open and slack. One of her front teeth has begun to darken and the others are stained with snuff juice. She reaches for the can to spit. "I know you're ashamed of me."

A big hurt has begun to grow inside me, at the bottom of my stomach, a knot drawn tighter and tighter. I whisper, "I never said that."

"You think nobody don't know what's in that head of yours, but I know. You think your mama is common and you'd rather have somebody like Frog Taylor for your mama, Frog Taylor with her big fat ass, that's what you want. As much as I love you, you treat me like this. Go on. Go on over there. I can't stop you."

"Mama, please don't be like this."

"Go on over there, I said." Tears are growing in her eyes. Her mouth trembles. The hurt in me gets bigger, catches fire. I ache all through.

So I stay, the one time. But mostly I do not stay.

Aching memories of my mother begin in those days, when I betray her in my thoughts. I feel the ache as bitterly now as I ever felt it then, when I began to stand in judgment of her. I see her in her thin dress, pinching snuff into her mouth, and I think: I will not live like this. She reaches for a pot to cook in, and I know the pot was not cleaned well, but my mother does not know or care. I sweep the floor carefully in the kitchen, and my mother drops biscuit crumbs onto the clean part of the floor and hardly pauses to notice. The feeling remains as vivid now, in the present, as if it had happened this morning.

JUNE FRANCES TOOK me to the little cemetery where graves were stuffed inside a broken wall. We glimpsed older graves we could not reach. I asked if her family was buried here and she said no, these graves had been abandoned when the land was part of somebody's plantation and then split up and sold. Negro and white graves were all mixed here, because the family buried the slaves right next to the family; and though I was already old enough to doubt this tale, seeing how few white people want black people anywhere near them, I nodded and allowed her to continue.

We had paused near the vault of a grave that had been shoved up out of the ground by tree roots, clearly visible all around the rectangle of brick. June gestured to the bricks and said, "Here is another example of the restless dead."

Alma Laura had joined us and was sitting on the top of the grave; given what June Frances had just said, I thought maybe she could see Alma Laura too and that was what she was talking about. "She's always around," I explained. "She never did die, really."

June looked at me like I had gone daft. "This is a man's grave," she explained with her patient voice. "Honor Jeb Leigh. See?" She nearly stuck her hand through Alma Laura to point at the letters on the tilted tombstone. "He was so restless in his grave he shoved it right out of the ground. This is evidence that he was perhaps buried alive."

I blinked and looked at Alma Laura, who gave me the signal to be quiet. Since June was not the type to accept contradiction, especially when she was telling lies so big and bold, I followed Alma Laura's advice. Though I knew from Alma Laura that, no matter how restless she was, she would never have made such a mess of her own grave.

"He killed a nigra slave with his own hands. He found the slave with a white girl."

"Doing what?" I asked, though I had my suspicions.

"Doing what a nigra ought never to do with a white girl," June shook her head sadly. "Then the farmer's wife planted a tree over the grave, and when the tree grew tall enough to shade the grave, the wife died."

"We lived in a nigger shack, in Holberta, one time."

"It is not the same thing," she explained, maybe a bit put out that her dramatic story had failed to scare me more. "And you should not say nigger, you should say nigra. It is not polite to say nigger unless you are talking about the very worst kind of nigger."

By the time she explained this to me, that same day of my first visit, we had left the graveyard where Alma Laura was sitting, and walked toward the barn to meet the milk cow.

"I have to visit Esther every day," June explained, "or else she gives only half as much milk the next day. Even Papa says so." She called her daddy "Papa," because it was more refined, though she explained this to me much later.

I UNDERSTOOD EXACTLY what she meant about the word to call colored people, and afterward, never used the word "nigger" again, speaking only of "nigras," until my daughter taught me to call them "blacks," or "Blacks," as, for instance, "Now we will have to go to school with all the Blacks." I made these changes in order to be considered a better quality of person than my own family, which has continued to call black people niggers to this day.

Even after June explained the idea to me, I never called my daddy "Papa." The word rang too gently in my head. When I talked to June about her daddy I referred to him as "your papa." But my own I named my daddy, always, when I talked about him, which was not often.

But I learned many other courtesies from June. I learned to eat with one hand in my lap, never switching the fork from one hand to the other, as I used to do at home. I learned to keep my elbows off the table and to sit up straight, never hunching over the plate. Eating soup without slurping or blowing across the spoon took me longer, because I only got to practice at her house when there was soup, or at Aunt Addis's when there was chicken stew. At my own house, I slurped and sucked and blew in order to eat faster, so I would get enough before everything disappeared. At June's house, Piggy ate politely or else his papa cuffed him across the jaw. At my house, the boys ate like hogs at a trough, and the girls hardly better. A person had to use both hands in order to keep up.

June Frances taught me that ladies wear gloves nearly all the time, a fact that I had noticed the few times I had ridden into Kingston to Kress's five-and-dime; June's own pair of gloves had been stained with yellowish cat piss and had a smell, but they impressed me anyway. She allowed me to wear them, and I put them on after she assured me they had been washed in the new wringer-washer. The fabric felt smooth and soft on the calloused skin of my hands.

"I got the stain when I tried to chop cotton with the gloves on," June confided. "Mama made me pull them off and the cat peed on them at the end of the row. They belonged to my mother's sister Bethany, who is loose and takes up with every kind of man."

From June I also learned about the behavior of girls with men and boys; and in this case, some of what I learned made me feel better about my own mother and family. A girl was not supposed to associate with boys until a certain age. In my own family, Nora, who was at this age or older, was still not allowed to date boys, talk to boys, or receive letters from boys, and when I told this to June, she seemed impressed with Nora's virtue. "You can't even have any kissing cousins," June explained, and I replied that we did not. "A man cannot be allowed to see a woman naked, even your brother," she added, and I added nothing to this, because I knew my daddy liked to watch Nora wash off in the tub.

"If a boy tries to kiss you, what would you do?"

"If it was Cob Granger, I would let him."

"Cob Granger is as handsome as pictures of Jesus," June agreed. "But what if it was somebody else? What if it was Piggy?"

We giggled into our palms, because we both thought the idea of Piggy doing anything like that was ridiculous. "I would turn my face away so he couldn't reach my mouth," I answered. "And if he reached for me, I would back off."

I AM IN the present again. The moment hurtles toward something out there, unseen. The illusion that the past still exists, that I can travel in it, surrounds me, but I know that the images of June and me are false ones. I am more real than they are, I tell myself so.

The reassurance helps, because this morning I found Mama in the kitchen of my house, stooped over, looking at the refrigerator, maybe hoping to pour herself a glass of milk. At once I thought to myself, you are dead, you cannot be here.

But she pulled the refrigerator door open even wider; the cold spilled out in tendrils of mist that licked up and down her body. She inspected the food in my refrigerator slowly, the carton of orange juice, the milk, the packages of boiled sandwich ham, the box of cheese. Mayonnaise, relish, mustard, a jar of salsa left here by my grandson, who likes it. Fresh vegetables and fruits. A freezer full of meat bought on sale and wrapped carefully. Canned biscuits, too, so that I would never have to mix another batch unless I wished. My mother inspected every corner of the refrigerator, opened every cupboard, peeped behind every door. I held my breath.

When she left I sat down at the table. She disturbed nothing, she left the kitchen neat. Around me, laid out in tidy squares and smoothly curved shapes, my clean kitchen gleamed.

I remember no expression on her face. I have been sitting here at the table trying to think whether she wore any. Was there disapproval? Could there have been envy? Maybe she was proud that I have achieved this much in my life, that I have a clean kitchen and enough food for months? Even a tiny bit proud would satisfy me. But I do not remember any expression at all.

UPSTAIRS IN THE Taylor farmhouse, June led me to the back of a closet where there was no wall. Inky blackness filled the space beyond, a blackness so palpable you could squeeze it with your hand.

"There's a coffin back there, somewhere," June announced, giving me a significant look.

"Is not."

"Is too. It is the coffin of Jacob Brown, the man who once owned this farm. He was my papa's cousin."

I stared into the black space, from which, suddenly, a dusky odor emerged, or I thought it did, like the smell of a dead bird, the musk of decay.

"He died of a mysterious disease," June intoned, "and the family buried him here, out of sight in the attic, in order to keep the germs from getting into the ground. The germs from dead people are stronger than most other kinds of germs." She leaned into the blackness. The closet was already dark, I could hardly see her. "We should go look at it."

"I don't want to go in there."

"All right," June tugged her skirt from under her thighs; she always pretended a hard time getting comfortable. "We can sit here then. But sometimes cousin Jacob walks around."

"He does not."

She nodded, and I watched the outline of her head in the murk. "Yes, he does," she whispered, and she made it sound almost sad. "One time I woke up and he was behind me and he had his cold, cold hands around my neck."

"You're a telling a story."

"You shouldn't call people a story like that. I woke up and he put his cold, cold hands around my neck, and he began to squeeze, and I could not breathe, but I knew who it was and I gasped, 'Jacob,' at the last second and was saved."

My heart had begun to pound, and I could have sworn, for a moment, that I felt icy fingers wrapping my own throat. This was her best story yet. I leaned even farther forward, and June gave me a little shove, and I squealed, "Stop it, June."

"You don't have to raise your voice." She shushed me dramatically. "Listen, there's something out there."

We both listened. June scooted over next to me and hid her face behind my back. "It's just like before," she muttered against my back, "when he tried to kill me by choking me."

But there was nothing to be heard except the distant radio. Till suddenly I heard a voice I knew.

When Frog Taylor called us downstairs, we scrambled out of the opening to the attic, and June hurtled down the stairs like a hound after rabbits. I heard my daddy and changed back into my church dress before I went down myself. "My wife needs her at home and so I come on up here."

"Well, we would have brought her home soon." Frog's voice rose to a high pitch of politeness. "Albert was planning to run her there in the truck before he laid down for his nap. Won't you, Albert?"

Mr. Albert had laid a toothpick on his lower lip and looked my daddy up and down. "Yep."

"Well, I can walk her on home now."

"We can give you both a ride."

Daddy fixed his eyes on me. From across the room I became afraid of him and wanted to hang back. I wished he would say yes to Mr. Albert and let him drive us home in the truck. But Daddy smiled at me and said, "Your mama sent me to get you, baby doll. She needs help with them younguns."

I nodded and then took a deep breath. "I had a good time, June Frances. Thanks for asking me to come."

She dipped her head, like a chicken going after corn, suddenly shy again.

"That was mighty sweet, won't it?" Frog smiled at everybody.

Daddy gathered me to him with a look and we left then, and Daddy never did answer Mr. Albert's question about the ride. We set out walking down their driveway, through the gray dirt of the front yard. Sweetgum balls from last autumn rolled underfoot. Daddy set a brisk pace down the road, and sometimes I had to trot a little to keep up. We headed along the road and then along a path through the woods, one I had walked with Addis once or twice. Soon we were all alone walking in the woods with warblers, sparrows, jays, and whatnot screeching overhead.

"You worried your mama." He looked at me piercingly as he squatted on his heels rolling a cigarette. "You know it?"

"Yes, sir."

"She didn't know nothing about you going to eat with the Taylors."

I looked down at the ground, but I could still tell he was watching me.

"You'll have to get a whipping," he said. He looked at me

for a long time, and I felt as if my bare skin were knotting and tightening. He licked out the tip of his tongue onto his lower lip. Then he smiled and lit the cigarette and smoked it.

Afterward, instead of beating me, he stood, and we walked down the path. I followed behind him at a careful distance, several steps, but not enough to be conspicuous, like I was trying to run away. We walked the long way, across Piney Creek onto the dry side. Daddy kept ahead of me and only looked back at me one time, when we were in sight of the African Methodist church. Some black children were playing in the churchyard near a juniper tree, and Daddy eyed them, then turned to me. Beard darkened his lower face. His teeth gleamed. Clouds and tree branches were moving behind his head, as if he had put them there. Then he turned and we walked again, without hurry.

We neared the house on the pond side, out of the woods, and Daddy stopped there, under a birch tree, to take off his belt.

He fixed his eyes on me. His voice lowered flat and toneless. "You move a muscle, I'll give it to you twice as worse."

He moved around me with the belt. I stood there while he lashed me across the legs and arms. I hardly felt anything while he was whipping me with the soft leather, though I knew he had cut my legs with the belt. I was too afraid to feel anything, because he was still there, moving around me. I hurt later, when he was finished. Beginning as he faced me, looping the belt through his everyday pants. I could feel tears sliding down my face and something wet slid down my legs as well, and I refused to look at him for fear he would take off the belt again. "If your mama had of done you, she would of done you worse," he said. "You ought to be thankful." He walked away, his dogs setting up a chorus under the house.

LATE AT NIGHT I hear Mama again, shuffling on the clean linoleum. I pull on my robe and tiptoe out of my bedroom, my king-size bed. Even before I round the corner I know she is there.

She has not turned on any light, she has not disturbed anything. But a flux of moonlight traces her iridescent outlines in front of my sink. She has been eating, I am certain of it, and later I will discover that someone has scooped out a new corner of the macaroni and cheese casserole. But now she simply stands in front of the sink, looking out at my flower garden in the moonlight.

All questions freeze on my lips. After a few moments I move into the sitting area from which I can still see her. I look out one window and she looks out the other, and we are faced with the whole garden, the pebble paths and the fish pool and the arbor where I trained wisteria to grow, the climbing tomato plants at the back, the scuppernong vine, the fig bush, and the young, short apple trees, for tonight they all blaze, all the flowers, and every branch bows heavy with fruit or berry, every place I turn. So I am hardly surprised when my mother walks outside, nor am I surprised even when, a moment later, I follow her.

Clouds roll in a high wind, and their mottling across the moon makes it appear the light is moving across my hands, my nightgown, and clinging to my steps. I button the robe at the front in case the neighbors should be watching. Discreet, I move along the slate path.

Ahead, my mother has stopped beside the Japanese maple in its bed of pine straw at the corner of the house. Out here in the dark she seems less substantial, as if she really is a ghost, as if I really might poke my hand right through her, without hurting her at all. But I am reluctant to step too close. I wait, I allow her to lead.

Once, by the hummingbird feeder, she turns and looks at me. I believe it is the first time our eyes meet. A chill sweeps me, and I remember, suddenly, sitting in the open square of blackness in the back of June Frances's closet on that first Sunday afternoon. The chill reminds me of that, made up of the air over a grave or from inside a tomb. My dead mother watches me for a few moments, then turns, and I follow her.

When I am aware again I am halfway across the bare field in back of the house. I do not so much waken there as regain control of myself, recovering my limbs, stopping my forward march. Mama still walks ahead, nearly across the field as I watch. She never hesitates, like my dream. She heads toward the river. She plunges into the woods in her white slip. Moving forward, through darkness, toward water. I glimpse her face slipping under the water. I have not seen the image so clearly for years. The white round pancake of her face slipping under the water, without expression.

I return to my house when I am sure she's gone. I lie in bed till dawn, even though I can hardly close my eyes.

I am beginning to understand. In that river I am moving, too.

NORA

NORA LIVED TO be a good age, sixty-eight, old for my family. She collected a little Social Security at the end, as I have.

I believe we were friends when she died, a relief, since she behaved as if she hated me when we were young. She hated everyone then, but especially me. I sat through her funeral while a high wind threatened to rip off my hat, a nice beaded black affair with a veil, something my second husband gave me. I clamped my hand there and tried to ignore the wind. I was thinking we might have to close the lid on Nora after all, the way the wind was whipping that lacy thing at her throat. She reclined there quietly, composedly, with a piece of a smile across her lips. Even dead, Nora could stir up a storm.

When we chopped cotton and when we picked it, I worked near her, and she kept her eye on me. She criticized the way I chopped, she claimed I skipped over patches and left the dirt in big clods. I took it to heart and chopped furiously, finer and finer, till my back and shoulders and arms burned. At times Nora whimpered and pressed her hand against her lower back, and I mimicked the pose. The pressure of my hand provided a bit of relief for sore, tired muscles. But neither of us said much about it, and we rarely complained to Mama, who had her own aches and pains.

We both grew thin as sticks, all those years, till suddenly one day Nora began to blossom into a kind of plumpness that Daddy kept his eye on.

He kept her close by him. She washed his hands at night, and pulled off his boots and socks, and rubbed his feet. She stirred the sugar into his coffee. At times he showed a softness toward her that made Mama arch her back and spit. But Nora never lost her fear of Daddy, and I understood why.

Daddy caught Lyle Yates propped against the corner of our house talking sweet to Nora, and Daddy blacked both his eyes and then raised welts on Nora's backside with a leather cord. When Mama got upset about it, he gave her a couple of licks to think about, too.

One day, when we returned home from school, Mama glared at Nora from across the kitchen. Her expression became so menacing that Nora stopped midway through the room; she trembled and became very afraid, knowing Mama's temper. "Your ass is going to get stomped when your daddy comes home," she hissed.

"What did I do?"

"You daddy is going to break every bone in your nasty body."

"Mama please," a flutter in her voice, "what are you talking about?"

Mama drew a letter out of her bosom. "You got this here letter. Carl Jr. told me this has your name on it."

A desperate longing, like nothing I had ever seen before, consumed Nora. “Give it to me! Oh please!”

Mama shoved the letter back into her bosom. Nora stood whimpering and my heart had begun to pound. “If this letter is from a boy, your daddy will wear you out.”

“Mama, please give it to me. Please don’t tell Daddy.”

Instead, Mama gave her a smack across the face and wheeled and left the room.

I did the same, leaving my schoolbooks on the table and carrying the water bucket outside. A patch of red spread across Nora’s cheek.

Daddy came home stomping mud off his boots and flapping his work gloves against the porch post. His hands were scratched and dirty and oozing blood in places. He had gone back to logging after a spell of tending fires in tobacco curing barns; the wood fires had to be watched all night. The money was better logging but the work was hard and he always hated it, especially that he scratched his hands up, and tore his fingernails, and blistered his palms. He mustered with the crews at Mr. Jarman’s store, and Roe Yates gave him a ride home every evening.

“Get over here and wash my hands.” He stopped by the water bucket and glared at Nora. When she failed to move instantly, he said again, “Did you hear me? I said get over here.”

Nora moved toward him, arms folded like a shield against her chest. She stood in his shadow and poured hot water into the basin, cooling it with water I had drawn from the well. She took his hands and soaked them in the hot water. “Goddamn, that stings,” Daddy said, and Madson, at the kitchen table, giggled.

"What the hell are you hooting at?" Daddy asked, and Madson shut up right quick.

Nora took a soft washcloth and ran it tenderly over the gnarled backs of Daddy's hands, one scar from a knife fight in Holberta, another from an accident opening oysters. She scrubbed so gently Daddy was surprised and blinked uncertainly, gazing at the top of her head. All four of their hands were submerged in the soapy water.

From the back of the house we could hear Mama barreling down on us. "Is that Willie?" she shrilled. "Is that your daddy? One of you younguns better goddammit answer me."

"It's me," he said flatly.

She loomed in the door and studied Nora.

"Did she tell you?" Mama asked.

"Did who tell me what?"

Mama jerked her head toward Nora. She looked like she wanted to spit. "This one. Did she tell you what she done?"

Daddy narrowed his eyes at Nora and pulled his hands out of the washbasin. He reached for a towel to dry his hands.

Mama pulled the letter out of her bosom, the envelope slightly moist and wilted. "This here letter," she hissed, "is from a boy."

"How do you know, Louise, you can't read."

"Carl Jr. read the name to me."

"That little son of a bitch was by this house?"

Carl Jr. and Daddy fist-fought over money Daddy owed Carl Jr.; Daddy threw Carl Jr. out of the house. He was living with Uncle Snookie, Mama's brother, at Willard's Fork.

"He come by to get some clean overalls," Mama said.

"That rat-ass son of a bitch ever steps foot in this house while I'm here, I'll fuck him up bad."

"I had to give him some clothes," Mama explained, slightly withered by Daddy's response.

But his curiosity about the letter defeated his anger against Carl Jr. Daddy snatched the letter away from her and peered at it. Daddy could read, and in fact got to be pretty good at it later in life when he was no longer working; he would sit in his house on the one chair he and Mama had left, and all day he would read pornographic books, girls prancing naked on the paperback covers, dancing with the tips of their nipples two inches long or more, stiff as bolts. Facing Nora, Daddy read the name on the envelope, then opened the letter and mouthed the name at the end.

"This is from that son of a bitch Lyle Bates," Daddy spat.

"I knew that's who it was from." Mama shook her head and all her chins. "She's been pining after that one."

"Hush, Mama," Nora whispered.

"Make me a cup of coffee while I read this letter." Daddy fixed Nora with a stare and spoke to her in a low, flat tone.

"That's why she's rushing down to that store two and three times on a Saturday," Mama kept nodding and eyeing Nora, a gleam of satisfaction in her eye. "She's been mooning over that boy."

Nora served Daddy, who sat peering at the letter. Lips moving the slightest bit. He read something and smacked his lips. "Oh, horse shit," he hooted. "When did you let him touch your titties?"

"I never done no such of a thing."

"It says right here, 'I love to run my hand up under your blouse where your titties are.' "

"It don't say anything like that."

Daddy glared at her. His smirk had slowly changed to something else, before my very eyes. "Did you let him stick his fingers in your pussy, too?"

Tears sprang down Nora's cheeks so suddenly it was as if a wound had opened. Daddy rose over her like a shadow, and she huddled without moving. Daddy's tone was low and cold. "Answer me, girl. You let him rub your pussy?"

"No, sir."

"You sure you hadn't?"

Speechless, she nodded her head. "I never done it," she croaked.

"So if I check it, I'll find out it's just like I left it."

Nora blushed to the roots of her hair. Mama stood behind them both with her legs planted wide. Nora's chin trembled and she spoke with a broken voice. "Daddy, I didn't do anything with Lyle Yates, I didn't do what he said, Daddy, I swear it. He's been after me, and I kept telling him to leave me alone."

"She's a liar," Mama swore. "She's been after that Yates boy since I don't know when, parading all up and down the road."

"Hush, Mama," Nora said, trembling, and Daddy struck out, once, fiercely, across her face. The crack was like gunfire, and Nora's head turned, her hair whipped around; I see it even now in such detail, as if it is happening in front of me, slow motion. She gave a small cry and her nose started to bleed. She held her hand up under her nose but stood still.

"Get out of my sight," Daddy said.

She stumbled through the door that led to the back of the house. A few minutes later I found her holding a wet cloth over her nose. She glared at me like a bird of prey. "What do you want?"

"Are you all right?"

She laughed. "No, I'm not all right. Daddy just knocked the hell out of me."

I twisted my toes all together and stood there. She lay on the bed and looked at nothing in particular. A question floated in the air between us, because I had heard what Daddy said, but I feared to ask it out loud, and Nora stared right through me. Then turned her face to the wall.

I helped with supper. Mama fried fatback black at the edges, boiled cabbage flavored with fat. I cooked a pot of soupy rice with black pepper. For once Nora was nowhere near to boss me, but Mama kept glaring at me which was almost as bad.

"You'll be getting boys to send you that love mess in a letter," Mama accused.

"No, I won't."

"Yes, you will, I know. You'll be dragging all around here like your sister, laying in there in the bed pouting because her daddy told her what's what."

"I don't have to do everything she does."

"Don't sass me, missy." Mama cuffed me across the face, hard.

Nora stayed in the bed through dinner, but the rest of us ate. Carl Jr.'s place sat empty, and we all felt it more so with Nora gone too. I had to feed the kids and Otis started to eat off my plate again, but I laid my fork against the tender part of his wrist till Daddy laughed and Mama made me stop. When Otis whined and Daddy smacked him, I was glad in my heart.

Later I slipped into the bedroom with a fatback and biscuit for Nora, and she ate it huddled against the headboard. She hunched over the biscuit like a field mouse. She licked every crumb from her fingertips and chewed the fatback rind last of all.

Next morning, Mama woke Nora and me and said to come to the kitchen, even earlier than usual, before dawn. Daddy sat in the chair with a cut on his cheek and another one on his arm. Carl Jr. sat next to him with one ear all bloody and his clothes tore up pretty bad. Him and Daddy had become the best of friends now. He looked at Nora and said, "We damn near killed Lyle Yates. Swore he wasn't doing a thing with Nora, lying bastard."

Nora blinked at him and never said a word. Mama had lit a fire in the stove. Nora sent me to the well for water, and I stepped fearfully onto the porch and down the steps.

We cleaned both of them up and bandaged the cuts. Mama dabbed alcohol onto Carl Jr., blowing on the wound to fend off the sting. Carl Jr. cooed and pumped his legs. Nora took care of Daddy and pronounced, "It's going to take stitches for you."

"It won't," Daddy spat.

"Daddy, your cheek is cut open."

"It don't reach that deep."

"It's nearabout all the way through."

"Oh, shut up." He pressed the cut back together, dabbing

it with alcohol himself, tears streaming down his face. "Pull off my shoes and wash my feet."

He looked her in the eye. For a moment, the tiniest flicker of rebellion flickered across her face.

Without a word she unlaced his boots, took them off. She filled a pan with hot water and peeled the socks down his white, veiny legs. He soaked his feet and she rubbed them. She knelt over the pan with her cheeks pink and flushed, dress wet and clinging to her back, her hands glistening, Daddy's toes curled back with happiness. She toweled the feet dry and pulled clean socks over the smattering of hair on the top of each foot. Daddy had a tuft of black hair on each big toe.

Daddy looked at Nora in satisfaction. "I like how you take care of me, little girl."

"I ain't so little anymore."

Whether she meant to be coy or not, Daddy took it as flirtation, and laughed.

That evening I found her in the bedroom with a paper sack; Corrine snored beside her, sleeping like a log. When Nora saw me coming she shoved the sack under the edge of the bed. I knew right then she was leaving. She looked at me and blinked. I pretended I had not seen anything.

We went to bed. She rested there in her dress with the covers pulled up to her chin, and I pretended not to notice that either. Near midnight, with Otis snoring and Carl Jr. sprawled across him, she slid out of bed. She sat there in the dark for a long time. A tap sounded on the window, and she opened it and handed out the bag. She stood over me for a moment, then kissed me on the cheek. Her lips were cool and moist. She whispered, "That letter never was from any Lyle Yates, either. I fooled Daddy this time."

She grinned. I grinned back. She slipped out the window and was gone. The print of her kiss remained on my cheek; if I close my eyes I can feel it still.

When Daddy found out she was gone, he spit a mouthful of coffee halfway across the kitchen, then fastened his gaze on me. "Were you in the bed with her?"

"Corrine and me was," I answered, and Corrine hid behind my skirt.

"And you didn't wake up when she got out of bed?"

"No, sir."

"You laid there asleep."

"Yes, sir."

"So you didn't see what jackass it was run off with her."

"No, sir. I didn't see anything because I was asleep."

He glared at me for a while. We all speculated who the boy or man might have been. Mama still believed she had eloped with Lyle Yates, but Daddy assured her Lyle Yates needed too much mending to be thinking about eloping with anybody right now.

"She was a strumpet," Mama said. "Strutting around here like she did. She acted liked she was the mama." But even as she said this, something sad and lonely filled her eyes.

"She probably had a boyfriend in every cornfield," Madson declared.

Daddy reflected on what Madson had said, chewing the end of a match. "She probably did, son." He hawked and spit in Mama's spitcan, and announced, "I don't want to hear another thing about it."

He sat there brooding. Now and then I could feel his gaze on me.

That night I slept between Corrine and baby Delia in the middle of the bed, with my head at the foot of the bed, and woke at the slightest noise in the room.

During the day I kept a wary eye. The work Nora had done fell on me, including all the cooking, since Corrine proved sorry help. I boiled grits, fried fatback, mixed biscuit dough, and stoked the fire in the stove. I pulled off Daddy's shoes and socks and washed his feet. I stirred the sugar into his coffee. By the time we learned what had happened to Nora, that she had married Burner Boyette and lived on the farm right down the road with the whole Boyette family, I had replaced her in nearly every way.

I discovered I made a better cook than Nora had affected, that I made the biscuits lighter and fluffier than she did, stirred the grits better with fewer lumps, and I fried a good chicken the few times we had it. I could make a gravy out of the least bit of drippings and flour.

At night, I continued to sleep upside down in the bed, staring at Corrine's, Baby Hob's, and Delia's feet. Hob slept with us whenever Daddy wanted Mama for his business. Often I hardly slept. I was listening for something, a step in the night. I would know the sound when I heard it.

I began bathing during the day when Daddy worked, or early in the morning, when he was still asleep. Even then he would find me sometimes. He would amble to the doorway without warning and I would freeze. "Excuse me, honey," he would say, and smile, and I would cover my breasts with my hands.

Once Otis walked in on me while I was washing. I slapped him sharp across the face and sent him squealing to Mama, who slapped him again herself when she found out what he had done. "I never meant to," Otis squealed, dancing, while Mama's blunt hand lashed at him.

"You little peeping tom son of a bitch," Mama hissed, "you stay out of that room when you ain't supposed to be in there."

At night I dreamed about Nora. In the dream we were sleeping together, only Nora and me, and she curled herself sweetly around me and kept me warm with her arms. Then I would wake up and see feet sticking out from under the blankets, and I would draw my legs under the covers and lie there missing Nora in the dark.

THE NEXT TIME I saw her she was expecting her first child. She had been living down the road at Maxie Boyette's farm all this time, when for us it had been like she flew to the moon. Mama and I walked to visit.

"Hello, Ellen. Hello, Mama." She spoke with the tip of her chin quivering, her voice quivering too, and led us to their tiny bedroom.

We sat on the bed. Nora held Mama's hand like a little girl again. Her eyes filled with tears and, to match her feat, so did Mama's. They sat sniffling and holding hands. The backs of Nora's hands were nearly as rough and brown as Mama's.

"You're going to have a baby," Mama said.

Nora rubbed her belly. "I sure am. If it's a girl, I'm going to name it after you."

Mama blushed and ducked her head a bit. "I was thinking you didn't miss me at all."

"Oh, Mama."

"It's the truth."

They sat together. They still held hands but their fingers had loosened.

"Who's looking after the younguns?" Nora asked me.

"Corrine," I said.

"Corrine is right smart with them younguns," Mama added, but that was a lie.

The moment becomes important and large when I look back at it. I am seeing Nora with new eyes as I look back on that room. She has become kinder, softer, at least on the surface. She smiles at Mama without that little twist to her mouth, that sneer. Her lips have learned to relax for the moment. When she speaks, her voice drips with affection. When she looks me in the eye, for a moment, the Nora I remember needles like a knot at the center of each pupil.

Her lip trembled, and she gazed at Mama with watery eyes. "I miss you, Mama. I don't like to be here."

"I know you don't, sweetheart. You'd rather be at home with me, wouldn't you?" Mama beamed, feeling herself so loved.

"They treat me kind of funny."

"Minnie Boyette is a funny woman," Mama nodded her head.

"I think that woman hates my guts. That's what I think. For taking her son away." She lowered her voice and ducked her head toward the door. She smoothed her hand over her stomach. "But I got me a baby coming. She don't matter."

"She'll be all over you when that baby comes. Minnie Boyette is one funny woman all right." She paused, as if she expected Nora to say something, but Nora watched the door.

On the walk home, Mama continued to weep and dab at her eyes with one of Daddy's stained handkerchiefs. We trudged along the side of the road. My shoes had begun to pinch again, and I resented it because Nora had two pair and took both of them when she left.

Mama said, "You won't ever leave me like your sister done. I know you won't."

"That's right, I won't, Mama," I answered, and petted her arm. But she gave me such a dull-eyed look, with such a flavoring of ash, that I hardly believed myself.

"She didn't say a word about the wedding," Mama sniffled. "My own daughter."

"She said it was a justice of the peace."

"That's so sweet," Mama said.

"She loves you, Mama," I added, with an ache of loneliness in my own belly. "She said how much she missed you."

"She did say she missed me right smart, didn't she?"

"Anyway, it was Daddy who run her off, not you."

She heard me but set her lips tight together and never answered. I had, maybe, spoken more bluntly than she liked. We finished the walk in silence.

BURNER BOYETTE SOON quarreled with his family over Nora and moved them both into a house outside of Pine Level, to help with another man's farm. The house leaned precariously, hardly more than a shack with a bed and a kitchen table in it.

Burner picked me up in his boss's truck and drove me for a visit, to help take care of their new baby boy, Burner Jr. Excited to be away from home, I actually longed to see Nora again, though the anticipation had its sharp edges. We drove over a bumpy dirt road, turning into a narrow, wooded driveway out of sight of the main farmhouse and the farm buildings. The house stood secluded in a narrow cleared yard and the woods bowed in from every side. An apple tree heavy with green apples grew to the side of the plank porch, where an old swing hung from a rusted chain. The apples had attracted some worms but enough remained whole that I ate myself a bellyful, raw and cooked, while I stayed at Nora's house.

Every morning Burner got up before daybreak to join the farmer and his sons bringing in the peanut harvest. Nora had been excused from that, for the first time in her life, because of the new baby; she was grading and tying dry tobacco instead, in one of the three rooms of the house where they lived. The dry tobacco took up most of the room, and each night Burner brought more.

I helped while I was there. We graded the leaves from golden to brown to trash, bundled the dry leaves, and wrapped their tops with another leaf, tight, like a head wrap, the lower leaves flaring out like skirts. We sat in the room or out in the yard with our piles of cured leaves, the dust working up our nostrils till we sneezed.

"I hate how this stuff gets up your nose." Nora rubbed hers with the back of her wrist. "But we sure God need this money with that baby in yonder."

"This tobacco's got a pretty color," I noted. "It's not all dark and dried like Mr. Taylor's always comes out to be."

"Daddy always did say Mr. Taylor burnt up his tobacco in the barn." The mention of Daddy made her thoughtful.

"There's spiders in dry tobacco, sometimes," I noted, to ease her thinking.

"I know. You remember when Mama found that wolf spider?"

"Good Lord," I nodded my head in a knowing way, and the gesture reminded me, without any warning, of the way Mama nodded.

"She like to jumped out of her step-ins. If she was wearing any." Nora fanned herself with tobacco leaves as she flushed red with laughing. She looked lovingly down at her own baby, dimpled and white in his nest of cushions, snug in a box on the floor. "I hope my younguns don't ever see me like we've seen Mama." She pursed her lips and set her jaw.

"You'll be good to your younguns," I said, watching her. "Like I'll be good to mine."

We sat in motion, hands sorting the fragrant leaves, though for a few moments silence and stillness clouded us over. The dimpled baby gurgled, and we smiled and looked down at him. We smiled together with the baby and with each other. We had seldom smiled together when we lived in the same house, not in this tender way, and shyness overcame us both. We worked till sundown.

In spite of the dust, I liked the smell of tobacco leaves, its acrid, sharp edges driving up the nostrils; I liked the dirt of the leaves, except the dust, and the bits of string, the tough stems of the leaves after they were cured. The rough texture of tobacco sticks pleased my hand, and I never got a splinter, though I drew many a splinter out of Nora's hand, or Burner's, in the evening when he came home and helped us work.

Nora's baby, when she let me hold him, smelled warm and sweet, like biscuit dough made just right; and when Burner lifted the baby, himself fresh from the fields, the warm baby smell mixed with the sour field sweat of Burner, and then he laid the baby on a towel and unpinned the diaper where lay a sweet, fragrant baby turd. I loved to hold the baby and wished for one of my own.

I stayed till Mama sent for me. The time was sweet, in the same way time had passed at Aunt Addis's house. I saw everything more vividly because I never knew how long I would be there. We woke up and started the fire early in the morning, as early as we would have lit the kindling at home; but here in Nora's kitchen we were alone. We did the dishes side by side, and Nora praised my hands, the shape of them and the texture of the skin. "You have those smooth pretty hands," she said. "Mine look like I soak them in lye twice a day."

"They do not."

"They do too. Look how bony my fingers are."

"They're not bony, they only have a few knobs on them." Her hands had large brown freckles on the back, the same texture of freckle that traced the sunny side of her arms and shoulders. My skin was clean and clear. I asked, "Do you ever hate me because I don't have freckles?"

Nora laughed. I liked the ease of the sound. "I don't hate you."

"I used to think you did."

"No. I don't hate anybody." But she glanced at her shoulders, the dusting of freckles along her upper arms. "I think you're stuck on yourself, that's all, but so is everybody."

"I am not stuck on myself," I squealed, but for years afterward she would say the same thing, as if it were really true.

"Besides," she added, "I don't even mind having freckles any more. Burner likes them." She blushed and refused to say more, though I was longing to ask what, exactly, she meant.

My first night asleep on the couch, when I had heard Nora's moaning in the bedroom, I sat up with my heart pounding, afraid for her. Then I heard the rhythm of her whimpering, and Burner's heavy breath, and I lay reluctantly onto the cushions, though my heart continued to drum against my ribs till they finished. I listened till long after they were done. I hardly slept.

For days when I heard their bed rocking against the wall, the mattress springs creaking and singing, and their giggling or even their harsher sounds, I wondered what this feeling was. I had heard similar sounds in my own house coming from Mama and Daddy, though Mama had never squealed with laughter the way Nora did. I ran my fingers over myself, inside my drawers, where my stuff was getting hairy and changing. Exploring there, I felt warm, as if the surface of my skin shimmered. As I listened to Nora and Burner I was floating in the feeling with them, as if what they were doing was a cloud and I lay enfolded in it.

I have moved toward unknown places in myself at moments like that, lost in the night hours in some strange setting, like that time, sleeping on the lumpy couch in the unfamiliar room in Nora's house with the scent of cured tobacco flavoring the breezes. What I understood exceeded any words I could provide to describe it, but the slight sense of nausea that overcame me, along with the pounding of my heart, the quickening of the blood in me, sufficed. Here was Nora making the same noise as Mama, and thinking nothing of it, right in the next room. I lay with the sheets pulled to my chin, feeling uncomfortable at the softness of my breasts under my hands.

Later by decades, in Nora's room in the hospital while she was dying, the memory of that particular moment returned to me. I could feel the closeness of the room, the bent spring of the couch jabbing against my shoulder blade, and my hands floating over my breasts, cupped around them, squeezing slightly. The headboard of the bed stopped hitting the wall. In the quiet aftermath of the ruckus they'd made, their murmuring voices lifted like a cloud; I could hear only the sound and none of the words, but the sound had a lightness to it. Their togetherness left me suddenly hollow and lonely.

MY FINAL MEMORY of Nora is this: When Nora was a little girl she had a blue-flowered dress with white buttons, none broken. On the day she died, she remembered that dress, last of all, before slipping away from us. Wearing the dress, Nora had stood taller, lighter, pretty as a cloud passing overhead and somehow spritely. Where did it come from, such a pretty garment? The answers lie buried somewhere in me, lost, but I have the impression that someone sewed the dress for Nora when she started school. Can I remember back as far as that? Mama's sister Rhonda was famous for sewing, but known to be stingy with fabric. Daddy's sister Tula had pedaled a sewing machine herself now and then, sewing a shift for Mama or a plain skirt for herself.

Nora put on the dress while Mama watched. The clean blue fabric slid across Nora's freckled back. Mama slipped the dress over the shoulders and adjusted it to hang. "That nearbout fits," she said, and smacked her lips. A moment later, without ceremony, she pulled the dress off Nora again, leaving Nora to shiver in her dingy drawers, her bony backside poking out.

On the first day of school Nora wore the dress. She washed her hair and let it hang clean around her face. There was no ribbon to tie it back and the barrette she prized so much was the wrong color for the dress. She walked around the kitchen in the dress as if the fabric were fragile. She sat carefully in a clean chair, smoothing the skirt over her knees. When she came home, she carefully hung the dress on a nail in the bedroom, smoothing out the skirt.

Because she had few good dresses, she wore it often, and began to come home with an expression on her face I had never seen before. Fear. A setting of the lips into a frightened line, and a slight flaring of the nostrils. She looked around our house as if she had never seen it before. Sliding the dress off her shoulders, she flung it into the corner on the floor.

After that, she wore the beautiful dress as if it were nothing. She might wear it to school two or three days in a row, and the fabric quickly lost its newness and faded from boilings in the laundry pot. When she outgrew it and I grew bigger, the dress became mine, and I wore it to school the same as Nora had. Even in its faded state it was far the prettiest dress I had ever worn, and I buttoned each button carefully.

I never threw the dress in the corner when it was mine. On laundry day I followed it anxiously from washboard to rinse water.

On occasion I caught Nora watching me, since she knew what I was up to. Sometimes she scrubbed that dress extra hard on the washboard, hoping the fabric would wear thin and finally shred in her hands.

When I outgrew the dress, a year or so passed before Corrine grew into it, and I dressed her in it with a feeling of reluctance. By then most of the color was gone and the fabric had grown dingy with age and wear. She wore it to play in the yard and soon it was as gray as the dirt around the house. She ripped the bottom of the skirt on the bobbed-wire fence around the Allison's cow pasture when we went fishing in the river near there. I hemmed the skirt and shortened it for Delia when she needed a play dress of her own. The buttons had remained intact all that time, except one that broke when Corrine used the dress to whip Madson and the button chipped on a corner of the chest of drawers.

Last I remember, Delia wore the dress into the chicken yard, the dress already tight across her shoulders, and hanging on her without shape or color, as she ran barefoot through the chicken turds.

So it all came back to me, that day in Nora's room in the hospital, sitting among her children amid the evidence of her good adult life, her strength fading on the bed, and I was there to hear her say, "I love my blue-flowered dress," in the softest voice; I was there to smile and remember the dress, exactly the one she was talking about, all those years ago, when it was the most beautiful piece of cloth that she or I had ever seen. Her children all wondered what dress she meant, and I told them; I gave them the gift of their mother as a little girl, and I remembered how I loved her then, when she was small and the dress was bright. I understood what memory was for, then. She and I remained there, those little girls lost in the river; we are together even now as I am remembering, and she is dead, and we will be there when I die, forever. I was glad to have come to sit with her while she faded, because now I could love her again. She lay with her wisps of hair arranged on the pillow, and we watched her die. We waited all night. Nora, who heard nothing by the end, finally added, in the most peaceful voice, "It has the prettiest flowers on it."

MY DROWNING

I DREAM OF my own drowning, and in the dream once again I fail to distinguish between the past and now. We are walking through the woods toward the pond, headed for Nora's funeral. I should be older than I am; this thought occurs to me as we follow Mama through the woods. Mama has come to Nora's funeral too, even though Mama is already dead; but Daddy is nowhere to be seen. We walk together, all of us, Otis and Carl Jr., me and Corrine, Madson and Delia and Hob, the baby whom I hardly knew; sometimes I even hear Joe Robbie's voice, and I look for him as if I need to pull his wagon and hold him upright in it, like before. We are eating cold biscuits from the sack I carry, and we push our way forward along the path, shielding ourselves from the underbrush.

Aunt Addis joins us at the edge of the woods and picks me up. I am suddenly very small and she lifts me without any effort. She slides her cool hands under my dress and the smooth tips of her fingers brush my legs, my lower back. She slides my dress over my head. I wear a yellow slip underneath, and Aunt Addis adjusts the straps that have slipped low on my shoulders. I stand at the foot of a cypress at the edge of Moss Pond.

In the black water Nora's body floats, her face partly submerged. Dark fingers of water lap into her nostrils. Behind me stands my family, and when I turn to look at them, Mama keens and sinks to her knees. Sorrow etches her face. But I feel nothing, and turn to study Nora in the water again. The image becomes familiar to me, not simply that this is Nora but that this is Nora at the age when she married Burner Boyette and gave him his first child. She wears a familiar dress, blue-flowered, but larger and simpler than the one she had as a girl.

I step into the water. Hands push me from behind, but whose? I try to turn to see but the hands are pressing me forward and I take another step into the water, so cold; my slip rises in the water, my feet sinking into the mud; and I go forward again, and again, and the water closes over my head, and the slip rises, and my legs, suddenly tiny, have sunk into the mud. I have walked near Nora, the water draining from her lips when she bobs high, her eyes open and fixed on the sky over her head. I wonder how she has become young again like this, and how I have become so small. Suddenly I stumble beneath the water, beneath Nora, and I am drowning, I can feel the water in my own nostrils, I cough and gasp and the water fills my throat. But Nora's hands lift me out of the water and cold air fills my lungs.

OTIS WAS THE last to die before I was left alone in the family, and before he did he told me the story of the river, and when he told me the events echoed, as if I had heard it all before. On my hearing the story, something akin to a memory unlocked within me, as if what Otis said were the truth and not simply the shadow of one more dream. So I nearly believed him, even if he was lying, and this may have been all he wanted.

Daddy wanted you born dead, Otis claimed, so he beat Mama something fierce when you were in her belly, more than once. If she said she felt sick he beat her, made her work, and took the money from her, bought liquor, drank till he was falling over. So Mama hated you, he said, and when you were born she took you to the pond, and she tried to drown you, and she would have done it, except Nora saved you. You didn't know that, did you?

Mama hated you, he repeated, with emphasis, she wanted you to be born dead. The idea of one more mouth to feed drove Daddy to distraction, at least in Mama's mind. He had been all right through the first three children and the ones that died, but now he had given up farming because he hated to work for so little money. So when Mama turned out to be pregnant again, Daddy knocked her around whenever he could. He beat her legs with keen switches, he beat her across the shoulders with a buggy whip, and he set out to work her to death, or to work her till you died inside her. She worked for every farmer around the pond, and every dime she earned Daddy slipped into his pocket, and if she threw up in the morning or acted puny or tried to get out of working, he gave her a beating on top of the sickness. So she trudged off to the fields every day, and me and the rest went with her.

Mama swelled up bigger than ever. Daddy hardly ever worked by then, and if there was any food in the house Mama had sneaked to buy it, till at the end of the summer when you were born we were eating wormy oatmeal and grits bought on credit from the Little Store.

According to Otis, I was born before dawn one morning, August 19, which has always been my birthday though I never knew Otis to remember it. I was tiny as a kitten, wet, cold, hungry from the very first moment. After I was born, Mama laid up in bed and refused to nurse me till her breasts were so sore she had no choice. Daddy stared stupefied at the cradle where I lay.

He disappeared after that, and we had nothing. Mama stayed in bed all day at first, then stirred in the house as if she could not quite believe he had vanished. One day she stared at me a long time with hardly any expression on her face. She picked me up and walked with me to the edge of the pond, near the old mill. She set me on the ground without even a blanket under me and then she pulled off her dress and lifted me up and walked into the water. She lowered me to the cold pond. But Nora and Otis had followed, and Nora waded into the water, took me away from her, and ran into the woods. Nora hid with me in her arms, till nightfall. Then she sneaked into the house and laid me in the cradle like nothing had happened.

The next morning Mama started to nurse me, and then Aunt Tula came by and we went to stay with them for a while, including me, and we lived there until Daddy came back. He made up with Mama like the Lord intended, according to

Otis, who by the time he died had become a preacher ordained by some church or other.

Had the story he told not resembled my dream, I would have paid no attention to Otis at all. He would have lied for meanness any moment of his life. But he had once told me he knew a secret about me, though he never spoke it.

Even so, there were places where his story was different from any version of my dream. He claimed the drowning had taken place in the pond, but in my dreams I had always seen Mama walking into Holcomb River. He claimed this happened when I was a baby, but in my dream I had always been older. He claimed to have been there, when I remembered only Nora.

"Why are you telling me this now, Otis?" I asked.

"My mama tried to kill somebody," he said, while his bloated wife, Naomi, rocked back and forth in her chair, at the same time using her thumbnail to dig some food from between her two front teeth.

"That's some mess you're making up, Otis," I stated flatly, with Naomi eyeing me and Otis struggling to sit up.

"I'm telling you the truth," he wheezed, and sank against the bed, and I folded my hands around my purse and watched him. Pretty soon there was a rattle in his chest and then his tubes filled with this or that and all his machines beeped at once, and the nurses ran me out of there, and he died, I suppose, in his wife's arms, if she could stand up that long.

But after he was dead I heard the words he had said over and over again. I could hardly help but wonder.

By then I had buried them all, there was no one left to ask.

Even the younger ones, Corrine and Madson and Hob and Delia, even they had died before me, along with the aunts on both sides, who might have heard some shadow of the tale.

FOR A TIME, while I was sitting with Otis listening to the moist rattle of his chest, it was as if I were sitting with Daddy again, watching him die. Nora and Corrine and I kept watch on him as he lay in the hospital. Everyone thought we meant to be dutiful daughters, but we three understood, without ever speaking the words aloud, that we were keeping an eye on him, to make sure he finally left the world. The boys had died or vanished; but Daddy had his girls to sit with him till the end, while he shrank to the size of a nut inside his own skin, complaining to the last about the way the nurses treated him and repeating his eternal wish for a drink.

He frightened us, even weak, dying, and hardly able to move. One day when I relieved Nora, I found her wide awake, sitting with her back perfectly erect in the chair, clutching her purse against her, staring at Daddy with her eyes wide open as if he were the Moss Pond monster.

Once when Corrine came to relieve me, I whirled at her when the door opened and startled her; she paled at my expression and asked, "Ellen, what's wrong? Did he do something?"

I shook my head. She understood my fear from the fact that I simply turned toward Daddy, and we stood side by side and looked down at him, him frightened too, wheezing, needing a shave and maybe even with his diaper soiled, needing someone to change it for him, and we watched, Corrine and I.

On the last morning, Corrine and I confused the schedule

and both arrived at the same time to relieve Nora; by accident, we thought, until Nora looked at us from the chair. Then we knew Daddy was finally ready to go, and we sat down and waited until he was done. He died with his eyes open and with an earnest wish that one of us would speak to him tenderly to ease his path, a sincere desire that one of his daughters lay her cool hand on his forehead to soothe his way out of the world; but we simply sat there in our straight-back chairs and listened to that rasp, like an old hinge, louder and drier until he died.

I HAD ALREADY been driving, visiting places. I had found the wreck of the house in the Low Grounds, the place in Holberta, the Little Store at the end of Moss Pond. After Otis's story, I went to Smithfield to check my birth records and saw, duly recorded, the fact of my birth, the date I had always known as my birthday, and no evidence of anything unusual. But his story set me driving more, and searching for memories wherever I went. I drove along county roads in Johnston County, I drove the streets of Potter's Lake where I lived with Bobjay. I drove the roads around Moss Pond and walked through tangles of branches that hid the wreck of the old mill. Then I climbed the path to Moss Pond itself, and I stood at the edge of the water.

Paper cups and rusted beer cans tangled in the weeds at the bank. A big, pillowy sanitary napkin wrapped around a branch. The surface of the water, pitch black, shuddered like skin. I stared down into it and waited. But no memory would come. I had felt drawn to this place, and I had come here and found nothing.

Kneeling, I slipped my hand into the water, warm at the surface then cold beneath, with a feeling of thickness and weight as if it were syrup. My hand vanished entirely, I could not even see its shape.

I closed my eyes. All the dreams were there, all those echoes of whatever real event had happened so long ago. Locked in some patch of my brain was a memory of every moment of every dream. Hidden as well was the actual memory of my mama and the river, or creek, or whatever body of water had drawn her down into it; hidden despite all the remembering I had done. Had she tried to drown me? And the memory had gotten twisted in my head? She had remained an enigma for me, maybe for all of us, you see; and even at this end of my life, even after all the remembering, I could still gain no clearer image of her.

SHE REMAINED A mystery through all the years that followed Nora's marriage. When I was gone, Corrine took over the work in the kitchen, with Delia to help her; and by then Carl Jr.'s daughter had turned up, and Mama raised her too, like the rest. After a while Mama never got pregnant herself again, that was the only change I can point to. But by then her daughters were having babies, and she had grandchildren.

When I brought my own children to visit her home, she gaped at them as if they were monkeys in a zoo. She made them kiss her on the cheek, that same tired, wrinkled patch of skin; giving me some sugar, she called it. She asked them whether they loved their grandma. She looked from them to me as if she would never have dreamed I could produce such offspring. She treated all my sisters the same way.

She made a special dinner, during one visit; she had no choice, by then, but to cook herself. She boiled a whole pig's head and baked fluffy white biscuits and boiled cabbage and cooked white rice. The biscuits steamed in the crisp autumn air, each arranged on the plate like the postcard of a mountain. In the old days we would have thought so much food a feast, and Mama and I set to eating with relish; she was pleased with herself for having laid such a table. She and Daddy stuck their forks into the white fat hanging from the side of the pig's head, tearing off strips, savoring the taste. I sliced whatever lean meat I could find for my children, who stared at the pig's head through the meal. The littlest sat almost at eye level with the pig. They chewed biscuit as fast as they could and hurried into the yard as soon as they could get free. Mama pretended not to notice the puny appetite they showed.

I ate more than I would have, sucking the white fat from inside the skin the way I would have done when I was a little girl. Mama and Daddy and I sat there, probably the first time we three had ever eaten alone. They hunched over their plates with their elbows propped on the table. They chewed in quiet. For the first time in my life, I could feel them as old and harmless and even benign.

Outside, one of my kids had stepped in a chicken turd and another was making fun of him. It might have been Otis and Nora from a thousand years ago. We glanced out the door at them and then at each other. For a moment there was warmth between us. I have never had another moment like that. For that instant I was safe to love them, and I did.

LEAVING THE POND, I drove to the Holiness Church and sat there for a long time. The congregation had prospered to the point of bricking up the old building and adding better stained glass to the windows, milky smears of green and gauzy brown; but I could recognize the old building where June Frances and I had played in the yard after Sunday School.

Horns blared behind me, and trucks wheeled into the dirt yard in front of the new gas pumps at the Little Store across the road. A lot of people were standing outside the store, sipping Pepsi out of bottles. I walked over there to buy myself a chocolate drink; I could already taste it as I headed toward the store.

Men jumped out of the trucks with rifles and shotguns. "Who seen it?" one man hollered to another; both men needed a shave and one was missing part of three fingers.

"Avery Taylor," the other man answered.

"That Piggy's boy?"

"That's who it is. He seen this creature down at the bottom of the pond, is what he said, not far from the mill. And you know, Piggy don't let that boy drink nor sniff no pussy, so he keeps a pretty clear head."

The fellows all agreed that it was so, and I slipped past. As I was headed into the store, I heard one of the men snicker and ask, "Why did they name that boy Avery, do you reckon?"

Inside the store I smelled pickle, salted crackers, black pepper, all the old smells that had soaked into the boards. The woman behind the cash register was nobody I remembered, though she smiled at me in a friendly, if mostly toothless, way. She stood next to the jar of bubble gum and atomic fireballs.

"Hello," she said, "what can I do for you?"

I opened the Pepsi cooler and lifted out a Yoo-hoo. "Looks like you got some excitement," I noted.

"This boy seen a monster at the pond," she said. "Everybody is just all upset about it."

"A monster?"

"It's been a monkster around here for years," spoke another voice, and that was when I saw old Miss Ruby, little and twisted, sitting by the coal stove with a blanket wrapped around her.

I opened my chocolate drink and stood by the stove with her. Miss Ruby looked me up and down. "I believe I know you," she said, and when I told her who I was, she patted my arm, delighted she had recognized me. "You know all about this place, then."

"I'd sure never have believed they'd see that monster again."

"It was always here, the monkster was," Miss Ruby said, "it was here when you were a little girl, and it was here when your daddy was a little boy." The strain of seeing had become too much. She closed her eyes. The exertion of lifting her head caused her to shake a little, and I knelt in front of her, to look at her face.

"It's hard to see the little ones when they get old." She lifted her hand as if she might touch me. Stringy blue veins shuddered inside fragile skin. She forgot me and settled back. "When they told me they seen the monkster again, I told them, take me down to the store. I want to be there to see everything. Nothing brings people around here together like that monkster does."

She blinked, trying to sit upright, though her eyelids were

heavy and drooping and she was nearly falling asleep. I remembered begging to charge a sack of beans and having Miss Ruby watch me fierce and sharp-eyed, without pity, answering no. My heart hardened at the memory but I stood there a moment longer, till her breathing deepened and she fell asleep.

I took my chocolate drink. The woman behind the cash register waved and grinned. One of her teeth was shaped like Idaho. "You better not drive in them woods where that monster can get you."

"I'll stay on the main road," I said.

"You reckon it really is a monster out there?"

"I don't know. That boy might have seen something up at that mill."

"I don't even like to go up there."

"You know it's haunted, don't you?" I asked.

"No!"

"It sure is. Old Man Oneal Jarman, who was Miss Ruby's father-in-law, killed his wife up there. He was widowed, and he took a young wife, and she tried to run out on him, and he killed her at the mill, back when they were still grinding corn. And then he put her body on the millstone, he ground it up with the corn and put little bits of her body in the corn and the flour for nearly everybody around here, and everybody ate little bits and pieces of his wife. My mama used to tell that story."

"Oh, glory to God," she said, her mouth hanging open.

So much information had stupefied her and she sat there with her shoulders slumped as I headed for the door. Outside, trucks were heading off in all directions, though a knot of folks waited by the gas pumps for fresh news of the sighting.

"You used to live around here?" the woman asked, as I reached for the doorknob.

"Yes, I did. A long time ago." I let the door close behind me and headed across the gravel. The people by the gas pumps were describing the monster to one another as if they had all seen it, and telling stories about how their daddies had seen it too, years ago, and maybe it had been seen even earlier before that, back in the old-timey days.

The voices quieted and the wind picked up as I trudged to my car. I drove away and have not been back there since. It occurred to me later that if Avery Taylor, June Frances's nephew, had taken to seeing things, he came by it honestly, since June Frances was prone to imagine more than she saw. It also occurred to me that, if Avery had actually been near the mill that day, it might have been me he saw there, through the tangles of branches, searching in the pond for my own ghost.

We buried Otis shortly after that. He had died as peacefully as he could, and Naomi laid him to rest in a casket the size of a small barge, dressed in his best black suit and thin black tie, with a Bible tucked between his hands and his stomach, riding there like a dinghy on a swell. I stayed after they closed the casket and removed the flowers to watch them lower the casket into the ground. Everyone else had gone, but one of my children stayed with me; everyone thought we were crazy, I guess, and Naomi never would speak to me afterward; but I stood there till they got his casket in place, and put the top on the vault, and began to shovel in the dirt. Otis's funeral was the very last funeral I meant to attend, except my own, and I stayed there till he was covered with dirt and the flowers heaped over him again. He was drowning in the flowers, I thought, and for some reason that made me smile. I took my daughter's arm and smiled at her. Relieved, she led me to our car and drove me home.